# The Adventures of Rustle and Eddy

Joseph R. Lallo

ISBN-13: 978-0999708163

# Table of Contents

## ACKNOWLEDGMENTS

I would like to gratefully acknowledge my editor for this title, Anna Genoese. Furthermore, special thanks go to ViiStar, the talented sculptor responsible for bringing many of my characters to life. Her fingerprints are all over this book. Eddy's visual design, and even the biology of merfolk within the setting, is based in large part upon some great fan art of him drawn while the story was developing. She is responsible for the cover of the book. Perhaps most importantly, her enthusiasm for the story was one of the main reasons I saw it through to completion.

# **Chapter 1**

A tiny patch of shore shimmered in the rising sun. Tucked between the eastern mountains and the crescent sea, these water-worn stones were as far from human eyes as one was likely to find. It was not, however, deserted. A tiny creature watched the foamy water flow into the shallow basin below him. He blinked away the salty spray and flicked his wings to dislodge the droplets that clung there.

He wasn't supposed to be here, watching the sea, trying to understand its motion. Elsewhere, his cousins and siblings would be searching for him. He would get an earful when he returned to his pond. There were chores to be done, things more suited for a fairy like him. But they could wait. The pond was so small, so still, little more than a puddle beneath a tree far from the shore. The nearest he would come to tasting the sea air back in his home was on the breeze before a storm. And even then, it would be only briefly, before he and the others huddled into the shelter of the weeds.

The water shifted, drawing his gaze. It wasn't the gentle ripple of the wind, or the powerful flow of the waves. This was smaller, more focused. This was a creature. He huddled down behind a smooth stone, ready to flee. The ripple abruptly stopped, easing back into the random motion of the waves, but the little creature squinted at the murky water. There was something there. He couldn't make out even a hint of its form, but there was something lurking beneath the surface.

The wise thing to do would be to escape, to fly away. That was what his kind *always* did. He'd learned never to face anything alone. A fairy among others could be formidable. But a fairy alone? Less than nothing. If it moved, it could kill you, so you should move faster, and hide better. But his curiosity was strong. He'd seen many things cause ripples in the home pond. They'd never come out of the water. Why should the ocean be any different? It was just a bigger pond, after all. If anything, it was home to the same little fish and frogs, only bigger.

He shuddered. No, not frogs. Frogs *did* come out of the water. And their lashing tongues made short work of things not so much smaller than the fairies themselves. Half of the bedtime stories he'd heard from his parents featured hungry frogs and foolish fairies…

He took a breath and found his courage. Frogs were noisy, and you could always find them hopping about at the edge of a pond where they made their home. If there were none along the shore, there were certainly none under the water. Whatever this was, it wasn't a *frog*.

The surface rippled again, precisely where the previous ripple had ended. He flicked a fresh coating of droplets from his wings and buzzed toward the thing he'd discovered. Just a quick look. Enough to see what it was. Then back home again. If he knew what he'd seen, he could ask the old wise ones about it. They would know. They knew *everything* that happened in the water.

He flitted along the surface of the water, his motion a collection of random zigs and zags, the better to avoid being caught by anything that might have been chasing him without his knowledge. When he reached a point above where the ripple had been, he peered down. The half-seen form wasn't any clearer, but it was certainly there. It was a whisper of paler color amid the dark blue green of the sea.

As he hovered, trying to make out what precisely he was looking at, he felt a worrisome stir in his belly. Something felt wrong. He darted up and away, mindful of the intuition that all-too-often was the only thing that could save someone so small and weak as he, but he was a heartbeat too late in heeding his instinct. Water erupted from the surface in a stinging spray, and concealed within, something very solid and very strong closed tight around his legs. He panicked and cried for help, but his musical voice was swallowed by the roar of the sea. A moment later, so was the rest of him.

Icy salt water filled his nose and mouth. His vision vanished in a rush of cloudy greenish water. He struggled and fanned his wings, churning up the water around him. The grip about his legs was too great, and he was moving too fast. All he could do was wriggle and flail about as the current made him its plaything and the pressure squeezed in around him. Down and down they went, he and the thing that had captured him. As they traveled deeper, the light from the cloudy sky faded. Soon all was black.

Though he'd not taken a breath, and indeed had wasted half of what he'd had on a fruitless scream, for the moment he was not in danger of suffocating. A fairy knew how to make the best use of air, regardless of whether that air was drifting through the trees or nestled in their lungs.

The current shifted. They'd stopped moving downward. Now they were moving forward, and quickly. He pushed and shoved at the fleshy digits clamped about his legs, but they may as well have been made of stone.

All at once, the water gave way to air again. He was thrust upward, into a place as pitch black as the sea had been. The grip loosened. He tried to flit away, but his wings wouldn't obey him. The water had folded and bunched them terribly. It would take time for them to recover. Instead, he dropped down to the water's surface again, where he floundered and splashed until he felt cold, slimy stone beneath him. He scrambled to the solid ground, slipping and sliding along in the darkness toward no destination more specific than "away."

From somewhere behind him, light suddenly appeared. It was terribly dim, a sickly green, and it revealed something that he wished it hadn't. He was in a small stone alcove, a pocket of air trapped somewhere deep below the rocky shore. He shut his eyes and felt for the motion of the air around him. The wind would always show the way, if there was even the tiniest crack leading to the outside. But there was nothing. The air here was dead and still.

There was no escape.

His heart drummed in his chest. Fairies did *not* cope well with captivity. To be trapped, to be cut off from the wind of his birth, was unthinkable, unimaginable. It meant he was lost, and utterly alone. But no. He *wasn't* alone. It was worse than that. Something had brought him here.

He turned back in the direction he had come. The glow was coming from a strange crystal bowl sitting just beyond where the water through which he had entered this prison lapped at the stone he now stood upon. It illuminated a towering figure, not so different from a fairy in some ways. His face, his arms, everything above the waist was quite fairylike. The only thing missing were a pair of wings. But he was *enormous*. At least as large as those humans his father told stories about. And below the waist, where legs should have been, there was only a silvery tail, like one of the little fish from the home pond. He'd slid up onto the stone a bit, but his tail fin still idly splashed in the water. The fingers of one of the bizarre creature's hands dripped with the same green glow, and where the drops touched the stone they traced strange ribbons of light before reaching the water and vanishing in a dim bloom of green.

The thing smiled at him, but in the mind of the little fairy, he was just showing his teeth. The fairy looked madly for a place to hide. His surroundings offered little in the way of shelter. Bundles of a strange, thin substance were bound with thread and stacked in neat piles along one wall. A few highly polished shells threaded onto a long string hung from a peg hammered into one sloping wall. All he could do was wedge himself into the far corner, hope this monster couldn't get far from the water, and watch for a chance to escape.

It watched him back. There wasn't anything obviously threatening about the creature's gaze, but just being that large was threatening enough. It rinsed the glowing green from its fingers, then reached for one of the bundled stacks and spread it open, leaving through the individual sheets. Each was covered with intricate black shapes. The creature seemed fascinated by the shapes, staring intently at them and running a finger along each column of them. It coughed and spat, clearing the water from its lungs and taking a breath, then slowly chanted something in a voice that sounded booming and clumsy in comparison to the fairy's own language.

The chant repeated over and over. The fairy felt the weakest glimmer of magic. He crossed his arms and gave a self-satisfied huff. For all this beast's terrible size and awesome strength, its magic was laughable. He himself had only *begun* to learn the way of the wind and water and he was *twice* as skilled with magic as this creature.

That said, there was *some* sort of an effect. After iterations of the chant, the beast would speak a few additional words. Each time he spoke, the words seemed a little less clumsy, a little more intelligible. Eventually, they had *some* sort of meaning.

"I speak now?" the thing said, in a thickheaded, mush-mouthed mockery of the fairy's own language.

"Y-yes," the fairy said, fearful of what might happen if his captor became frustrated. "You speak now."

"Ah, ah, good, good! I try. I try have talk with you. You fairy, yes?"

"Yes. Water fairy."

"Yes, yes! Water fairy! I know this. You small. Little wings. Move in air like we move in water. Yes. Water fairy. As the book say. So happy to see water fairy. I merman."

"Merman? I have n-never heard of a merman."

"No. Not many hear of merman. More know mermaid, but still not many."

"I don't know that either. Mermaid. Merman. W-what are they?"

"They are me! I am they. See? Strong swimming tail. And water as air. I learn water as air."

"What? I'm s-sorry, but you don't make much sense when you speak, merman."

"I know. Spell not easy. Not easy for me. We try though. Try to speak. I have questions. So many. But you. Do you have question? Question for me?"

"A-are you going to eat me?"

He released a horrific, booming laugh. "No! No eat water fairy. Happy to *find* water fairy! What does water fairy *call* water fairy, please, so I can call that?"

The fairy shook his head. "I'm s-sorry but I didn't understand."

"I am Eddy. That is the merman that is me. What is the water fairy that is you?"

"You want to know my name?"

"Yes! So I can call you that!"

"I'm The Damp Nourishing Wind That Rustles the Pebbles and Carries the Mist."

"… That is many words, water fairy. What part of that is the name that is yours?"

"All of it. That is all my name."

"Many words… I call you Rustle. Rustle is easy to remember and say."

"F-fine. If you like. W-will you let me go, Eddy?"

"Yes!"

Rustle's heart leaped.

"But not soon."

He slumped. "P-please! It is *awful* here. *Awful* to be away from my home wind and water."

"Is bad? So sorry, Rustle. I know. I know is bad. I take you from shore, and I not ask. That is bad. I put you in place you don't want to be. Also that is bad. But if I do not do this bad thing, I do not meet water fairy Rustle! I do not meet *any* but more merman and mermaid. And I want to know more than them. You want this too! You came to water. You looked for something new. And you found! Now is time to learn about merman." He sagged in dismay. "This last time you meet merman. We not go place or do thing except in water. Not like mermaid…"

Rustle, looked at the defeated expression of his captor. There was something familiar in it. Something he'd felt far too many times.

"You don't get to go far from home?" he asked.

"Not far. Not far at all. We don't know the things to make that a thing we can do. They don't teach us. Those things aren't for merman. Only mermaid."

"What don't they teach you?"

"They do not teach water-for-air, air-for-water. That I have to learn for me. And the magic for easier words. Some mermaid, they say, do not *need* magic for speaking. They meet people and learn to speak with them. But merman? No. Eddy meet no one."

"Why don't they teach you?"

"Merman stronger than Mermaid. Go *deeper* than mermaid. So merman go down, mermaid go up. It is equal, they say. But is *not* the same…"

"No, it *isn't*," Rustle said. "Fairy *men* aren't supposed to stray far from the home pond *either*."

"I see this! I see that sometimes there are fairymaids. But never *never* fairymen! Why this?"

Rustle shrugged. "There aren't very many of us. We are supposed to stay home and teach. We're the keepers of the home pond, the defenders of it. But how are we supposed to teach if we never learn anything? If all we have are stories that the women bring home?"

"Yes! Yes! There is *much* below, but also there is much above! Mermaids with magic, they can go below if they wish. But mermen? Never above! Because no magic, that is why. And so, I take a book." He tapped the bundle of pages. "I take the book that my sister had. She did not know. She didn't need it anymore. But I can use it. I can learn. And you see? I meet you! Already I learn about the above, I learn water fairymen have the same problems as mermen." He furrowed his brow. "But if fairymen do not get to see the world, you cannot teach me much *about* the world."

"And you can't teach *me* much about it either," Rustle moped.

Eddy scratched his head and ran his fingers through his wet hair. "Not terrible, though. You know things, fairy things. And I know merman things. We can learn those, yes! That is not nothing."

Rustle crept forward and stood. His wings were feeling better. They'd more or less returned to their proper shape. He could probably fly. And with a bit more effort, he could probably swim. But now that the terror had faded, the opportunity was dawning upon him.

He paced forward and tapped the book.

"This is magic?"

"It is not magic, it is *filled* with magic. A spell book. It has all the magic the mermaids need to go upward. My sister even used it to have land swimmers like *those,*" Eddy said, excitedly pointing at Rustle.

"Those are my legs."

"What did I say?"

"Never mind. We fairies, we are good at magic. I might be able to help you cast some of these spells better."

"Good! This is good! Better spell casting means better talking and better breathing and all of the other better things. And with the better things, I can have *adventures* like the mermaids." He clapped. "New things to see and do! Other people!"

"I'll help you. And I'll forgive you from bringing me here against my will, but you have to do something for me."

"I will do anything you need me to do, Rustle the fairyman!"

"I want you to show me something. Something no fairy has ever seen. Something that I can teach the other fairies. I want a new story, Eddy."

"I can do this. We have many things for making good stories."

"Good. But none of it can work unless we find a way to help me to breathe in the water."

"Water-for-air! Air-for-water! Yes, this is the first spell. The only spell I learned well."

Rustle looked at Eddy uncertainly. "*You* learned it *well.*"

"Yes, yes. See?" He took a few deep breaths with a theatrical flourish. "Breathing air, just like a surface person. I can do this for you, only backwards. Very easy. As easy as talking."

"Are you sure it isn't *easier* than talking?"

"Maybe it is? But it does not matter. I can do this for you now. Do you want this?"

Rustle weighed options. On one hand, this was quite likely the only opportunity he would *ever* have to learn things about a world the other fairies had never dreamed of. He could return to his people with *real* knowledge, real teachings. New stories and lessons. On the other hand... Eddy was a bit clumsy and thickheaded. The merman had already trapped him in this awful place, and did so in a terribly unsettling way. Everything he'd ever been taught as a fairy was telling him to fear this creature, not trust it. It was a difficult decision one that he would have to weigh very carefully…

"Too much thinking, I must not have asked right. I'll just do."

"No, no! Wait, I'm not sure I—"

"Don't try to hold breath. It is easier that way."

Eddy snatched Rustle before he could dart away. The fairy took a last, panicked breath before he was once again plunged into the water by the graceless merman, who joined him in submerging entirely beneath the surface.

The light from the glowing bowl barely penetrated the first few inches of the water, leaving him in near pitch black surroundings, blinking in the salty water. His mind raced, and he angrily scolded himself for being such a fool. The one bit of relief was the knowledge that a nice deep breath and his innate fairy magic meant he could last the better part of an hour without taking another breath if he really needed to.

All around him, he could hear the muffled thrum of the merman's booming voice filtered through the water. He couldn't make out the words, but it was clear he was repeating the same words again and again.

A tiny, itchy sensation prickled at his skin. Flickering points of light crept over him like ants on a log. Then, all at once, his lungs *burned* for breath. He struggled and tugged, desperate for air, but Eddy held firm. Finally, chest heaving and eyes wild, he released the air and took a raking breath of the sea water.

The burning in his lungs eased. He took another tentative breath. It wasn't the same. The water felt heavier, thicker. But a lungful of sea now did the work of a lungful of air."

"Wow…" he uttered, his voice oddly deep and subdued as expressed through the water rather than the air.

"There, you see? It is good," Eddy said.

"Can you let me go, please?" Rustle said calmly.

"Yes, of course. You are my new fairyman friend."

The fingers holding Rustle loosened. He darted as quickly as the combined flutter of his over-worked wings and kicking of his tiny legs could manage. When he was level with Eddy's face in the dim light, he reared back and punched him in the nose as hard as his tiny arms could manage. It wasn't hard enough to do any damage, but it certainly got his point across.

"You could have *warned* me it would feel like I was drowning," Rustle snapped.

Eddy rubbed his nose. "What you mean? It feels how a merperson always feels when leaving the water or coming back. Until they are better at water-for-air and air-for-water."

Rustle scratched his head. "Really? Well… Now you know… Us people who breathe air don't like it when we have to take a breath under water."

Eddy nodded. "Yes. Yes, good! You see! Already I learn! We will do *so much* together, Rustle the fairyman." He snatched the spell book from the surface and tucked it under his arm. "Come. We will learn and do many things. But I was almost out of time to do this when I found you. I have to go back to my village. You come! But when I say hide, you hide. You can hide, yes?"

"Fairies are very good at hiding," Rustle said with a nod.

"Great! Then we go now!"

Eddy thrust with his tail and darted off. Rustle tried to keep up, but he was certainly no match for the merman's speed beneath the waves. Fortunately, Eddy realized and looped back, snatching Rustle and holding him up so the fairy could grip his hair. Once he was holding tight, he darted off again, and Rustle watched with anticipation as the distant lights that could only be an undersea village slowly approached.

This was going to be amazing.

# Chapter 2

Eddy swept downward, mindful of the tiny form clinging to his flowing hair. He'd awoken and begun his routine the way he had so many times before. He'd never imagined that this would be the day he would finally find someone from the surface to talk to. The last thing he wanted was to spoil it any worse than he already had. There were so many things to think about. So many little things that air-breathers might have trouble with that his fellow merfolk wouldn't.

As the pressure upon him began to return to what he was accustomed to, he paused and gently untangled his new friend Rustle from his perch. They'd traveled far enough from the surface that there wasn't quite enough light from the sky for even *his* sensitive eyes, so the fairy would not be able to see anything at all. With one hand lightly clutching Rustle's legs, Eddy rattled his bracelet of shells to conjure a bit of light. The little shells, harvested from snails along the sea floor, took on a blueish glow. He chuckled at the sight it revealed.

Rustle's eyes were wide and searching, almost transfixed by the glow of Eddy's bracelet. His hair was an utter mess, and his clothes were twisted as though he'd been tossing and turning in bed.

"Are you well, fairyman friend?" Eddy asked, holding Rustle close to his face.

"You move too fast!" Rustle said. "The water is so *thick* compared to the wind. I can barely hold tight enough to not be swept free."

"I am sorry for that, Rustle. But we have far to go, and not much time to get there. I have many things to do. I will be missed if I don't go to the places and do the things. But I worry for you. I know, when sometimes mermaids come close to where I work, they have to go slow, or the deep starts to hurt."

"The deep starts to hurt?" Rustle said.

"Yes! In the head, sometimes. It presses harder when you are deeper. For me it is the other way. I feel wrong when I go shallow. And *very* wrong when I go above the water."

Rustle twisted a finger in his ear. "I *do* feel a strange ache."

Eddy nodded. "This is the deep. The water-for-air magic should help with it, but it needs more time maybe. We can wait here some until the ache stops. It should not take long."

"That is good." He rubbed his head. "So, it hurts for you to go up to the surface?"

"If I go too fast. And without magic, I almost cannot go at all." He shrugged. "Like mermaids, only up instead of down."

"I wonder why it happens?"

"More water pushes harder."

"Why doesn't air do it?"

"Air doesn't do it? I did not know! I thought the high things, like the fairies and the… sky fish—"

"Birds."

"Yes, the birds. I thought they had to stay high, and the bottom things with the land swimmers, they had to stay low. Why else would they stay so low all the time?"

"Most things can't fly."

"Fly. Fly is like air swim?"

"Yes."

"Ooh. So land swimmers are like crabs and snails and things. Always on the bottom. I learn so much so fast!"

Rustle gazed down into the murky depths. "What are those lights down there?"

"That is my home! It is still far to go, though. If I go fast, and don't stop, we will get there in an hour."

"It's odd you know a word like hour, but not legs."

Eddy shrugged. "I cast the spell bad. Big missing pieces in the talking."

"If it's so far away, how can we see the light? We're not an hour from the surface, and we can't see the sun. Even on a cloudy day I'd expect the sun to be brighter than just about anything."

"Here and above, the water is cloudy. Has many things in it. The things the big fish eat. Further down it is *very* clear. You can see light for a long way."

"But where does the light come from?"

Eddy held up his bracelet. "There are many things. Things down deep, they make their own light. Even me!"

"You make light?"

"When down deep enough, I do! Eyes and fins. No way to see, otherwise. Unless you bring shells or other glow things. Do things not glow in the air?"

"Some things do. Fireflies. And when we stir up our magic, fairies glow. But we usually keep our glow subdued if there might be someone else to see."

"Why?"

"Because if we don't, they might catch us." Rustle crossed his arms. "Like you caught me."

"Didn't need glow to find you though."

"I wasn't being as careful as I should have been. Still, I suppose getting caught by something else isn't something *you* need to worry about. There aren't any frogs or birds or fish big enough to eat something as big as you."

"No birds or frogs, no. But very much fish."

Rustle blinked. "There are fish big enough to eat you?"

Eddy nodded, his long hair billowing about. "Big enough to eat me, and others big enough to eat them. There are *many* big things here."

The fairy glanced nervously about. "My head feels better now. Maybe we should go."

"Good! I will move fast, get there soon as I can."

Rustle tried to flit back to his place atop Eddy's flowing locks. The motion showed a considerable improvement in his navigation of the water compared to earlier, but it was still a little more sluggish and imprecise than Eddy supposed was his intension.

"You are getting better, little fairyman. Soon you will be as good in the water as in the air."

"I hope so. I *am* a water fairy. I thought I'd gotten good enough. But I was only just starting to get the feel for water."

"You stay with me, Rustle. You'll get the feel for the water in a way no fairy ever has." Eddy briefly rummaged in a small bag slung behind him. "Good. The book is safe. Come, we go!"

#

Rustle held tight and folded his wings flat as the powerful, wave-like paddling of Eddy's tail thrust them effortlessly through the water. He tried to shut his eyes and feel what the water told him. Though he was no longer trapped within that little pocket of air, the terrible feeling of closeness and isolation never truly left. The wind that covered the world was, for the most part, one continuous blanket. This part or that could be as different as night and day, but it was still a seamless whole. Being trapped, unable to flow with it, was bad enough. But here, beneath the waves, he had lost contact entirely. It made him feel so terribly alone. The older water fairies, those he was to someday join and even replace as the teachers of the young ones, said the water had the same flow, the same connection. But he'd only ever had to feel for it in his little pond, where there wasn't much to feel at all. Here in the sea, it was at once too much and not enough. The motion was subdued and heavy, but the scope, when he could get a sense of it, was nearly as dizzying and immense as the wind and sky above. And it was far more *full*.

Not having to worry about knowing where he was going and, until Eddy's recent comments, the lack of concern about large predators had left Rustle to observe what little there was to see around him. Now that he knew there could be things lurking in the darkness that might make a meal of even something as large and powerful as a merman added an extra level of intensity to his gaze.

Here and there, felt more than seen, a massive form would slide beneath them or over them. Sometimes the glow of Eddy's bracelet would catch the silvery sheen of a darting shape that was gone before he could fix his eyes upon it. Eddy casually rolled and bobbed around something truly massive, dragging his fingers along its slippery hide before chuckling and quickening his pace.

"What was that!?" Rustle yelped.

"A whale. A small one."

"Would that eat you?"

"Not *that* whale. Things that big only eat things smaller than you."

"There isn't much smaller than me, back up on the surface."

"Here there is more of everything. More of the very big. More of the very small. We are close now. Look," Eddy said.

Rustle hauled himself forward. What had not so long ago been little more than some half-seen lights in the indistinct distance now revealed itself to be something much more interesting. It was a city, but it seemed to have more in common with the pond and trees where the fairies made their home than the stories the fairies told of human villages. The light came from a variety of sources, but most were sea creatures either living or dead. Finely woven nets held wobbly, translucent blobs that cast warm, torch-like illumination. Elsewhere, spongy bundles gleamed with the green glow Eddy had used to light the air pocket where he'd first spoken to Rustle. Little shells like the ones on Eddy's bracelet were embedded in the ground and around openings, tracing out what would have been paths in a more earthbound race.

The homes were elegant structures of bright pink and yellow. They looked like they'd been grown rather than built, though the way heavy stones had been embedded in the colorful tissue connecting them suggested their form had at least been guided, if not outright *designed* by the merfolk. The shapes reached high into the open water, openings scattered irregularly about and glowing with more of the warm light from within. Near to the sea floor they ran together into a complex formation. Higher up they separated into what looked like the stout, inverted roots of a massive tree.

Though Rustle wouldn't have called the town bustling, there were perhaps a half-dozen merfolk out and about. Two of them seemed to be arguing about small bundle of fish that one of them held. Others were idly chatting. The water carried their voices much farther and more clearly than the air would have. Another was smearing a thick paste of some kind onto one of a handful of fractures running along the surface of their reef-like homes.

"We call it Barnacle. Other villages would not still be there, but we are still there," Eddy explained.

"Why would other towns be gone?" Rustle asked.

"The ground shakes sometimes here. Breaks our homes a little. It shakes more now than before."

"Why not leave?"

"Because this is home! My farm and mine are near here. My family was born here. My family *will* be born here. But we talk later. You should hide now. People shouldn't see you," Eddy said in a hushed tone.

"Are your people dangerous?" Rustle asked, huddling a little lower in the billowing thicket of Eddy's hair.

"No. But I didn't *ask* about taking the spell book. My sister would get mad if she saw I used it. She thinks it was lost. I'll say when it is safe. My sister, when she yells, yells *hard*. Come, though. I am already late."

#

Eddy pumped his tail a bit more furiously as he approached the edge of Barnacle. Merfolk were not beholden to the rising and falling of the sun, not directly. The moon, however, and the tides that followed it, dictated their schedule in a similar but far more rigid way. As useful as it was to wake at the break of dawn, few things truly required one to be precise about it. When it came to tides, some places may not be accessible if one waited too long. His sister was thus justified in the stern look she gave as he darted through the narrow doorway of their home.

"Eddy, *really,*" she snapped.

Her arms were crossed against her shimmery bodice, and her thin eyebrows were drawn into a withering glare. Like all mermaids, her skin and features—at least those of her upper body, were much more like the land-dwellers than those of the males. That was useful, as the men who served upon the boats and the docks seemed far more willing to interact with someone they considered beautiful than otherwise. Her hair was a deep brown, in contrast to the more aquatic coloration of Eddy's. She'd decorated it, oddly enough, with the skull of some sort of rodent. On another creature it would have looked grim or morbid, but she managed to make the intricate, bleached white artifact look positively artful. Her skin had the deep tan of a mermaid who spent a good deal of her time in the sun, a sign of just how much of a hard worker she was.

"I know, Mira, I know," he said quickly. "I have the things you asked for. And more besides. Truly exceptional specimens."

It was nice to be speaking his own language again, without having to rely upon a translation spell of questionable quality. From the way Rustle responded at times, he worried he might not sound as coherent as he would like.

He reached into his bag, careful not to reveal the book hidden within, and fetched a small mesh sack of brightly colored orbs.

"Here you are! Good ones today," he said, holding it up to her. "Some *very* fine pearls. I was worried it would be another year before this batch would be ready, but I think it will be an *excellent* harvest."

13

Eddy held out the sack, but Mira reached past it and instead touched his face. There was concern in her eyes as her thumb rubbed his cheek. He knew what she'd found, even before she said it.

"You've got some blossoms... And look at your eyes," she said, tugging at his eyelid. "You're bloodshot. You've been heading toward the surface again, haven't you? Is that why you're late?"

"I only went upward briefly," Eddy defended.

"Eddy, briefly is still too long. It is *bad* for you. I've told you a hundred times. And mother told you a hundred more! If you need something from above, ask me. Just as I ask you for things below."

"I know..." Eddy said, looking away.

"What were you doing up there?"

"I was just... testing myself is all. A merman who can stand a bit more of the surface than the rest can get a lot more jobs." His eyes darted to a fracture that had split the curved roof of their entryway. "Maybe *then* we could afford a place that didn't need to be patched every time the ground shook."

"No amount of money is going to find us a place like that in Barnacle. But these will fetch us more than enough to afford a proper patch and plenty left over besides. *Oh,* but I've got to be going or the tide will take the trade ships with it!"

She gave him a hug—causing the hidden form of his fairy friend to scurry in a panic to avoid being found out.

"Now you be careful. And no more going up, you hear me! You remember what happened to Father."

"I know. I know. I'll see you at dinner."

Mira dropped the mesh satchel into her bag and hurried out. Eddy watched her go, and when he was certain she was too far to turn back and surprise him, he put his mind to the spell again and spoke to his friend.

"It is clear now, Rustle. You can see the place I live if you wish."

The fairy untangled himself from Eddy's hair and swam out in front of him.

"Who was that you were talking to?" Rustle asked.

"That was sister Mira. She is older. Still I am a child to her. Even though she is only a year more old than me."

"Why couldn't I understand either of you while you were speaking?"

"The spell is between me and you. There is better spell for more easy speaking, but I do not know it so much yet."

"Maybe we can work on it. It might be nice to know what people are saying to you."

"We can! This we can do, yes! Oh! But not soon. I must go to my farm, and after that my mine. If I do not go now, the current will be against me. I bring with me the book. The work is not *all* day. Plenty of time for you and me to do things, and lots of talking and things for you to see the whole time! But I need to be ready. Please look around my home, if it can teach you things you wish to know. It is not much, but we are proud we have it."

#

Eddy swam from the entryway into the heart of his home. Rustle hurried to keep close, glancing about as he went. Eddy may have claimed the home was not much, but it was still the most remarkable thing Rustle had ever seen. The largest room, roughly in the center of the home, was well lit with a netted jellyfish. The walls, ceiling, and floor were covered with a mosaic of shells. Here and there, hollows hosted colorful sponges or fronds of seaweed as decorative accents. He followed as Eddy swam to an adjoining room, a pantry of sorts. Bundles of fish, eels, and assorted other treats were tethered to the floor with green twine.

"These are fresh! Mira knows the things I like best!" he said, tugging another fine mesh bag from a small chest of carved stone. "Do you eat eels? If you do, you will never taste a finer one than this!"

Rustle nearly ran face first into the offered sea creature. He darted backward to avoid it.

"Ugh. No," Rustle said. "I don't eat creatures."

"You should try! It is a new thing. You want to know new things! I will bring with me an extra that you can enjoy if you like."

He stuffed them into the bag and swam the next room to grab a small roll of strange cloth before returning to the better light of the den. Perhaps he was too frightened when they'd first met, or his eyes hadn't adjusted to the weak light, but Rustle realized he'd never taken the time to really observe his new friend. There was a *marked* difference between he and his sister. Admittedly, Rustle had only gotten a fleeting glimpse of her through Eddy's hair, but she didn't look so different from a fairy woman, save for the size, the lack of wings, and the fishy tale. Eddy was overall more aquatic in appearance. His skin had a blue tinge, shifting subtly to silvery gray scales on his tail. His build was wiry, with spindly arms and a lean chest and midriff each looking like they'd been threaded with iron-hard muscle. His eyes were a bit larger than seemed proportionate, dominated by an opalescent gray iris and a slit-shaped pupil.

Noticing that he was being observed, he stopped his preparations long enough to offer a smile, revealing teeth that were a measure more serrated than one might have expected. Spiny fins flanked his face on either side, and similar spines gathered in clusters in places like his forearms and his waist. Even his fingers were tipped in claw-like nails. Taken individually, his traits should have made him monstrous, but they'd somehow arranged themselves in a way that was curious, friendly, and enthusiastic more than they were fearsome. Though perhaps Rustle would feel differently if he were to find himself on Eddy's bad side.

15

"We won't be back until nearly time for sleep. Most of a day. If you don't want eel, what *do* you eat? We'll need some."

"I eat nectar, mostly."

"Nectar?"

"From flowers. It's sweet."

"Oh! Sweets. Like for children. I have some."

He swam into the pantry and returned cupping some shiny, grape-sized balls in his hands.

"Take one. Try!" he said, urging them forward.

"What *are* they?" Rustle asked.

Eddy plucked one between his thumb and forefinger. It was squishy, revealing a thin layer of something resilient and clear around a purple interior.

"They are sweets," he repeated. "Like for children."

"So you said, but—"

"Try!"

He poked the little ball in Rustle's face. It was the size of his head, so rather than popping in his mouth, the covering ruptured and Rustle got a face-full of the filling. At first, he pulled back and spat it out, but when the flavor fought its way through the surprise, he found it was actually delightfully sweet. It was a more complicated flavor than violet nectar—his personal favorite—but it was rather tasty. Even getting a mouthful of seawater along with it didn't ruin the flavor.

"It… isn't bad," Rustle said. "What is it made of?"

"Things that grow along the shore. I do not know what they are called. Mira buys these for after we eat sometimes, as a treat."

"I think they'll do as a meal."

"Then I bring it for you."

He disappeared into the pantry and returned with a glass jar to pop them into before stowing them in his bag. With that done, he commenced tightly rolling up a peculiar outfit made from the same material as the bag, then slipped his hand into a tool that looked like someone had tried to fashion a mole's claw out of a handful of shiny white stones.

"Ready to go to work?" Eddy asked. "You will see my farm, and my mine. Many things no fairy has seen! And you can tell me of things that no *merman* has ever seen. Such fun!"

"I'm ready when you are—*whoa!*"

Eddy hadn't waited him to finish answering, reaching out to snatch him by the legs and position him atop his head to hold tight to the hair. With that, he swam happily out the door and into the darkened depths beyond.

# Chapter 3

Rustle held tight to Eddy's hair and watched the little circle of sea floor illuminated by the merman's bracelet. When he'd agreed to come along with Eddy, he'd imagined his discoveries would be a bit more… substantial than they were turning out to be. It was true that his brief appearance in the merfolk town of Barnacle had given him a wealth of fresh knowledge, the primary lesson he'd learned since then was that the sea was very big and very dark. There was also the "deep" that Eddy had warned of, a pain that would creep up as they ventured further downward. No less than five times during their journey, Eddy had to stop to let Rustle's pain ease. The final time had required a few careful recitations from the spell book to chase the last of the pain away.

"We are close," Eddy said. "My farm is not very much, like my home, but you shall see it all."

"What sort of a farm can you *have* beneath the sea? I only know that humans and such have them, but they need sun," Rustle said.

"Not sun here. Just warm. The good warm water is what it takes. From below."

"Good warm water from below," Rustle said. "Maybe when we get a moment, we can work on that spell, so you can speak more clearly."

"Yes, yes. But not soon. Work first."

He swept lower and slowed his pace. Rustle experimentally released Eddy's hair and worked his legs, arms, and wings. At this speed, he could just about keep up. Though it took much more effort than simply hitching a ride, it felt nice to have a bit of control over where he was going. At least until he felt a stir of motion in the unseen water around him that flashed images of predatory creatures waiting to gobble him up. He darted a bit closer to Eddy for the sake of safety.

It was subtle, but his host was clearly more at ease in this part of the ocean than he had been even in Barnacle. The smile on his face was wider, and his motions had a more confident, smoother, more graceful quality to them. Another sign that he was entering the depths better suited to mermen than mermaids was the glow that was beginning to form at the edges of his irises and the tips of his fins and spines. It wasn't enough to illuminate their surroundings even as well as the jellyfish lamps in his home, but it provided enough light to give form to sea floor around them.

"Here. This is my farm. Stay far from the pointy piece in the middle. Very hot. It will burn if you go close."

Rustle strained his eyes to see the tableau opening beneath him, but with only Eddy's natural glow, he could only make out the faintest hint of wafting forms and angular, gnarly rock formations. He *could* see that the farm was tucked nicely into a little rift in the sea floor. Hidden and protected as it was from the open water, Rustle decided it might be acceptable to take the measured risk of summoning some light of his own.

He shut his eyes and fluttered his wings. For a fairy, glowing took little effort. Indeed, most times it took more effort to avoid it. The smoldering blue of his own light swelled and pulsed, and slowly the 'farm' revealed itself to him.

A tall, narrow spire jutted up from the center of a strip of waving red fronds. The density and variety of the life here almost made up for the sparseness of the journey here. Back in the forest, most things were variations of blue or green, gray or brown. Here, every color in the rainbow seemed to get equal consideration. The stone was marbled with turquoise and yellow. The fronds ran the spectrum from pale yellow to brilliant red. Long, narrow tubes jutted up from the waving seaweed and winked with wriggling green and white forms. Scattered among them were fish and things which Rustle didn't even know how to classify. Some looked too perfectly painted with brilliant, contrasting color to have been anything but the daydream of an idle artist. Others had the rocky, misshapen visage of something the gods knew most would never have to see. They did not scurry and hide at the arrival of the merman or the sudden appearance of light. It was as though they knew that they belonged here and anything else which might arrive was of no concern to them.

"The pointy bit there, in the middle, is where the good warm water comes from," Eddy said.

He pointed to the milky white plume of water gushing from the top.

"Don't go close. Very hot. The pointy things with the rushing water will burn. But look around. There isn't much here that will try to eat you, I don't think."

"I would prefer a bit more certainty than that," Rustle said.

"Me too!" Eddy said brightly.

Without further elaboration, he disappeared into the waving fronds and the slow, steady scrape of his claw-shaped tool on stone commenced. Rather than rely upon Eddy's weak assertion of his safety, Rustle joined him among the fronds. The merman looked up from his work and smiled.

"You want to know what I do?" he asked.

"Yes, please," Rustle said.

Eddy held up the claw tool.

"Scraper, from worm teeth. Big worm teeth, from down low."

He pointed to the stone, where assorted little snails and other hard-shelled creatures held tight to the stone and burrowed among the silt.

"Little clingers. They eat the bottom parts of the fronds, and then the fronds float up and I can't have them. No good. So I scrape."

It was oddly beautiful to watch as Eddy worked. These were the same snails whose shells adorned his bracelet and provided light when jostled. As a result, each scrape across the stone caused a sweep of glowing points to appear where the snails were hiding. Though the ones on his wrist were small, many along the stones grew much larger. The merman pried one free. It was about half the size of Rustle if he were to curl himself up.

"Such a pain, these. Always scraping and sifting. But once they are off the bottom, they have a soft bit, see?"

He pointed at the underside, then raised it up and slurped the snail from its shell.

"Good eating," he said, juicily chewing it. "Enough of these and I don't need lunch. And a good hard shell. Mira uses them. She makes things to sell. They don't glow as good as the small ones, but very pretty in the right light."

Rustle winced a bit as he watched Eddy snacking on the creature. The merman popped smaller one off a stone and offered it up.

"Try one?"

"No."

He scratched his head. "You say you want new things, but you don't want any of the new things."

"I want to *learn* new things. I don't need to taste them to do that."

"You do if you want to know what they taste like." Eddy tossed the snail into his bag and continued to maintain the roots of his patch. "What *do* you want to know?"

"What is that spire that sprays the hot water?"

"It is connected to way down deep. Water goes way down deep, where there are things that aren't up here. Then it gets hot, because it is *hot* way down deep, and it makes it spray up and bring the new things with it. And here and there creatures eat the new things, and they grow up bigger stronger. Also, lots of different colors! Here, come, come."

He swam through the forest of fronds until he reached what at first glance was a stretch of the rift covered with polished stones, but they fluttered now and again, causing stirrings of silt and puffs of water.

"These here, these are our shellfish. They have been in the family since my father's father. They make pearls. Big ones. And they make them faster than anyone else's *I* know." He moved a stone to reveal a little bag of them. "These are ones I found that weren't nice enough for selling. But look at them."

He tugged the bag open and dumped them out into his hand.

"Pearls?"

"Yes! You don't know them?"

"No."

"Little, pretty, hard things. Air-breathers pay much for them. And most are white, but we have blue, yellow, red, mixes of colors, colors that are different if you look in different light, or in a different way. Very special. Only in farms like this."

Rustle picked one up out of Eddy's hand. It was tiny by merfolk standards, and a bit misshapen. It was about the size of Rustle's fist and had a unique and gorgeous luster. The fairy was astounded by the piece.

"May I have this?" he asked.

Eddy smiled. "Yes, you can have. Maybe when you go back to the surface, you will bring *me* something special, yes?"

"I don't know if there is anything that would interest you."

"You bring the thing. It will interest me. To me, that pearl is a small one I can't sell, but you look at it like treasure. This is why we help each other, yes? Show each other the trash the other will treasure! I have much work to do, but maybe we'll find more trash for you."

#

Much of what Rustle reasoned must have been the morning was spent tending to the roots of his frond patch, weeding out those too small to be of any use and harvesting those that had grown large enough. When that was through, Eddy donned the odd garment he'd packed away. It was a thick, rough gray hide, like some manner of leather but with a rubberier texture. It covered him along the front like a smock, and was paired with a skirt of sorts to protect his tail and thick mittens to protect his hands. It even had something of a backward hood with tiny slits in it to see through, such that when fully dressed the wasn't a scrap of flesh exposed from the front.

"What is this all about?" Rustle asked.

"The hot thing, it is best if it does not grow too tall, and that it does not clog," Eddy said, fitting the claw over the mitten. "So I have to shape the top sometimes."

He glanced left, right, and up, then lowered his voice and whispered. "Also, I need this for getting into my mine. We go there next."

He swam up while Rustle watched. Curious as the fairy was, the heat from the water plume was already as much as he could handle. Perhaps sensing Rustle's curiosity, after Eddy had chipped away a bit of end of the spire, he caught the removed piece in his gloved hand and swam back with it.

"This is very special," he said, holding bit of stone, still so hot it made the water around it sizzle and shimmer. "These bits have very much of the same new things that are in the water. And they are *lucky*. If you bury one of these under a new home, that home will be a place of wealth and happiness. I will leave it here. Maybe you will take it with you. Not so much trash as the bad pearl, but still interesting. That is for later. Now we go to the mine. Inside we will have lunch, and then more work. There are *many* new things for you there. Things even mermaids never see. Come!"

He grabbed his bag and swam deeper through rift. Rustle buzzed along as best he could, but a mixture of his own fatigue and Eddy's enthusiasm caused him to fall behind. He wasn't terribly concerned about it. In all of the time they had been in the rift, nothing particularly large and frightening had reared its head. A few of the more grotesque denizens of the deep he'd seen could probably make a meal of Rustle if they tried, but they were all far too slow to catch him even at his diminished speed. And with the glow of his fins and spines, Eddy was simple enough to spot at a distance. So, Rustle moved at his own pace and gazed at his surroundings.

Beyond the grounds of Eddy's 'farm,' the rift was a much wilder and more chaotic place. A few threads of the same feathery seaweed grew here or there, but they were joined by prickly or spongy growths of various types. Other hot water spires jutted up, each with their own bloom of life around them. Through time and practice, Rustle found his connection with the water *very* slowly developing… though sometimes he could swear he felt a hint of the crisp, lively energy of wind and air even here in the water. He stopped and touched his fingers to the stone. It wasn't possible, of course. How could there be anything more than a little trapped pocket of air like the one near the shore? And even something *that* large didn't seem likely. Still, knowing that didn't change the fact that he could feel the shadow of a whisper of a breeze somewhere beneath him. So strange…

"Come!" Eddy called. "Nearly there!"

Rustle set the consideration aside and fluttered along after the merman until he reached what was easily the least inviting patch of sea floor he'd yet encountered. A section of the rift wall had eroded away somewhat, and in the inky blackness within the scoured-out tunnel, scalding hot water and cloudy silt swirled and churned. The more jagged and horrid-looking growths and creatures he'd spotted along the way seemed utterly enamored by the opening, gathering around its perimeter and giving it the look of a snarling mouth ringed with teeth.

"I found this one day, looking for good stones," Eddy called, the rush of water making it difficult to hear him. "Most times the hot water comes up through the stone. I see this here, with the water *in* the stone, and I think, maybe there is more tunnel behind. And there *is*. So much good things behind it. And because it is so hard to get to, no one else ever comes. No one even knows it is there."

"You have to swim through that?" Rustle called.

"Yes! But I have these clothes. If I am fast, it does not hurt at all."

"What about me?"

"I have this bag!"

"Eddy, I don't like being—"

"It will be fast!" Eddy assured him.

Before he could object further, the merman snatched him and tossed him into the bag. Eddy launched forward, pinning Rustle to the bottom of the satchel amid the glass jar of sweets, a few eels, assorted shells, and other loose ends. The bag shook and a few errant spritzes of hot water made it past the flap, but it was over after a few seconds and a mitten-clad hand reached in to free him.

"See! Quick! … Did I do wrong?" Eddy said.

Rustle's eyes, fists, and teeth were clenched tight.

"Eddy, how many times do I have to *tell* you? Fairies don't like to be shut away in tight spaces! It is bad *enough* I'm in the sea, away from the wind and sky, but then you throw me in a *bag* and drag me into a cave without even waiting to see what I have to say about it?" Rustle raved, buzzing about.

"Calm! Be calm! Don't hit," Eddy said, flinching when Rustle buzzed close. "There is room here. Lots of room. I am sorry about the bag but there is lots of room, and many things for you to see!"

He tugged at his outfit and slid it free, tucking it into his bag. They were not far from where the billows of hot water gave way to the marginally cooler water of the cave. With the outfit shed, the glow of his spines and eyes, when combined with Rustle's glow, illuminated the walls adequately to reveal a remarkable amount of detail. And indeed, despite his lingering anger, once Rustle allowed himself to look upon the walls he was rendered speechless by what he saw. Scattered liberally about the walls were strange, organic shapes set into the stone. He recognized the curl of shells like those of the snails, clams, and other odd creatures Eddy had shown off farther up in the rift, but these weren't quite the same. They were larger and seemed to be made from the stone itself. Veins of glittery stone threaded among them, catching the light and making the walls seem to shimmer as he moved.

"What are they?" Rustle said.

"The shiny bit is silver and gold. The stone creatures? I do not know. There are more, other places in the mine. Some are things I have never seen beyond the walls of this place."

"Amazing…"

"You see? I show you things no one else sees. Very nice, yes? Now you!"

"Now me what?"

"We have lunch. You see all of this because of me. Now you tell me things I don't know."

He dug out the jar of sweets, then unfurled one of the eels and gingerly held it into the swirling, scalding water for a few moments.

Rustle took an offered sweet and nibbled at it as Eddy continued.

"Already I know that a fairy can glow, and that a fairy is afraid of small places even though a fairy is small. And they punch harder than a little thing should be able to punch and have bad tempers. These things I did not know. What are more things?"

"Um…" Rustle began, rubbing the back of his neck. "It is hard to say. When you're surrounded by something all your life, it's hard to know it's special. And if you don't know *anything* about me, then where do I start?"

Eddy pulled the eel from the hot water and messily crunched into it. Rustle grimaced and looked away.

"Wherever you want, Rustle. It is all new to me!" Eddy said, munching happily. "Maybe we look at the book, and you teach me better magic? I bet even Mira doesn't learn *fairy*-style magic."

"I think that may be a good idea. If I am breathing water because of a spell you cast, I would like to know that you could cast it again if you need to."

"That one I can cast very much. But I want to know the others."

He pulled the book from his bag and spread it out on the flattest bit of cave floor he could find. Rustle looked over the pages briefly, but there wasn't much reason for it. Though the book had the subtle but undeniable aura of a thing of mystic power, the looping shapes spiraling across the page may as well have been random smudges for all he knew.

"You know… I can't read this. Fairies *speak*. We tell each other things. The marks we leave are simple. Circles of stones and leaves. We don't have spell books. I cannot read this."

Eddy nodded. "This I was afraid of. But still. You say fairies are good with magic, and you are good with it even without spell books. I am *bad* with magic, but even *I* can do magic *with* the spell book. So, a fairy that can use a spell book would be *very* good with magic, and that would help me to be better!"

Rustle flitted down and stood atop the page, eying the complex shapes. "I suppose. But that would mean I'd have to learn to read this. That will take time. More time than we have, probably. What if I try to help you in different ways?"

"Like how?"

"How do you cast the spell?"

He slapped a finger down on the page at the beginning of a spiral, nearly bumping Rustle from the book. "I say this word here, and all of the others after it, very much times. Over and over. And then something happens maybe."

"You don't focus?"

"Focus? No. Only read. I should focus?"

"You *must*. That's all magic is, at least for us. You reach out into the power of the world around you and… *ask* it to do as you wish. But to do it, you have to be aware of it, to feel it."

"You show me how to do this."

"You may as well be asking me how to show you to breathe."

"Yes! You show me how to breathe! I do not do this to air without magic, so that is a help."

"No, that's not what I… Fine. Close your eyes."

Eddy nodded happily and shut his eyes, though their glow was still eerily visible through the thin skin of his eyelids.

"Now just *feel* the air… er… the *water* around you. Feel how it moves, and—"

Eddy took another noisy bite of his eel and munched happily. Rustle glared at him, a pointless gesture since his eyes were still shut.

"If you are focusing, then you are *only* focusing. That's the point of it!" Rustle said.

"So, no eating at the same time?"

"No!"

"This will be less fun than I hoped."

He let the eel float beside him and dedicated himself wholly to the task.

"Just feel the way it moves around you. When you move your hand or fin, feel how it curls and swirls."

"I do this. I know how the water moves."

"I don't want you to *know* how it moves. I want you to *feel* it. To sense it with more than your skin. Sense it in your mind."

Eddy nodded again and shut his eyes tighter, as though exerting physical effort would somehow bring enlightenment more quickly. Rustle tried to open his mind as well. Water had a different nature to it than air, but they had much in common. The others back home said the truly talented water fairies found a way to use their innate knowledge and affinity for wind to connect to the water as well, and then they became much more powerful. They lived longer; they were able to venture farther from home and take greater risks. They were *legends* among their people. He himself had never gotten the knack. To him they had always been two different things. When he reached out with his mind, inviting the energy of the water to mix with his, inevitably he found his will and thoughts drawn toward the air, distracting him from the water.

He paused for a moment… Even now, it was the feeling of *air* that drew the focus of his mind… Air that was *quite* near.

He turned toward the darkened tunnel ahead. There was no mistaking it. Somewhere out there, tantalizingly beyond his fingertips, there was air. No. Not just air. *Wind.* It had the life and stir of a breeze along the surface, but the surface was so very far away. How could that be?

Without an explanation, Rustle buzzed through the water toward the source. He had to know. Being cut off from his home wind had been steadily bothering him more and more. The promise of a real breeze felt like he was being offered a cool drink of water after wasting in the desert for days. He needed to feel the air on his skin again.

He drifted deeper and deeper into the darkness. His own dim, natural glow lit the way. The veins of precious metal twisted away, following other branching paths. The tool marks left by years of mining became sparse and scattered. The tunnel walls had a sharper, rougher texture here. The stone caught his glow with a glassy sheen. Little open voids covered the entire tunnel around him, like a churning foamy sea had been instantly turned to stone, the bursting bubbles now forming razor sharp edges. But as he traveled, the feel of the air drew nearer.

He came to a stone that was unlike the others. It was the same dull gray as the entrance of the mine. The edges were too smooth and precise to have been caused by a break. This was crafted and moved. He could not conceive of the amount of effort it must have taken, as it reached from floor to ceiling, truly massive. From Rustle's diminutive point of view, moving it would have been like moving a mountain. He investigated all around it and found that it fit quite snuggly against the wall of the tunnel. There wasn't a crack or crevice large enough for him to squeeze though—not that he would have risked it with the harsh texture of the walls in this section of tunnel. But there was no question in his mind. Somewhere not far behind this stone lay a drifting, vibrant wind.

"Rustle! Little fairyman!" called Eddy's voice in the distance, flavored with concern.

"Here!" Rustle called.

The distant glow of Eddy's eyes and fins approached from the darkened tunnel behind him.

"Rustle! I tried to focus and when I stopped you were not there! You must tell me when you go!" Eddy said.

"What is this stone, Eddy?"

Eddy looked the stone up and down. "I do not know. A stone where it does not belong."

"That was my thinking. Have you ever seen it before?"

"Did you pass anything but black stone on the way here?"

"No."

"Then why would I have come this way. There is much good stuff in the mine, closer to the opening. I never needed to come so deep." He swam a little closer. "Someone *made* this stone…"

"I thought so, too."

"How did you find it?"

"I felt air behind it. More than just a few bubbles."

"No… Air so low? That does not happen. Never that I've seen."

"I am *certain* of it. It is a shame the stone is impossible to move. I wonder if we could see where the air is."

Eddy ran his fingers over the stone, then clapped away the silt.

"I will move it."

"But it is enormous."

He crossed his arms and threw his head back proudly. "I am a merman. We go down deep, and we are strong. It is what we do. Wait here, Rustle. I will get my things.

#

After a few moments, Eddy returned. His heart was soaring at all of the new and exciting things that had happened already. For years, his days had been largely the same. Collect some pearls, give them to Mira. Tend to the fronds, tend to the shellfish, tend to the mines, and back with the final tide to sleep and more of the same the next day. Even having someone to talk to, to *explain* the tedium to, had brightened his day enormously. And now, right here within his own mine, there was something *new*. It was wonderful. It was a sign that seeking someone from the surface was the right thing to do.

He found his way to where Rustle was waiting beside the stone.

"Move aside, Rustle," Eddy said, setting down the things he had fetched.

In addition to his bag, his outfit, and his claw, he'd brought some of the tools he usually left here in the mine. Right now, the one that made the most sense was his pick-rod. He pulled on his mittens and took the rod in hand.

"What's that?"

"This is my pick!"

"It looks a bit crude."

Eddy gripped it with both hands and looked rather defensive. It *was* crude, little more than a slightly crooked length of metal with a blunt, hammered end. More than anything else, it looked like a spear of all metal construction that had been horribly dulled, or perhaps never properly sharpened.

"It is a fine pick. Things of metal, bigger than bits of jewelry, are very hard to get for merfolk. The merfolk who work metal must be near the Glowing Pools, or else they must trade with those from above. Surface people do not make many tools that are good for the water. This is a *fine* pick. It belonged to my father. You will see how fine. Move away."

Rustle helpfully flitted to the far side of the tunnel. Eddy swam back a fair distance, gripped the rod tightly, then pumped his tail madly. In no time at all he was cutting through the water at an incredible pace. He reached the stone and hurled the pick with all of his considerable might. With his strength and speed combined, it penetrated the rock easily, wedging firmly between the black of the tunnel and the gray of the unexplained blockage.

Eddy looped back and grasped the pick handle, but it didn't budge. He smirked and adjusted his mitts, then held firm and started to work his tail. The current of the powerful strokes kicked up bits of stone and silt that hadn't been

26

disturbed in ages. The water turned murky. Rustle darted farther and farther away to spare himself the rushing water and stinging fragments of sharp stone. Then, with a long, slow grind, the stone started to move. It barely budged before coming to a stop, but that was enough. The merman wedged one mitt through the gap he'd created and held firm to the wall, then grasped the stone and heaved. Thus anchored, and therefore able to depend upon his raw strength rather than the thrust of his tail, he started to make real progress. The gray stone slid, rolled, and finally tipped forward, sending up a final, monumental rush of stone and silt.

He shielded his eyes as the *whoosh* of water swept his long hair back. When the dust cleared, he blinked the silky, fine silt from his eyes.

Rustle darted back to join him. There was a fresh branch of tunnel, nearly as large as the one that had led this far. But unlike the rest of the tunnel, in this portion the walls had been smoothed, the only roughness coming not from viciously sharp, ancient voids but instead more of the crusty green growth. And ahead, just visible at the edge of their glow, the tunnel curved upward. They swam along, following the curve of the tunnel up and down, left and right. The smoothed portion abruptly stopped, with a few very-clear merfolk words etched into the stone.

Beware. Danger.

"What does it say?" Rustle asked.

"Just telling us there is more ahead to watch for," Eddy replied.

It wasn't *so* far from the truth.

They continued forward, where the walls returned to their razor-sharp texture. The crusty green growth tapered off sharply, and the water had an oddly stale feel to it. Eventually, at the peak of a final upward slope in the tunnel, they could just barely make out the silvery, churning refraction of the water's surface.

Both fairy and merman wordlessly approached the surface. They blinked at each other, then at the surface again. Eddy was the first to brave it. He stuck his head up, but once he left the water, the glow of his eyes faded, leaving him staring into pitch blackness. He squinted his eyes as a warm, constant wind whistled against him.

Rustle darted up out of the water, then flopped down upon the smoothed stone near the surface. The gentle lapping of water over untold centuries had smoothed it sufficiently that the fairy didn't injure himself, but he seemed unable to lift his own weight with his wings. Rustle coughed and gagged. Eddy spat and coughed until his lungs were clear, then croaked the words of the water-for-air spell. The fairy shook his head and staggered to his feet.

"Until you learn your own water-for-air, you have to tell me when you want to leave," Eddy said.

The fairy spat a mouthful of water, then flicked the sea from his wings and buzzed into the air.

"You could have *warned* me."

"That is what I *said* to you."

Rustle glared at Eddy for a moment, then turned and let himself drift on the wind, barely fluttering his wings.

"It is so *wonderful* to have the wind about me again!" He flitted in a loop. "I feel light as a feather again. But this wind... it's so *different*. It's nothing like the wind of home. Like they haven't touched and mixed in *years*. Perhaps they've never touched at all."

They each strained their eyes, but their light didn't penetrate more than a few feet from the small pool at the mouth of the tunnel. It felt like they were a little island of reality at the edge of an endless void of oblivion.

"What is this place?" Rustle said.

Eddy grinned wide. "I will tell you, Rustle the fairyman. This... is *adventure.*"

# Chapter 4

"An adventure, Rustle! Finally, an adventure! Wind and air, down in the sea. I've never heard such a thing! And I know you haven't. Adventure!" Eddy crowed.

"I'm not so sure…" Rustle said.

"You wanted something new, a new story to tell. This is as new as there *is.*"

"But you can't follow. I would have to go alone."

The merman scratched his head. "That is true… If only I knew how to give myself some land swimmers."

He dug into his bag and set down the book. A bit of leafing through brought him to the page. Or rather, the *pages*, with the spell for conjuring legs.

"There is a lot of these words… This is very much spell…" he muttered. "Maybe there is more water further. I can crawl a little on land. Maybe if there is more water not far, I can crawl from here to there. Go look!"

"But we don't know what is out there."

"*I know,*" he said eagerly. "And we will learn! Together! You just have to go first is all."

"That's not how we are taught. Fairies don't go alone. They don't venture out to unknown places by themselves."

Eddy crossed his arms. "You'll never learn anything without being brave sometimes, Rustle. This is a time for *adventure.*"

Rustle grumbled. "Yes, Eddy. It is an adventure. You've said. But having an adventure isn't *everything.*"

"No, but it is something!"

"Why don't we head back to the mine. I'm sure you can show me something else, and I can tell you more things about the surface."

"Rustle! *This!* Don't you understand? The sea is a big place. There are a *lot* of merfolk. No one out there knows the name of Eddy. And why would they? What has ever Eddy done? Nothing to *remember.* You know who gets stories told? You know who people sing songs about? The ones who go places and do things that no one else would or could. And for the merfolk, that is the surface. When I was new, and my mother and father still looked after me, do you know what they told me each morning before I would go out into the sea? They would tell me one of the five big stories. They would tell me of Torrent, who was the first mermaid to walk on land. They would tell of Rina, who seduced an elven prince and trapped him in the sea until his people agreed to stop fishing in her people's shoals. They tell of Krista, who sought the great crystal along the southeastern shores. Even Calypso, who ventured to the churning cliffs and never returned.

"These are names that will never die, Rustle. They are names that lived more than the rest of us. I want that for me! I want to see the thing, to do the thing. I want to bring back the thing no one knew was missing, to fight the thing no one thought could be fought!"

"I *don't*. I just want to know about it, so I can tell my people about it."

"Then we are a team! You see the thing and tell me. Then I go to the thing and do the thing. And then you tell the people about the thing! But you go first."

Rustle glanced out into the darkness.

"I don't—"

Eddy clasped his hands together. "*Please*, Rustle! Just look. If there is nothing to see, nothing to do, then we go. No harm. And if there is something scary, you come back very fast and I will tear it to pieces. *Please!*"

The fairy chewed his lip. Exploring this place was a bit tantalizing, but finding exciting new things seemed a lot more desirable when it was simply an idea and not something he actually had to *do*.

"Fine. But just a look."

"Yay!" Eddy clapped. "You call back, tell me what you see!"

Rustle buzzed forward and upward. The wind was strange and constant. On the surface, it was always a bit chaotic, whorls turning this way and that. The best fairies could bend the wind to their whims. The worst could at least *read* it and know from where it had come and to where it might go. But here… it was different. The whisper in his ears and around his wings that he'd craved to be reunited with was certainly back, but it felt as though it was speaking a foreign language. It didn't feel like proper wind at all, but he couldn't put his finger on just what it *did* feel like.

As he buzzed deeper, the pocket of air proved to be *quite* large. It looped up, then down again, and opened into a yawning emptiness. After a few minutes of flitting about, he looked back and realized that he could no longer see Eddy. That he was alone in this place sent a jolt of concern through him, but to his great surprise, it was tempered by the feeling of anticipation. The merman's words must have sprouted the same seed of curiosity and wonder that had led him to meet Eddy in the first place. This *was* something entirely new. For each nook and cranny of the black stone walls, his were certainly the first fairy eyes to behold it.

It was thus with a mixture of relief and disappointment that, for nearly ten minutes, his buzzing and exploration turned up very few things of interest. The place was enormous, yes, but filled with little more than the foreign wind. Unlike in the rocky tunnel and practically everywhere else he'd seen on the sea floor, this place had no crusty glaze of tenacious life clinging to the stone. Indeed, it was gleaming and perfect, with the same perilously sharp texture. He *did* find more water. It covered nearly the entire bottom of the massive void in the sea floor. It was some distance below where they had entered, far farther than he suspected Eddy was willing or able to crawl across the land, particularly in light of the vicious sharpness of the stone. Other than that, there was nothing. He flew along the roof of the place, buzzing against the flow of the wind. No matter how far he flew, its strength never wavered. How could he have gone so far and not felt some inkling that he was nearing its source, or at least where it entered the current cave?

When his curiosity was no longer capable of overruling his survival instinct, he turned back, this time dropping low and following the surface of the water. Mindful of what had gotten him into this situation in the first place, he gave himself a bit more distance than when he'd investigated the half-seen form that had turned out to be Eddy. The relative friendliness of his captor was a profound and unlikely stroke of luck. He didn't trust such good fortune to come his way again any time soon.

The time in the darkness, lit by his own subtle glow, had allowed his eyes to adjust. Below him, the water rippled gently under the influence of the constant wind. It created little rolling waves, all propagating in the same direction. They caught and bent his glow into rings and loops of light. The water spread outward into the darkness in all directions, vanishing at the edge of his glow. He could almost imagine that it had no end. If not for the wind, and his innate skill at using it to navigate, it would have been impossible to be certain he was heading in the right direction.

He gazed down into the water. Unlike the higher levels of the sea, where it was a murky soup, here the water was eerily clear, offering fleeting glimpses of rock formations beneath the surface as they caught a glimmer of his light. Not far from the foot of the steep wall leading up to where Eddy patiently awaited his return, Rustle finally spotted something worth noting.

It was beneath the water, at the very limit of his vision—which thanks to the clarity of the water, meant it was a *long* way down. At this distance, he couldn't make out precisely what it was, but there seemed to be intricate designs of a pearly white material inset into an oddly smooth and rectangular slab of stone. He drifted closer to the surface of the water and strained his eyes, but the ripples kept him from getting any more detail. The smoldering spark of curiosity flared again, and he swept his eyes anxiously about. He'd yet to see anything that suggested there was any life in this cavern. Perhaps, if he was swift, he could risk a quick dip beneath the surface. Without Eddy's water-for-air spell, he would have to hold his breath, but he only needed a minute or two, not the *hours* he could hold his breath if he set his mind to it.

Rustle drifted down and risked a toe to the water. It was warm. Not scalding hot, but warmer than any natural body of water he'd felt before.

Before he could talk himself out of it he buzzed up his wings and plunked below the surface like a dart. He'd gotten a great deal more practice in the water in the past few hours than he'd had in the rest of his life, so making the switch from fluttering to swimming was swift and smooth. He shrugged off the light squeeze of additional pressure as he swam deeper and finally came to the unusual artifact.

It wasn't very large, a bit smaller than he was, and sat in a carefully smoothed recess in the floor of the cave. He ran his fingers across the stone and its mother of pearl inlay. It must have taken a profound amount of effort to create such a thing. The shapes were familiar, not so different from those on Eddy's book. More of the merfolk writing, he supposed. He stepped lightly on the smoothed stone and reached down. The slab was thin, and though it wasn't exactly *light*, he found that with a bit of effort he could lift it. He heaved it free and swam for the surface. Hopefully this would satisfy Eddy's thirst for adventure.

#

Eddy's eyes darted across the page of the spell book detailing the complex spell to conjure up a pair of legs. The incantation was an extremely long and complex one, and the procedure for casting it was liberally sprinkled with warnings against novices casting it. That much didn't concern him. The same warnings had been applied to the much simpler water-for-air spell, but *that* one was at least fit on a single page, and most mermaids knew it by heart. If he'd miscast it, he would only have needed to find the nearest mermaid to set him straight. He would have had to do it before he *drowned*, but fortunately that hadn't been necessary. This one would be reshaping his body, and he was a long way from anyone who could help him if he didn't do it correctly.

"Why do all of the interesting things happen where there isn't any water…" he moped, slamming the book shut and huffing out a sigh.

"Eddy?" called a tiny voice.

He instantly perked up. "Yes! I'm over here! What did you see for me, Rustle the Fairyman!"

The glow of his friend approached from the distance. Rustle was bobbing low to the floor of the tunnel, his flight clearly labored. When he arrived, Eddy held out a hand to receive the odd tablet he was carrying, but instead, Rustle landed on it and sat down on Eddy's palm.

"It is enormous," Rustle said. "It is like there is no end to this place. But in all of my searching, this is the only thing I found besides wind, water, and stone."

Eddy took the tablet with his other hand. Though quite clear and legible, the words inlaid on the tablet were of an incredibly ancient dialect. It was nearly unreadable, but after a bit of puzzling he worked out what it said.

*To all foolish enough to venture to this place. The doors above and below are sealed. The Bandits cannot leave. We cannot know what the years*

32

*ahead may hold. There may come a time when Bandits are second to a greater threat. For those times, we offer this key. May it be used only by the bold.*

Following this inscription, rendered with even greater care, was a brief sequence of words. He'd never seen them before, but they had the same shape and structure as the words covering the pages of the spell book.

"You're just staring, Eddy," he said. "What is it?"

Eddy looked to Rustle, then back to the tablet. "It is… I do not know for sure what it is. It is very old."

"Can you read it? That *is* writing, isn't it?"

"I can. Yes, I can read it."

"Well? What does it say?"

Eddy grappled with himself. On one hand, he was quite sure if he spoke those final words aloud, something would happen. On the other, he wasn't quite sure *what* would happen. That sounded wonderful to him, like the beginning of a hundred exciting stories from his youth. It also sounded like the sort of thing that Rustle would not like. … But then… Rustle didn't know any of that…

"It says Oorow Ho-own Willwoon."

Eddy's eyes darted about as he watched for some sign of the effects. He was a bit disappointed when nothing seemed to happen at all. When he looked back to Rustle, the little fairy had quite a different look on his face.

"Something is wrong," Rustle said, huddling down and looking over his shoulder.

From his posture and expression, one would think he was certain he would find a hungry creature breathing down his neck.

"What? Nothing happened?" Eddy said.

"You can't feel it? The wind! It's blowing the other way."

Eddy scratched his head. "I know currents change. Does wind not change?"

"Not like this… Wind flows and weaves. It eases this way and that. Even in a storm it doesn't move like this. First forward, now backward, nothing between. That isn't right."

"Odd…"

"Did the tablet say anything about wind?"

"Nothing about wind." He glanced down. "And it didn't say about water either! But look!"

The edge of their little pool was edging up along the slope.

"I don't like this… What if the water is rising down there, too."

"Then look please! Down there! *Please look, Rustle my friend!*"

"Fine! I'll go. But if there is anything bad happening, I want to leave this place, immediately."

"Yes! We go if anything is bad. But look now!"

Eddy tossed Rustle in the direction of what was now a *quite* audible rush of water below. The fairy gave him a hard look, then buzzed off into the distance. In no time at all, he was on his way back.

"What do you see?"

"I think the water is rising. Slowly, but it *is* rising. "

"This is *very good*! If it gets close enough, I can explore as well! We can explore *together*."

"Eddy, you said three words, and it reversed the wind and caused the cave to begin flooding. That is powerful magic." Rustle said firmly. "We should go. We don't know what else will happen."

Eddy crossed his arms. He tried to scrape together some sort of argument that might convince him to change his mind, but Rustle's steadfast expression made it clear he would not be budged.

"Yes. This cave will not go anywhere. If it floods, then tomorrow, or the next day, I can come and explore."

He gathered his things together.

"Thank you..." Rustle said, profound relief in his voice. "There is already *so* much for me to learn elsewhere."

"It is no problem, Rustle my friend. If we are friends, we cannot always do the things that *I* want to do. You are small and afraid. That is not bad. It is *good*. Keeps you safe."

"I am not... Well, I *am* small. But I'm not... I... I *am* afraid. ... But that's not a bad thing!"

Eddy furrowed his brow. "I said this. I *did* say this, didn't I? Is the spell working less now?"

"You *did* say that, but... It felt like..." He sighed. "I suppose sometimes seeing big brave things makes me think maybe it isn't always good to be small and... cautious."

"If you say so. Get ready for breathing water again."

He grabbed the fairy, murmured the spell again, and plunged down into the water. Once there, he released Rustle and swam along the darkened tunnel.

"It is best if we wait until tomorrow for adventure. Today there is more work to do. Almost we are out of time for lunch, and then there is mining."

They swam along, working their way back through the tunnel to the main mine. It was taking a bit more work to do so than he'd expected. There was a current now where there wasn't one before. That stood to reason. If the water was rising, it must have been coming from the tunnel. And quite quickly at that.

He worked his tail harder, but the current was getting stronger by the moment. They'd barely reached the midpoint of the tunnel they'd uncovered when it was all he could do just to keep from losing ground.

"What's happening?" Rustle called out, holding for dear life to Eddy's hair.

"I said it was good to be small and afraid." Eddy gritted his teeth, the water beginning to draw him backward. "This time, it was better than being big and brave, I think."

Bits of stone and silt were rushing along the tunnel toward them, striking Eddy's face and chest painfully. He worked his way toward the wall of the tunnel and tried to hold tight to it, but the jagged surface cut his fingers. He reached back and grasped his pick. A mighty thrust wedged it into the floor of the tunnel and provided an anchor point.

"What do we do?" Rustle said.

"Do not worry! We learn about how to handle too strong current when we are young."

"Then what do we do?"

"Get in shelter."

"But we can't do that!"

"Then you get up and away from anything solid that the current can hurt you against."

"But we're *surrounded* by that stuff."

"Then you find a thing to hold tight to. Like I do now!" He turned his head, offering an exhilarated smile to the fairy clinging to the end of his fluttering hair. "You see? Nothing to worry about. We know *all* about how to stay safe."

It was entirely possible Rustle did not hear this final assurance. The current had reduced Eddy's hearing to little more than a mass of current and turbulence. He shut his eyes and lowered his head, streamlining his shape as best he could to keep from being swept away and to help avoid being *too* badly scoured by bits of jagged stone.

Eddy had faced a strong current before. Being in the wrong place during a tide or being too near to a mudslide when it happens could cause the water to become dangerously churned up. And sometimes, where warm and cold water mixed, or two currents met, there could be a whirlpool. But all of those reached intensity like this only very briefly.

His hands were shaking, but he held firm until the pick itself suddenly shifted. He risked opening his eyes long enough to see the wall where he'd embedded the pick's head was beginning to crumble.

"Rustle!" he cried.

The fairy did not answer but the painful tug at a lock of his hair assured him where the fairy was. He released the failing pick with one hand and snatched Rustle, then held the terrified creature close to his chest.

"This will be bad, Rustle. If it is very bad, I am sorry. But I will try to make it worse for me than for you."

"What are you going to do?"

"I will tell you after. If there is an after for me."

#

Eddy's fingers tightened around Rustle. The fairy couldn't see what was going on, but a heartbeat after the merman had clutched him tight, he felt them both lurch into motion in the direction of the current. Eddy curled himself as tightly into a ball as he could, his thick tail folding up, his head curling down, his arms pulling in tight.

The pair thumped and bashed into the walls with punishing force but protected as he was in the center of ball Eddy had made of himself, Rustle was spared the worst of it. He could hear Eddy grunting and wheezing as he smashed and slid against the walls.

All at once, the bashing, pummeling journey changed to a tumbling, flailing arc, as the tunnel ejected them in a geyser. They struck the steep cliff twice on the way down, then splashed into the water below.

"Eddy?" Rustle said, dizzily recovering from the journey.

The merman didn't answer. His grip was still painfully firm around Rustle. That was a good sign.

"Eddy, are you awake? Are you hurt?"

"Ugh…" he groaned.

The grip loosened and Rustle flitted out to see what had become of him. All things considered, the merman had faired remarkably well. His entire body was checkered with scrapes and gouges, but none seemed particularly dire. His eyes were half-lidded and looked unfocused.

"Where are we?" he said, blinking and feeling a lump that had formed on his head.

"We came back out of the tunnel. We're down in the cave again."

"Do you see any rays?"

"Rays?"

"Big fish. Like the sail of a boat. Are there any here? Golden? Pulling a shell behind?"

Rustle glanced around. "No, I don't see anything."

"Any… black crabs?"

"No, there is nothing."

"Good…"

"Why? What would it mean if there were?"

"They say when we die, if we are good, a team of rays will bring us down to the heart of the sea. If we are bad, big black crabs will pull us to pieces and put our souls into oysters to become a black pearl. If they are not here, I am not dead. Or maybe the crabs and rays cannot find us here. One is the same as the other, I guess."

"We had better not die here. When fairies die, the seventh wind sweeps us up and brings us to the rose garden of eternity, and the wind *won't* reach me here," Rustle said.

"Funny how fairies and merfolk go different places. Maybe this is the first time a fairy and a mer went somewhere together."

"Right now, I just want to know how we're getting *away* from here."

Eddy nodded and swam up toward the surface, which was churning much more than Rustle remembered. They each peered through. Once again, the only light was their own, but they scarcely needed it to see that they wouldn't be going back the way they'd come. Water was pouring down the face of the cliff, and they could hear the intensity of the geyser that the entrance had become.

"This… this is not all bad," Eddy said.

"How is it not all bad, Eddy? We're trapped!"

"Only a little."

"A little!?"

"Yes. We are trapped in a *big* place. Not so bad. And the water is rising. When it gets to the pool, there won't be much more water to add to the cave. So, it will slow, and we can escape, probably."

"Probably?"

Eddy nodded with a smile. "Probably!"

"I don't like probably, Eddy. I like definitely."

He shrugged. "We don't have that. But we have probably, and that's almost as good. Much better than not at all."

"What are we supposed to do until then?"

Eddy turned and gazed, eyes twinkling, into the inky depths below. "Explore…"

# Chapter 5

Rustle flitted about, trying his best to bolster his own glow to see his surroundings. From the moment his new "friend" Eddy had grabbed him and dragged him into the water, he had been bobbing back and forth between terrified and excited at the flood of new experiences. Currently, he was mired firmly in "terrified." Being flushed through a rocky tunnel into a mysterious air-filled cave at the bottom of the sea had a way of darkening even the most adventurous creature's outlook.

"Rustle my friend! Here, I found the bag!" called Eddy, nothing short of unwavering enthusiasm in his voice.

The fairy moved as swiftly as he could toward the ghostly glow of the fins and eyes of his companion in this ongoing disaster. Rather than the very understandable feeling of impending doom and barely suppressed panic that was gripping his own mind, Eddy remained unfailingly upbeat. It didn't seem to matter in the slightest that he didn't know where he was, didn't know for certain if he would be able to escape, and was still bleeding from his unexpected trip through the tunnel. To look at his face, you'd think that he was sifting through the rubble along the cave floor expecting to find gifts.

Perhaps the most adventurous creature *could* keep the darkness at bay…

Eddy held up the bag. "The book is not broken. Still in the bag. And here, I found your sweets. Plenty of them. And my claw and pick. That is almost everything."

"*Almost* everything?" Rustle said.

"Most of the fronds I picked are gone. Just one left. And my eels are gone too."

"So, we don't have any food for you?"

He shrugged. "I had most of one. And many snails, remember? I am not hungry. It is fine."

"But we don't know how long we will be here. At the rate the water is rising, it might be a long time until you can swim back out."

"I am sure we will find *new* things to eat."

"How can you be sure?"

"We are in the sea. The sea provides."

"We *aren't* in the sea. We're *under* it."

Again, he shrugged. "Under the sea provides, too, probably."

"How do you *know?*"

"You worry too much, Rustle."

A distant sound, somewhere between the grind of stone and a rumbling growl, faintly reached their ears. They each looked to the source in the inky void.

"I think I worry the right amount, Eddy."

The merman didn't answer. He was too busy swimming *toward* the sound. Though Rustle didn't very much like the idea of investigating, he liked the idea of being left behind even *less.*

"Wait for me!" he called, darting forward and grabbing the end of the metal pick Eddy carried.

He climbed it like a tree, then scrambled up Eddy's arm and perched himself behind his fin-like ear.

"This is a bad idea," Rustle said.

"My best ideas are bad ideas," Eddy replied.

The fairy held tight and tried to get his bearings, but their combined glow didn't cut very far into the water, so he mostly saw little more than the floor of the cave as they swept along just above it.

"I hope your eyes are sharper than mine. I can't see where you are going at all."

"We are going forward. That is enough for me to know it is the right direction."

The fairy looked at the side of his friend's face. His manic expression of excitement and exploration was completely unhindered by the scattered scrapes and gashes he'd received as they were washed into this place. All things considered, though, he didn't look very much the worse for wear.

"You can take quite a beating, can't you," Rustle said.

"Oh, yes. Mira tells me, if there is one thing I do good, it is bounce." He glanced aside, trying to look at the fairy who was a bit too close to his head for him to see much more than a glimpse of. "When I was young, always I was bouncing. Bouncing off walls. Bouncing off rocks. Bouncing off other merfolk. But what I do *most* is bounce *back.*"

"It sounds like you should have spent more time watching where you were going."

"Mira said this too!" he said. "I hope someday I can think of a way so you can meet Mira without her getting mad at me. She gets mad at me very much, though, so it will be hard not to make her mad. But you are very like her, Rustle. You *think* more than you *do,* which she does too. Me? I think *after* I do. Mira, she says that's backward. She says that's why I have so many scars."

He held up his arm and eyed the trickle of blood and the assorted scrapes and cuts. For the first time, his smile faltered.

"I will have many new ones after this. Mira will worry. She will want to know why."

"Only if we get out of this alive."

He grinned again. "That is right, Rustle! If she sees me and I have many new scars, I will just remind her that at least if she *sees* me then the scars did not *kill* me. That is reason to be happy, not angry."

"I don't think that will work."

He shook his head and chuckled, almost dislodging Rustle. "No, it will not. But maybe that is good too! If she is angry that I did a thing and got scars from it, I may as well let her meet you, too. She can only get *so* angry, right?"

"I suppose."

"Then this is all good. Just so long as we get out of it alive. And we don't take too long. If we take long, she will be worried. I would rather her be angry than worried."

"If I had a brother like you, I suppose I would be worried an awful lot, too."

"Maybe, but probably you would worry as much as her only if you had *parents* like mine also."

"Did your parents bounce a lot, too?"

"No. Not as good as me. They both died. Left with the tide, but the tide didn't bring them back."

"Oh… I'm sorry. What happened?"

"Mother went off to do trade in Deep Swell. A very long way away. She did not make it there. No telling what did it. Father was looking along the bottom, not far from where the farm is. Sometimes deeper down there are better things, so he was always looking deeper down. One time, when he was deep, the ground shook and things fell. He didn't come back."

"That's terrible."

"It was terrible. But the *was* part is the important part. Father taught me that when I was very small. Lots of things people think keep being terrible, but they only keep being terrible if you let them. Let terrible things be *was* and not so much be *are*. Good things should be are. And will. Bad things should be was. Very smart merman, my father. A good way with words."

"It lost something in the translation, but I think I understand."

#

Time passed and Eddy continued swimming, thrilling at the sheer *size* of the place he'd discovered. It was a little disappointing that so far all they'd really found was a tablet with some magic words on it and a lot of air where it didn't belong, but any moment that could change. He'd covered an astounding amount of distance, swimming a swift and steady pace to avoid tiring too quickly. It was difficult to be certain, as he wasn't sure how loud it was to begin with, but the source of the odd sound that had drawn them this way couldn't be *much* farther along.

"Wait," Rustle said from his place behind Eddy's ear. "Do you feel that?"

"No. Is it more air where there shouldn't be air? Because there's still a lot of that, I can see it."

"No… No, it's different than that. I don't know how to explain it. Do you know how I told you it was important to focus when you use magic?"

"Yes. And then you wandered off when I was trying. And found this place."

"I didn't… That's not… Listen, what I'm saying is I can feel that over in that direction," Rustle said, pointing.

"There is someone focusing over there?"

"No. There is just… There is *focus* there. It is like the *world* is focusing there."

Eddy scratched his head. "That does not make very much sense, what you are saying, but it is better than chasing a sound I don't know is still there. You lead the way!"

He snatched the fairy from behind his ear and held him where he could see him, then swam dutifully off in the direction Rustle pointed. Nothing felt different, but there was no denying Rustle's reaction. The fear and caution that he'd been showing thus far was replaced by raw determination to find the source of whatever it was he felt. They wove down and up, navigating side tunnels.

"This is getting very mixed up," Eddy said, gliding deftly through narrowing gaps in the rock. "If we go much deeper, it might be smart if we leave marks to find our way back."

"Please, it's just a little farther," Rustle said. "There! You can see it!"

Eddy squinted his eyes. It was subtle—he wondered how Rustle could have noticed it at all, in fact—but there *was* something odd about the next curve in the tunnel. The glossy black of the volcanic rock had the faintest glimmer of its own light, a warm yellow gleam different from the blue of Rustle and the teal of his own light. He swam onward and, upon turning the corner, swam headlong into a stout metal grating with a clang.

"Ouch," he muttered, releasing Rustle to rub his head. "I hit a place where I already bounced once."

He blinked away a bit of blurred vision and looked over the grate he'd hit. It was made of metal, and unlike his pick, it was of *very* fine make. There was none of the telltale roughness of a crudely fashioned tool. There was a layer of greenish coating, probably the result of centuries of enduring the elements, yet a smear of his finger caused it to flake away to reveal a gleaming amber metal beneath. It was almost mirror-smooth. The grating was hinged at one side and had a stout lock on the other. The individual bars of the gate formed a grid so tight he could barely fit two fingers through its openings.

"This is from the Glowing Pools… No one else could have made something that would stand the sea for so long, and so well. But the Glowing Pools are *very* far away. I wonder how it got here."

"Forget the *gate,*" Rustle said, buzzing about before the grating. "Look what's on the other side!"

Eddy leaned against the grating aligned his eye with one of the holes. Rustle stuck his whole head through another.

The grating seemed to have been installed to block off a large room. And *room* was certainly the word for it. Whereas elsewhere they had traveled through tunnels and caverns with jagged natural walls, this place was shaped by hammer and chisel. The walls formed a precise dome inlaid with intricate symbols and small, faintly glowing yellow gems. The room extended off to the left, with most of it hidden from view from this vantage.

"The whole *room* is like… one big… *cage* for magic," Rustle said, his voice hushed. "Look, see the gems? My grandmother talked about them. She said *wizards* use them."

Eddy rattled the grating. The years hadn't weakened it much, as the lump on his head could attest. He poked at the lock, probing it with his finger. It was fairly solid as well, and quite large, another indication of its age.

"I think this is a problem. A very heavy gate and a very heavy lock. But there is room for you to squeeze through. You can go see. Maybe while you look I can see if I can get this open."

"I don't want to go in without you."

He rattled the gate. "Then you will have to wait until I can break this."

Eddy raised his pick and jammed it into the gap in the grate. He threw his weight against it, then propped his tail against the wall to shove harder. The metal of both pick and grate groaned, but neither did more than flex a bit.

"Come on! You are strong!" Rustle said.

The merman huffed a bit and pushed again.

"Why… *ugh*… are you so excited about… *urgh*… the glowing rocks and the fancy roof?" Eddy asked as he struggled against his pick. "Many things glow. You and I both glow. And there are places in Barnacle with a fancy roof."

"It's *magic,* Eddy."

"So? Already you know about magic. More than *me*. I can see why *I* would be excited about the magic, but why you?"

"Magic is *so* important to fairies, Eddy. You talk about being able to go up to the surface, and how the higher and more often a merman can go in the sea the more choices he has. For us, magic is *so much* more than that. Even the weakest fairy has *some* magic. But the more we know… the more we *are*. Fairies with better magic are stronger. They are better. They live practically forever. At least compared to weak fairies. I'm young. Still learning. But even

*I* know that this place… this place with such strong magic… This is the sort of place *made* for making people stronger."

"Really…" Eddy said, peering through the grating again. "Being stronger at magic is something I want, too. You help me. Now I want to get in there very much, and this pushing is too slow."

"How can I help?"

Eddy tapped the lock. "This here. I have seen the inside of a lock before. There are little parts. Little moving parts. They need a key for all of them to move at once, but when they do, this part here—the big bar that goes from the gate to the… outside of the gate. That will move."

The keyhole was just big enough for him to reach his finger into, so he stuck a clawed fingertip inside and rattled it about. "I can't get it. But you? You could almost fit in there. Take a look. Try to get the things lined up."

Rustle buzzed down and stuck his head in the hole.

"Wow. It's complicated in here," he muttered.

The fairy worked his arms into the keyhole, fluttering his wings and kicking his legs to wriggle himself as deep into the workings as he could manage. He grunted and a quiet squeak sounded from within the mechanism, followed by small waft of green dust rushing out the keyhole around him.

"Yuck!" he coughed. "There's all sort of… *stuff* in here."

"Can you move the things?"

"A little."

"Good. There should be little bits that don't line up now, but do line up when you move them."

"I see them. Three of them." More squeaks and creaks sounded. "I can't get them to line up. No matter how much I move one it never lines up with the other two."

"All of them need to move at the same time, by different amounts."

"That's *hard*."

"It is supposed to be hard. This is a thing for keeping people out of places."

"Let me… just…"

Rustle struggled and grunted, kicking his legs as little squeaks and creaks emanated from the mechanism.

"There! They're lined up… Did anything happen?"

"No."

"What else needs to happen?"

He rubbed his chin. "That should be… *Oh!* Of course."

Eddy grabbed Rustle's legs and gave them a twist. Rustle made sounds of startled complaint, but as his body pivoted in the lock, the brace slid aside.

"It is good. You are done," Eddy said.

Rustle wriggled back out of the lock and darted up to Eddy's face. "You *always do things like that!* Warn me if you're going to grab me!"

Eddy flinched and braced for a bop on the nose. "But you did good, see?"

He leaned on the gate and, after grinding away some of the grime clogging the hinges, it creaked open.

"Oh! I did! *I* did that! Er… part of it. *We* did that! Come on! Come on!" Rustle proclaimed, buzzing forward.

Eddy smiled as he grabbed his pick and swam inside. "You and me, Rustle. We're a good team. You can feel things and go places I can't. I can move things and do things *you* can't. This will be a good story, the one about us."

"Just so long as we are careful. It is only a good story if we live long enough to *tell* it."

"We survived rushing water, we cast spells, and found new things. We picked locks and found whatever this magic place is. What could stop us now?"

"That's one thing I'd rather *not* find out," Rustle said.

The pair entered the chamber and gazed about. Though only a few glowing gems were visible from the entryway, a constellation of them revealed itself as they crept deeper. The entire domed ceiling was spangled with gems of various sizes, each smoldering with a weak but clear yellow glow. They were arranged along lines of carvings, separating the roof into irregular angular fields. The carvings along the lines weren't writing. At least, not any sort of writing Eddy had ever seen. They didn't even seem to have the complex shapes of some of the older runes one saw on ancient artwork and texts. As far as he could tell, they were just a fancy design. Between them, though, in the larger stretches of roof, engravings of recognizable forms created a sort of tableau with sweeping, curving designs as a background.

"Look at them…" Eddy said. "The pictures here. That's a mermaid. And these are mermen. That's a shark, and those are whales. This is a story. … I don't *know* this story. … But I think it starts here…"

He reached toward the largest of the gems. Rustle flitted up and threw his weight against Eddy's palm, pushing it back.

"Don't!"

"What?"

"There is so much magic here, you need to be *very* careful. Who knows what could happen?"

"Well… If we make it happen, *we'll* know what will happen, right? Besides, why come in here if not to make something happen?"

"We *will*. We *will* make something happen. Just… keep your hands to yourself for a moment. Let me look things over before we do."

Eddy nodded. For now, there was plenty to see, even if Rustle didn't want him to *do* anything. He made a game of trying to identify the various carvings. Seven mermaids and seven mermen, with a many-armed mermaid between them. That was a goddess from the old days: Tria. A long stretch of curling shapes extended out before her. They seemed too random to be a pattern, but too precise to be the natural texture of the rock.

"Rustle, do you know what these shapes are, here?"

Rustle darted up and investigated.

"They look like flames."

"Flames? Is *that* what flames look like?" Eddy said.

"You don't know what *flames* look like?"

He shrugged. "Things don't burn down here. How *would* I know? … And why would there be a carving of Tria with *fire* in front of her."

"I don't know… Who is Tria?"

"This here is Tria, with her fourteen attendants. Always she has that many, and six arms. She is the maker goddess."

"The maker goddess?"

"Yes. Not the maker of the world. That is Mer. Tria is the maker of… things you have to make. Machines. Buildings." He pointed to an engraving of a chain. "Chains. Probably Tria made this chain in this story."

"A goddess," Rustle mused. "And there's a dish or something there in the middle of the room. Great-great-grandmother said she knew of a place where there was much magic, pictures of gods and goddesses, and a dish. She called it a… an *altar?* Does that sound right?"

Eddy nodded. "Sure. There are altars. But this wouldn't be that. Not for Tria, anyway," Eddy said.

"How do you know?"

The merman followed the engraving of the chain up along the ceiling as he replied.

"Altars are for offerings. And Tria doesn't *need* offerings. Not like you would make at an altar. For Tria you make little dolls. Altars are for Tren. And there is no Tren on these walls."

"What would Tren look like?"

"Like a merman, but with a tail like a… small, soft shell, tasty… a *lobster*, not a fish. He is the god of… It is hard thinking of the words now. I think it is time for the talking spell again. He is the god of *bad.* "

Eddy found where the engraving of the chain ended. It was a shackle of sorts, carved around a long, curving shape. When he followed *that* shape, he found it crisscrossing with others. It almost seemed as though he was too close to see all of whatever it was the engraving was supposed to be. He drifted backward, looking about. The weaving, curling shapes converged, and he realized that what he'd at first thought was a simple background to the rest of the carving was in fact all part of a single, *massive,* tentacled creature.

Something about the form, now that he could see it for what it was, chilled Eddy to the bone. It was… wrong. He had seen many tentacled creatures. The octopus, the squid. This was not one of them. There were pieces that were not so different from merfolk. The tentacles emerged from where a merman's tail would be, and from the torso, thin arms with spindly fingers. There were four arms, though, each with three fingers. The head was more like a gar or an eel, but carved with the angular lines of a crustacean's armor. It had three eyes. One on either side of its head, and a third in the center of the forehead. It was a thing comprised of mismatched parts, familiar shapes combined into something wholly other. Something that simply should not be.

He was still coming to terms with the primal dread that crept in around the edge of his mind at the sight of the creature when he realized he was hearing an odd trilling noise from beside him. He turned to Rustle and found that the little fairy was quite obviously speaking—and becoming visibly agitated at that—but Eddy could no longer understand him. The poorly cast speaking spell had worn off entirely.

Eddy fetched the spell book from his bag. The cover was lightly tattered from the tumble he'd taken when he'd been washed down here, but the pages were all intact. He found the spell and carefully pronounced its individual words for the first of what he assumed would be at least half a dozen readings. No spell but water-for-air seemed to take hold in a single reading. Nevertheless, he had no sooner had he spoken the final syllable when the trilling resolved into the clear, distinct voice he'd come to associate with his new friend.

"Goodness…" Rustle breathed, eyes wide and fingers twiddling in the water around him. "Do you *feel* that?"

"What is wrong?" Eddy asked.

"Nothing is *wrong*. Something is so, *so* right. The spell… it swept over me like a *wave*. I can still feel the power of it crackling around me. And all without you *focusing*."

"Oh, yes, yes. The focusing. That is a thing I was supposed to do." He tipped his head. "I think maybe still I said some words of the spell wrong. The words I am saying do not feel as smooth as the words I am thinking."

"Never mind that," Rustle said. "Is there another spell? See if you can do more. I've been trying my magic, but it doesn't feel much stronger here. I think maybe this is *specifically* for focusing merfolk magic."

"Maybe? Maybe! Let me see. Something short."

Eddy flipped eagerly through the book. Much of the magic was very complex, but one page was remarkably sparse.

"What is that one?" Rustle said.

"Oh, that is not an interesting one."

"What is it? What is it?"

"This makes cold, hard water."

"Ice?"

"Yes."

"Try it! It would be useful for me to know ice magic. My grandfather was the last one to cast ice magic at our pond."

"If you want."

Eddy turned his eyes to the page.

"Don't forget to focus. Pay attention to the words, gather your mind."

"Yes. Yes. You also pay attention. Maybe then you can cast the spell after."

"Excellent idea!"

Eddy nodded and once again looked to the page. He still wasn't entirely certain how one focused one's mind on something as basic as speaking a few words, but he did his best to follow Rustle's directions. He set the book down, held his palms forward to the center of the room, and spoke the words with slow and deliberate care. As he approached the end of the spell, he felt a peculiar and intense sensation he'd never noticed before. His mind and body tingled, like his soul was humming with power, and with the final word, a lance of white energy spiraled forth. As the light faded, the water it rushed through revealed itself as a crackling, complex looping shape of solid ice.

"I cast the spell! I did the thing!" Eddy crowed, grabbing the helical bit of ice. "So cold! Never have I done magic like that so well."

"Now me, now me!" Rustle said. "Quick, before I forget the words!"

Eddy nodded enthusiastically and swam around behind Rustle, crunching idly at the ice like a stick of candy. As difficult as it was for Eddy to understand *how* to focus, it was abundantly clear that Rustle was quite good at it. The same humming, tingling sensation of growing power began with the first few syllables of Rustle's casting, seeming to radiate out from him. He was barely halfway through the spell when the temperature of the water started to drop sharply. Little crystals formed, wafting and swirling in complex patterns as he neared the end of the spell. Then, with the final word, a blinding flash…

#

Rustle blinked and shook his head, little flakes of ice drifting from his hair. The light from the spell was quite intense, filling his vision with blobs of purple and blue that very slowly receded. When they did he was awestruck by what he saw. Unlike the neat coil of ice that Eddy had managed, great columns of ice had been conjured in a radiating pattern, like a star burst of glass-clear ice crystal. Where the ice met the walls, it formed great, blue-green mounds of frozen seawater. Some of the thinner tendrils cracked free and drifted up to the ceiling. Most remained braced against the walls and hung in the water like a wondrous sculpture of some sort.

"Wow…" he said, voice hushed and eyes wide. "I know it's just this chamber, the way it's bottled up the magic, but it is astounding to feel such power all the same. You see, Eddy? That is the sort of thing that can happen if you properly prepare your mind before casting. Reason enough to learn to focus, wouldn't you say? … Eddy?"

The fairy turned to find, much to his dismay, that the scattered nature of the spell had not been limited to in front of him. Despite Eddy having the foresight to take cover behind the fairy, a bolt of ice had struck him directly. His lean body was encased almost entirely in the water-clear ice. Only his head and one of his hands had escaped being entombed it the frigid coating. His serrated teeth were tightly clenched, and one eye was twitching a bit.

"Y-y-you are v-v-very good at m-magic, Rustle. L-less good at aim…"

# Chapter 6

Rustle flitted and darted about the room, his voice raised in a squealing cacophony as he looped around irregular columns of ice.

"What do I do! I killed him! I killed my friend and I'm trapped in a strange chamber in a strange tunnel in a strange cave in a strange mine in a strange rift at the bottom of the sea! I'm going to die here. Why did I do this! I should have known better than to try anything like this! I should have stayed near my pond. That's what the males are *supposed* to do!"

"C-calm d-down!" Eddy said. "This isn't b-bad."

"It *is* bad. You're frozen! You're going to die! Only the best water fairies can survive freezing."

"It is different for us. Th-the ocean gets cold. W-we have to not freeze, so we d-don't."

"So, you'll be fine?"

Eddy blinked again, slowly. "W-what?"

"I said you'll be fine? Tell me you'll be fine!"

"I'll b-be fine. I just… Can't breathe much… So, I'll s-sleep…"

"Until when!?"

The merman blinked again, even more slowly. "Until the ice is g-gone…"

"But that could take forever! The water is warm but it's a *lot* of ice! And the bag with the food is frozen in there with you! Eddy? *Eddy!*"

The merman's eyes fluttered shut as he drifted into a trembling doze. Rustle flitted up to his face and grabbed him by the ear.

"Don't fall asleep! You're strong! Break the ice!"

Eddy didn't stir, too far into the slumber now.

For a moment, Rustle let the panic have complete control. He buzzed in tight circles, tugged at Eddy's hair and slapped his face. He flipped back and forth between desperately trying to wake his friend and simply darting about like a lunatic.

"No! No. This helps no one," Rustle said, placing his hand on his chest to try to steady a heart that was buzzing faster than his wings. "You caused this, you can fix it."

He looked about. Encased in the mound of ice along with Eddy was *most* of their equipment. The pick—not that he could lift it—was sticking out the top of the mound a bit behind Eddy's head. The bag was practically it its core. On the floor of the chamber, however, his 'claw' had been jostled free at some point. It had a crust of ice, as almost everything in the chamber did at the moment, but the warm water had already fractured it. Rustle darted down and tugged at the ice, hauling free big flakes of it until the sharp gauntlet Eddy used for scraping and shaping rocks was free.

Rustle gave the tool an experimental tug, grabbing hold of one of the rubbery hide straps that held it together. He found that by working his wings and his legs for all they were worth, he could lift it. He placed his tiny feet on the floor of the cave, crouched down and hefted the glove over his head. Without a hand inside it, the thing flopped down over him. In fact, no amount of shifting or juggling could maneuver the glove into a configuration that didn't either block his vision, foul the motion of his wings, or leave the glove dangling uselessly below him.

His frustrated search for better handholds did, however, dislodge one of the pointed teeth that extended from one of the fingers.

"No! Now I broke it! I'm spoiling everything!" he muttered, throwing the tooth aside. "I was the *careful* one. I was the one doing everything right, everything the cautious way, just like the elders teach, and look at the mess I've made! Think… What *else* do the elders teach? A fairy is small, but a grove of fairies is big. A job is big, but the pieces of the job are small. With enough fairies, a job is only as big as its smallest piece, and any fairy can handle the smallest piece of a job."

He huffed and kicked one of the glove's straps.

"All of our lessons are only good if there are *lots* of us."

Rustle turned aside and eyed the bit of glove he'd thrown. It was lodged in the bottom of the mound of ice that held his friend. He buzzed over to it and levered it back and forth. The motion not only dislodged the tool, it caused a chip of ice to float free. He hefted the single tooth and looked at the veritable mountain of ice.

"The job is still made of small parts…" he mused. "Parts small enough for one fairy."

He tugged at the straps that had formerly held the tooth to the glove and, with a bit of effort, managed to tie them into a loop he could grip with his hand. The single tooth was half as tall as he was, but quite light. Holding it by the strap, it looked as though he were equipped with a vicious and barbaric-looking shield. He flitted back, angled its angled tip, and darted forward to drive the tip into the ice. With all of his weight behind it, it bit considerably deeper, and a few shoves and yanks fractured a larger chunk of ice free.

"I don't have a lot of fairies once…" he said, tightening the loop and buzzing back for another blow. "But I've got the same fairy lots of times. I guess today I'll learn if that's just as good."

#

50

The Adventures of Rustle and Eddy

Quite far to the southwest, Mira was patiently waiting just below the surface. It was tempting to give up and leave, as she'd lingered for several hours without so much as a glimpse of a boat, but she knew better than to do that. Reliable, consistent, and *fair* contacts among the surface people were vanishingly rare these days, and having developed a mutually beneficial trade relationship with a Tresson woman, she wasn't about to risk it by letting her impatience get the better of her.

She peeked her head above the waves and shook the water from her hair, scanning the horizon and squinting at the brightness of the sunset. A smile lit up her face as she saw the distinctive patchwork sail of her trade partner. She ducked beneath the waves again, worked her tail, and breeched, sending a sparkling cascade of water into the air to catch the attention of the enterprising mariner. The sailor dropped her sails and Mira swam eagerly to the edge of her tiny, single-person fishing boat.

"I am so sorry to have taken so long," remarked the Tresson woman in a thick accent.

"You need not apologize, Disaahna," Mira said. "I am only happy that we didn't miss one another."

The woman pulled back a flowing hood to greet the mermaid with a smile. Mira had met precious few humans in her time—it was seldom wise to linger near them, lest she risk encountering some of the more unsavory aspects of the species—but those she *had* met all had the same dark skin baked darker by the sun. Some of the other merfolk of Barnacle had a similar complexion, but none of the humans seemed to be as fair-skinned and fair-haired as she.

"I had a very hard time finding what you wanted, but I think I have something you will like," Disaahna said.

She carefully tugged a small bag from the deck of her boat. A bit of fiddling with knots and rummaging through the contents revealed a small, sun-bleached skull. It was perfectly white, with the distinctive, wedge shape of a lizard of some kind.

Mira gasped and tugged at the edge of the boat to pull herself higher. "It is *gorgeous*… What sort of creature is it?"

"A rock gecko, or so the shaman in the neighboring tribe said. I have three of them, and many other bones besides. Take it, see if it is what you wanted."

Mira reverently cradled the intricate skull and swam back from the boat, holding skull first where a pendant might hang, then against her head where a bow would normally sit.

"I can think of dozen ways to use it. And that's assuming there isn't just a collector who wants to have it."

"So strange," she said, shaking her head and holding out the bag for Mira to return the skull. "No *gold* for you. No silks. None of the things everyone else trades for. You want bones."

"They are so exotic, Disaahna. And there simply isn't any other way to *get* them. Besides, is it really so different that you want these?"

Mira offered up the small sack of pearls. At the sight of it, Disaahna's eyes widened and she eagerly traded her bag for the pearls.

"You want the little impurities from our oysters and clams, I want the skeletons of your desert animals." Mira sifted through the bag and turned up a tiny snake skull. "Imagine it… these things live in a place with no water at all… It is almost mythical."

"I suppose for you that may be… Oh, there are some *lovely* ones here… It is good you had so many, because I warn you now I may not be here for a week or two."

"Why?"

"There was an earthquake in my village. Three houses fell, the church is badly damaged, and also the well. We must do what we can to rebuild quickly. And also, the terrible waves did much damage to the pier. I am lucky my boat was spared."

"Really… Disaahna, does that happen often? The shaking of the earth?"

"Sometimes. But never so often as this and never *nearly* so badly."

"We have had trouble with such things as well. My home has *always* been coping with such things, but I'd never heard of it reaching the *land…*"

"There are those who say it is an omen. That we have angered forces beyond us."

"But how? I cannot imagine anything that those of the surface *and* the sea would do to bring the wrath of the gods upon us *both.*"

She raised her hands. "We cannot know the intention of the gods. We can only pray for their mercy and thank them for their bounty. *Oh!* As I speak of their bounty!"

She shuffled from the edge of the boat into the small bit of shelter beside the till.

"You spoke of your brother and his appetite. If you are so fond of things we have only here on land, I thought perhaps he would like this."

Disaahna emerged with a strange, leathery coil.

"Oh? It looks like an eel."

"No, no. Dried sausage. Most dishes call for it to be soaked for three days before using it." She held it out. "I think, for you, that will not be a problem, eh?"

Mira took the sausage, but the sailor's words stirred something in her mind.

"Something wrong, Mira?"

"No… No… The tide is ready to turn back, and so should I. Two weeks, you say? Until we meet again?"

"Two weeks, from this day. A friend of mine tells me he can get a good price for more of the shell bracelets you made. And that bone knife fetched a fortune."

Mira nodded. "I shall see if I can have more of each for you."

"And as for you?"

"I wonder… Have you heard of this thing… a… Ki-oh-tay?"

"A coyote, yes. Not so rare."

"Excellent! I had a chat with someone from Deep Swell and they said they had the most beautiful bones. The teeth especially."

"You have a buyer?"

"No. This one will be for me."

"I shall do my best to find one with *all* of the teeth then. But as you say, the tide shall leave soon, and I have more fishing to do."

"Until next time," Mira said.

She plunked down into the water, sausage in one hand and heavy bag of bones in the other. The return trip at this time of day would be a simple one, the flow of the sea taking her out with little effort if she let it, but nevertheless she worked quite hard to quicken her pace. All of the talk of the trembling ground had brought terrible thoughts to mind. Every day her brother toiled in the mine, in the same stretch of the sea that had claimed their father when the sea shook. Eddy was skilled, alert, and resourceful. But he was also clumsy and foolhardy. There was no reason to suspect anything had happened. The sea hadn't shaken since she'd seen him last… but all of this talk of damage and collapse had made her eager to see him again, and soon.

#

Rustle stopped to catch his "breath," if such a word applied in his curious situation. He'd been chiseling at the coating of ice for longer than he thought possible. Flakes of ice lifted away and melted quickly in the warm water, leaving an oddly smooth little crater in the crust that held his sleeping partner. His efforts thus far had been dedicated to exposing Eddy's other hand. Rustle wasn't entirely sure what he thought he would achieve by doing so, but it seemed as good a target as any. He was tantalizingly close.

With a final, mighty charge, he launched himself into the carved divot and drove the tooth home. It shattered through the last of the ice and, to his dismay, nicked the back of Eddy's hand. He pulled back and bit his lip in concern as a thin ribbon of blood curled forth, but to his relief it was only a tiny nick. After a moment or two the bleeding stopped.

Having achieved his task of the last few hours, Rustle took some time to consider what to do next. At this rate it would take *days* to chip through enough of the ice to free Eddy, even *with* the warm water helping melt it away. But what other choice did he have?

If his mind had not been so through twisted up in uncertainty, he might have been struck by the odd motion of Eddy's blood. Thickened a bit by the cold, it clumped together into a curling, undulating orb rather than spreading and mixing with the water. The dark red blob drifted slowly downward until it finally plopped against the stone of the floor.

Or more specifically, the stone of the dish in the center of the room…

The effect was immediate. Mystic energy, the same focus that had drawn Rustle here, intensified. Rustle flitted back and took shelter behind his sleeping friend's ear, tossing his tool aside as though it were evidence of some crime.

All around him the gems pulsed and intensified. The water was crackling and alive. The columns of ice that still hung in the water around them fractured and burst. Even the mound of ice that held Eddy cracked, though not sufficiently to free him.

Rustle shut his eyes, but there was no use in doing so. The things he was *seeing* weren't the most terrifying. It was the things he was *feeling*. The strange thing about this place had been the focus without a mind, without a will… But he felt the will now. It was powerful, crystalline in its clarity.

He opened his eyes again. The glow of the room was blinding, and rose, it had been joined by a radiant form in the center of the chamber. This glow was independent of any gem. At first it was simply an indistinct haziness, but before his eyes it became more defined. Arms resolved out of the light. Then a lashing, fish-like tale. Finally, a piercing pair of eyes opened.

The figure before him was a merperson… or at least the general shape of one. It wasn't defined enough for him to know if it was a mermaid or a merman. All he knew for certain was it was a figure of terrible power. Power that persisted even in death.

Its eyes swept across the walls, and previously unseen lips curled to reveal the fainter interior of a mouth. It looked to be admiring the carvings that had so enthralled Eddy upon their arrival.

All Rustle wanted to do was escape. It was precisely what he had been taught to do in times like this. It was the wise thing to do, the safe thing to do. But two things stopped him. The lesser of the two was his curiosity. As a creature of magic, this figure was a being of awe and wonder. The *most* important factor in keeping him from fleeing was Eddy. It was his fault Eddy was trapped here. He didn't know how he would protect the sleeping, frozen merman, but it was his duty to do so.

If he couldn't run, and he couldn't hide. That left just one option, something that went against everything he'd ever learned or felt.

With a hard swallow and a final moment to steady himself, he flitted forward.

"H-hello…" he said.

The radiant figure turned to him. Little more than bright eyes and a dimmer mouth, it was difficult to read its expression upon seeing the fairy.

Interest, certainly. But was it the interest of a scholar presented with a fresh curiosity? Or the interest of a predator presented with fresh prey?

"I… I am sorry that we invaded your… *home?*" he continued.

It did not answer, its eyes now sweeping slowly to the sleeping, frozen figure of Eddy. Rustle felt a sting of concern and darted in front of Eddy, placing himself in the creature's line of sight again.

"We didn't mean any harm. We were just… We were having an adventure," he said.

Its eyes focused on him again. The tail curled and it darted forward, but before it could reach either Rustle or Eddy, the chains carved into the relief pulsed with light and the figure was drawn back to the center of the room.

Rustle gazed at the smoldering chains in the relief, then thought back to the heavy door with its complex lock. A lock that was fastened from the *outside*.

"This isn't your home…" he said, realization and fear flavoring his voice. "This is your *prison…*"

# Chapter 7

Rustle's mind practically rattled about in his head. He was trained from birth to scrutinize the world around him, moment to moment, to discover anything which might be a threat to him. At home, this meant watching for the twitch of foliage and imagining the hawk that might be swooping above. Confronted with a glowing embodiment of raw magic, locked away in what could only be a mystic prison, his mind was aflame with the possibilities. What had this being done to be locked away here? What would it do now that it had discovered him and his friend?

The sheer weight of the horrific scenarios would have paralyzed a normal creature. Fortunately, the same highly trained instinct for spotting trouble also provided instructions for how to react to said threats. Those instructions were always the same. Run and hide.

He darted toward the still frozen merman who had gotten him into this mess and hid behind his fin-like ear. Logically, he wasn't any safer there—it wasn't as though Eddy could defend him—but just being concealed made him feel worlds better than charging out into the tunnels and caves that, as far as he knew, held even greater threats. And he couldn't leave Eddy behind. Fairies are stronger when they are together.

"Why did I have to be curious? Why did I have to leave the pond? Why didn't I listen to the others? Why did I come here?" he muttered to himself, eyes wild and voice on the brink of madness.

The golden form before them leaned forward again, testing the limits of the strange spell that kept it in the center of the room. As it drew closer, Rustle could feel his hair stand on end. This being was nothing *but* power. The piercing glow of the eyes swept along Eddy, then fixed on Rustle where he'd taken shelter.

"How long…"

Rustle didn't know how he became aware of the words. He didn't hear them. Not with his ears, at least. He simply… knew that they were intended for him. They slipped into his mind, skipping all of the pesky steps of perceiving them.

"How long have I been imprisoned…"

"I-I don't know. I don't come from here. I come from the surface," Rustle said.

The being thrust a finger toward Eddy, causing a fresh flare of the chains in the ceiling.

"*He* does not come from the surface... He is from very near this place..."

"B-but he's sleeping. I used magic, and I didn't mean to, but it was so strong here, and I froze him and he fell asleep and as *soon* as he wakes up and we get him free we will leave you be and you'll never have to worry about us again because—"

Rustle's rambling picked up speed as he continued, like his assurances were a stone rolling downhill, unable to stop and accelerating out of control.

The being raised a hand to silence the fairy.

"I will wake him..."

The radiant eyes shut and the hands pressed together. Up until now, the general level of magic around him had caused Rustle's skin to tingle. Now it became more acute, the force of will gaining a focus and edge. The magic clashed and sparked against the mystic barrier that kept the being in place, but a lance of energy pierced through. When it struck the ice encasing Eddy, the thick mound of crystal shattered around him. A galaxy of flakes burst outward and filled the water. Currents of magic pulled the twinkling crystals into complex whorls, tracing out sigils and runes in the water around them before the rising temperature caused them to dwindle and melt.

"Eddy!" Rustle cried, flitting about the face of his sleeping friend.

The merman was floating free of the ice now. His breathing was still quite shallow, but Rustle could see that the icy blue tinge his skin had taken on had begun to return to the healthier teal he'd come to expect from the creature. Gradually the glow restored to the tips of his fins and spines, and finally his eyes fluttered open.

Rustle buzzed just in front of Eddy's eyes, watching as they fought to focus on him.

"Good morning, Rustle the Fairyman..." he said thickly. "What has..."

His eyes shifted to the figure dominating the room.

"What has happened..." Eddy finished.

"You will *tell* me what has happened..."

Again, the words wove their way into Rustle's mind, and from Eddy's reaction, they'd found their way into his thoughts as well.

"We explored a cave in my mine and you were in it," Eddy said.

Though he visibly and audibly shared the same feeling of awe that pushed Rustle nearly past the point of logical thought, he did *not* show even the most cursory evidence of fear. Did *nothing* frighten him?

"What of the world? How long since the clash? Since the Thieves and the Great Ancient?"

"Too long, I suppose. I do not know of that tale."

"You do not… And the names. Stuartia. Merantia."

He shook his head, dislodging a few stubborn flakes of ice. "I do not know them."

"Dangerous… terribly dangerous… To allow it all to be forgotten…"

"What has been forgotten?" Eddy asked excitedly. "Tell us the story. We are here for adventure, and to learn. Tell us what has been forgotten, of this place and of you—whatever you are. We shall tell the others! I will tell the people of Barnacle and they shall tell everyone beyond. My good friend Rustle will tell the people of the surface. Everyone will know!"

The figure's eyes shut. Its glow dimmed ever so slightly, as though it was focusing on something distant. Eddy, showing the foolhardiness that Rustle had come to expect from him, swam through the magic circle keeping the being in place and inspected its form.

"Eddy, be careful!" Rustle called, carefully moving no farther than the edge of the being's unseen prison.

"If we were careful, we would never have found this place!" Eddy said. "This is a mermaid. Or maybe this *was* a mermaid? But I do not know where from…"

"How can you be certain it is a female? The features are so indistinct."

"Do you not know a fairymaid when you see one?" he said.

He leaned forward. His proximity to the radiant figure's power caused his hair to billow, yellow sparks coruscating along the locks. He either did not know or did not care that it was occurring. Rather than backing away to a safe distance, he leaned closer to the motionless mass of power. Slowly he extended a finger.

"Don't *touch* her," Rustle warned.

Eddy pulled his hand back.

"Why should I not?"

"You don't know who or what she is! All you know is that this place was built to lock her inside."

"How do we know this?"

"Because she can't cross this line. Here on the ceiling and floor. And because the door was locked. Pay attention, Eddy!"

He scratched his head, but looped around her to join Eddy at the perimeter.

"It is not always a dangerous person who is in a prison, Rustle. Mira says they have stories on the surface about princesses in towers. And people like *us* rescue them. And when I was growing, father would tell me about mermaids who were trapped in shallow pools for the entertainment of bad people. Do you have those stories?"

"*We* have stories of fairies trapped in jars. Fairies used to power spells. Mostly we have stories of fairies being… *collected.*"

"So maybe this is one of those stories."

"Or maybe it is the story of a terrible witch who the heroes couldn't defeat, so they locked her away."

Eddy nodded. "It could be *many* stories…"

He crossed his arms and watched the being as it remained motionless but for the pulse of its glow. He flicked the edge of his tail fin in little circles. Had he toes, he would be tapping them impatiently.

"What are you doing, please?" he called.

The eyes opened and fixed upon him again. Words flowed once more.

"A heartbeat… I feel it… The Great Ancient…"

"What is this, the Great Ancient? And also, the thieves. The tablet my friend found mentioned thieves."

"What!? You didn't tell me that!" Rustle said.

"You would have said we should not say the words after that," Eddy explained.

"*And I would have been right!*" He darted up to Eddy's face. "This is even more of your fault than before!"

The words continued. "You come from Barnacle…"

"I do! My sister, my father, my mother, and theirs and theirs and theirs. Always from Barnacle."

"It would be a fine prison for it… the depths near Barnacle… Has the ground been shaking?"

"Yes!" Eddy said in fascination.

He started to drift forward again, but Rustle buzzed forward and urged him back behind the safety of the line.

"Very much the ground has been shaking. Always some, but now very much! How do you know this?"

"The tale is told…"

The figure turned and raised her hands to the carving. She swam toward the barrier, and up toward the ceiling. The carved chains pulsed with power, but now, the pulsing glow spread outward. Perhaps it was an enchantment of the chamber itself, or some spell cast by the mysterious being, but the carving slowly began to shift and churn. Like a shadow play, the carvings moved and flowed, acting out the tale they'd been carved to represent.

Two brilliant glimmers appeared at either end of the domed roof, so small they at first had escaped notice. One shone yellow, the other blue. They looped and fluttered in place, sending out waves of like-colored light. The light danced and shimmered along the ceiling, until finally two waves of opposing light met in the center with a crack and clash. The two points drifted toward center and met where their light had. First the blue pulse. Then the gold. Then the blue more brightly, then the gold brighter still. Without words, it told the story of two figures testing themselves against one another.

The pulses continued until they were blinding, neither seeming to be any brighter than the other. No sign of which was stronger, gold or blue. So there came other acts. A blue spire conjured forth, curling up one side of the dome and down the other.

"That almost looks like Steep Mountain!" Eddy said excitedly.

A gold pool grew and spread, seeming to smooth away and burrow down into all that surrounded it.

"And that's Deep Swell!" he cried, pointing enthusiastically.

"What are those things?" Rustle asked.

"Seamarks! Steep Mountain is… Wait. We watch the story first…"

Light of alternating colors now had shifted to forming complex and astonishing shapes. They were so intricate the detail seemed to fold in upon itself, never truly reaching an end. But each time some feat was concocted by one of the colors, the other matched it. Until finally, blue light wove and curled along the looping forms of the creature that dominated the background of the carving. The beast then moved, sliding along behind the details of the other lights and carvings until it came to rest behind the blue point.

There was a moment of stillness, then a faint gold haze pulsed, seemingly from everywhere along the dome. It moved like smoke, gathering into a brighter cloud behind the yellow point of light.

Eddy swam up to investigate.

"It is many small points. Like glowing dust…" Eddy said.

He recoiled backward as the massive, shifting behemoth surged across the carving and the cloud of yellow wafted toward it.

A new clash, infinitely more violent than what had been illustrated before, played out across the dome. Everything that had been created or depicted to this point served as little more than dry grass to be trampled by the behemoth and the haze of light. The tower Eddy called Steep Mountain fractured and tumbled. The magnificent shapes conjured in each color were wiped away. The destruction grew and spread, but there was no sign the battle would end.

Then came white light, the glowing figure of what Eddy had identified as the goddess Tria. Her many arms rose and with them rose a shimmering wall of white, completely encircling the battle. It continued to rage, sundering everything within the wall. Soon the actual temperature of the water around them began to rise. The water in front of the carving simmered, then boiled. Eddy finally retreated to a reasonable distance as the water at the top of the chamber entirely boiled away and, behind it, flames broiled and charred the stone, swallowing all else.

The flames died away. The golden haze was still now, tracing out chaotic, marbled lines across the walled section of carving. The massive behemoth lay motionless, though its eyes were still open. The figure of Tria waved her arms and the six attendants surrounding her whisked through the wall into the blackened wasteland beyond. The three mermen tugged at the limbs and tentacles of the beast, maneuvering it into the position of the original carving and forging the massive chains. The mermaids gathered the haze of golden light just as it began to churn again. The original points of yellow and blue drifted toward the wasteland, flaring to brightness once more, but Tria thrust her arms up and down. The chains pulsed again, and the lights were snuffed out.

With that, the glow of the wall faded, the blackness and char wafted into the water and dispersed, and the carving was as it was when they arrived. The glowing figure turned to them again.

"Do you understand…"

"I understand much," Eddy said.

"I don't understand very much at all, but what I do understand, I don't like," Rustle said.

"The tall thing. That was Steep Mountain. Very near to the center of the Crescent Sea. It reaches almost to the surface. The top is strange and sharp. It looks like from this story it was even taller, tall enough to be above the surface."

"You mean like an island?"

"You call them islands. We call them mountains. I suppose this big creature—there is just one of it, so I guess that is the Great Ancient—broke the mountain. That is why there is the jagged top. And then Deep Swell. It is a very low, very flat area. That is the home of the great council. It is our capital."

He squinted his eyes and gazed up toward the dome of the chamber.

"Steep Mountain was there. And Deep Swell was there… And all of that… *fire* happened all about here… That would be the Broken Fields. A very large place where the ground is sharp and pointy. Like broken glass. Does fire make glass?"

"I don't know, Eddy, but we shouldn't be wondering about that sort of thing while *she* is still here staring at us," Rustle said.

Eddy looked to the glowing form, waiting patiently within her prison, watching them.

"You are right, Rustle." He addressed the glowing figure. "Does fire make glass?"

"That's not what I meant!" Rustle hissed.

"Fire turns sand to glass…" came the reply. "And so it shall boil away the sea and turn the sand to glass again if you do not heed my words. In life, I was the mage Stuartia. Many of the feats depicted here are my own. My foe was the dread wizard Merantia. I can feel the heartbeat of the sea… I can feel the waning slumber of the Great Ancient. Each time it stirs, the land and sea shake. If it wakes… The sea will boil and burn…"

Rustle's blood ran cold at the words of ill omen dripping into his thoughts. He saw images of ruin. This mysterious, freshly discovered undersea world torn asunder. His own forest washed away by a wave sweeping in from the sea. He didn't know if the images were the products of his own imagination, messages from Stuartia, or some horrid premonition. He turned to Eddy.

The merman's eyes were twinkling, his face utterly dripping with raw excitement. He reached out and grabbed Rustle by the legs and shook him.

"Adventure, Rustle! Adventure!" Rustle raved.

He turned to Stuartia.

"What do we need to do, Great Mage!" he said, his posture straightening like a soldier preparing for orders.

"I cannot speak with certainty…" the deceased mage replied. "But if the Great Ancient stirs, then Merantia's spirit must cling to this place as well. You must find it. You must do what can be done to end its influence, to shatter its will, to release its control over the Great Ancient. And you must do it quickly."

Eddy looked about and swiftly set about collecting his things.

"Quickly, Rustle! We have a job to do! A call to adventure!"

The fairy attempted to form the words necessary to even *attempt* to convince Eddy to think it through, but the merman's excitement was impenetrable. He grabbed his pick, gathered the spell book and both pieces of the glove Rustle had used to try to chisel him out. In a flash he was fully equipped and ready to go. He streaked by Rustle, who barely had time to grab his flowing hair as he swept past.

"Eddy! Eddy please, wait!" Rustle called.

"We know the way the Broken Fields were made, Rustle! And how Steep Mountain and Deep Swell were made. I've never heard those stories! And we are going to save the day! A good mage and an evil one. A mission to save the world. It will be the greatest story. A story to tell children for the rest of forever!" He glanced back at the fairy entangled in his hair. "They will write songs about us, Rustle!"

"Fairies don't do this sort of thing alone. We should get help!"

"You aren't alone. We are together! It is the two of us. A team! And we cannot get help. We cannot *leave* until the water is high enough. At least, *I* cannot."

"Fine. Fairies don't do this sort of thing at *all*."

"Neither do mermen. But we do now! We are the *first*. Except for maybe the merman attendants of Tria. And they did not even have their own names. They were just Tria's Left Hands!"

"But what are we supposed to do?"

"This is *our* story. *We* decide what we do. Think of what we've done. You are curious about things you don't know, and you find me, able to show you *so much* you don't know. And I am curious to find people who can teach me things as well, and I find you, able to teach me so much I don't know. I show you the place I spend all my time, and you find something new! We venture to that place, and you find something *amazing!* You freeze me to a wall, and I wake to find a mission to save the sea! It is all falling into place, Rustle. It is *our adventure*. Whatever happens, Rustle and Eddy can do what needs to be done! And this next piece is easy. We find the other wizard. You found this one. Just look for the same."

"I don't know, Eddy…"

"Neither do I! Let us find out together!"

# Chapter 8

Eddy drifted gently along in a mild current, trying to let his tail recover a bit. His enthusiasm for the adventure ahead hadn't cooled in the slightest. His body wasn't holding up nearly as well. His tail burned with fatigue, but the smile had yet to leave his face. This was all in spite of the fact that it had been hours since they'd left they mysterious chamber of Stuartia and little of interest had presented itself since then.

He held Rustle gently in his hands as the fairy did whatever it was fairies did to sense the magic of the world around them.

"You are searching, right, Rustle?" he asked. "Not just hoping to spend all of the time until we can leave?"

"Even though that would be a *good* idea, I'm doing my best. It isn't easy. I can still feel that first chamber. It's so much more powerful than everything around it. You've got me looking for a specific drop of water in the whole of the sea."

"If it was easy, it wouldn't be an adventure. Chores are easy. Adventures are hard! Keep trying."

"I *am*. Just try to be quiet. It takes a great deal of concentration."

Eddy nodded. He flicked his tail a few times to keep them moving. Doing so must have jostled him a bit, because his stomach released a churning grumble that, in the relative silence of the tunnel, was enough to startle Rustle.

"What was that!?" the fairy yelped.

Eddy took one hand away to rub his stomach. "That was the sound of hungry."

"Uh-oh…" Rustle said. "There isn't any food here for you!"

He shut his eyes and shook his head. "Do not be silly, Rustle. Always the sea gives us what we need. If you cannot find something you want to eat, it means you aren't hungry enough."

"You should eat some of the sweets," Rustle said, tugging himself free of Eddy's grip and darting into the bag.

"No, no, no." He retrieved his friend. "You are not an eater like me. You need the sweets, and one or two won't do me much good. You keep the sweets. And keep looking for the evil wizard! I will look for something tasty. That way we are both doing something we are good at."

He glanced about, seeing little but the endless black volcanic stone that formed the rest of the tunnel and the rippling pocket of air above him.

"Strange that there is *nothing* alive here. It is not easy to find a place in the sea where there is not something alive, and this place is very much not alive at all. Even the wizard was not alive."

"Which is another good reason not to take orders from her."

"Ah, but you are *wrong,* Rustle. Because dead people at least know what killed them, and they can tell you not to do that. Also, she is the *least* dead dead person I have ever met."

"That's only because we accidentally… Uh…"

Eddy tipped his head. "What did we accidentally do that made her less dead?"

"Uh…" Rustle repeated, looking a bit anguished.

"Come to think of it. She was only less dead when I woke up." He grinned. "Did you do a dumb thing to make the adventure move forward?"

"I *said* it was an accident. I was trying to get you free and I spilled some of your blood. That dish in the middle of the room *was* an altar. It was… we sort of did a ritual, I think."

Eddy nodded slowly, a knowing smile on his face. "A ritual by mistake. That is a very 'adventure' thing to happen. It proves we are on the right track. Always things like that happen. That is fate making sure we turn the page. So, is that what it takes? Some blood on an altar to make people less dead?"

"I think? These are all stories I've heard from fairies who heard them from fairies who heard them from fairies."

"Stories from long ago. *Also* a very adventure thing."

"You make it seem like we can't make a mistake."

"We *can't.* This is *our* adventure. You never hear a story about adventurers who make a blunder and fail, do you?"

"That's because those adventurers died, and no one ever heard from them again, Eddy."

He scratched his head. "… I do not like that sort of thinking, Rustle."

"But it's true, isn't it?"

"It's too true. Too true is not fun. *Maybe* true, that is fun."

Another rumble rolled through the water around them.

"We really need to find you something to eat," Rustle said.

"That was not the sound of hungry," Eddy said, glancing off into the darkness. "Oh, yes! We were looking for a sound before we found the wizard! Since we can't find the *next* wizard so easy, let's look for that again!"

"Eddy, can we please stay focused!" Rustle snapped. "You can't just go charging off after every shiny thing you see!"

"Did you see something shiny?" Eddy asked, craning his neck and glancing about.

"No. I mean we can't let ourselves get distracted or we'll never get anywhere."

"I am not distracted. This is what you were teaching, right? The wizard, and whatever *you* are looking for, is a *maybe* true. I like maybe trues, they're fun! But the sound we just heard? That's very true. Too true. And *you* think those are better, right?"

"… I suppose there is some logic to th—"

Eddy grabbed him and thrust his tail. "We go!"

#

The burst of excitement energized Eddy enough to bring him a fair distance off to the side of the cavern. As they'd traveled, the sheer size of the place became increasingly awe-inspiring. By now they'd probably traveled as far *under* the sea floor as they'd traveled to get to Eddy's farm.

Their detour from the admittedly aimless search Rustle had been conducting had revealed yet another mysterious and distinctive feature of the cavern. There had been no shortage of tunnels thus far, but all of them had the meandering, jagged quality of things crafted by the whims of nature. As the dim glow of the fairy and the merman cast upon the floor of this stretch of cavern, they found a branching series of tunnels that were anything but natural.

"Look at them…" Eddy said, running his hand over the smooth surface of a tunnel that was a bit wider than his arm's width and perfectly circular. "Even when I try very hard, I cannot make the walls of my mine this smooth."

"They're like glass…" Rustle said, flitting up to the shiny black surface.

His distorted reflection stared back at him and reflected his light back in hypnotic ringlets all around.

"It is polished," Eddy said. "Not like with chisels and sand and cloth. Like what heat can do. More Glowing Pools things."

"Are we getting close to this Glowing Pools place?" Rustle asked.

"No, no. That is very far. But I suppose there can be places *besides* the Glowing Pools that can do such things. If we find a place like *that*…" Eddy looked aside. "The *things* I could do if I had a Glowing Pool of my own…"

They swam forward. The tunnel was much more direct than the others they'd explored. It had no sharp turns and ran in a straight line with a broadly downward trajectory. There were only minor deviations upward or downward. After having the whole of the cavern open around them, the tunnel felt oddly cramped to Eddy.

"Most of my own tunnels I make when I mine are only a little bigger than this," he said. "But the big cave is much nicer."

Rustle nodded. "I don't like it here. It feels closed in. I don't like closed-in places…"

"Lucky for you you're so small. Smaller places feel bigger for you."

Rustle shook his head. "It doesn't work that way. Big or small, once I'm trapped someplace, all I can think about is how I can't get away if something comes along to try to get me."

66

The fairy was still oddly transfixed by the glassy wall. Eddy looked ahead.

"So things in tight places are scarier for you than things in the open?"

"Yes."

"You should not look forward then."

Rustle's head snapped around and his glow flared. Ahead, *something* had caught their glow. It was smooth and metallic, but in all other ways was more deserving of the label 'monster' than machine.

They couldn't see much of it. The thing was almost precisely a match for the size of the tunnel. Its form was composed of bronze or brass plates, marbled with a green patina but otherwise smooth. They joined with impossibly complex linkages, such that it looked as though this might be a suit of armor for a horrible beast, or maybe the scales of a fish or dragon that was never meant to exist. A stout, tuna-like tail hung limply against the floor of the tunnel. It had six legs, each built of metal segments and tipped with pincer-type claws composed of a dark, stone-like material. The segmented legs joined to the hexagonal body smoothly, just where the tail thickened to nearly the diameter of the tunnel. Its body blocked the path ahead, and thus hid the rest of its form.

"Is it dead?" Rustle asked, peeking out from behind Eddy's ear.

"This is a thing someone built. Things you build don't die. They don't *live* either."

"Built?" Rustle leaned out further, curiosity starting to edge past fear. "But it is so complicated. You can build something that complicated?"

"*I* cannot," Eddy said, tugging at the blunt edge of the fin. "But *someone* can."

Eddy leaned closer, bringing Rustle along with him. The fairy's curiosity was piqued, but not yet to the degree that he was willing to get as close as the merman wanted to be. He flitted out and watched from a safer distance as Eddy grabbed hold of two of the legs and gave another tug.

"It is *very* heavy. Fins aren't so good for pulling things backward," he said.

"Be careful," Rustle advised. "… But what does the front half of it look like?"

Eddy pulled himself forward between the two legs and just barely managed to ease his head between the wall and the metallic body.

"There is not much body left. It is very stubby. There is not much *tunnel* left. Just a little ahead. The tunnel ahead is *very* rough. I think maybe this thing was digging it."

"A digging machine? I've never heard of such a thing."

Eddy glanced over his shoulder. "I know. Isn't it great! I think maybe I can push it out if I get ahead of it. Watch the bag."

He wriggled back into the clear section of the tunnel and dropped his bag far enough back to give him room to move the mechanism. As the tunnel had taken a slight up-turn in this section, the bag slid quite a way along the glassy floor before coming to a rest. He took his pick in hand and darted back up to the widest gap he could find. It took a bit of lashing of his tail and tugging with his arms, but he managed to cram himself into the space ahead of the mechanism.

"What does it look like!" Rustle called.

From the echo of his voice, he'd retreated quite far. Eddy carefully ran his fingers along the wall.

"The wall is sharp here. And there are all sorts of chips and flakes down on the bottom." He squinted and poked at the flakes with the pick. "The ones near the machine look round, like they were half-melted. Yes… Yes, and there are lines here on the walls. Like the marks I make when I dig, but deeper and very much the same to one another. A pattern. Definitely this machine was doing the digging."

"What about the machine? What does the front look like?"

He turned and analyzed the previously unseen bit of apparatus. A somewhat blunt beak of sorts jutted out from center. Little flecks of black had been driven into the metal there, and it was a bit more polished than most of the rest of the surfaces. Six perfectly round, amber-colored domes were set into a stout ring around the beak. Most were fractured or rendered cloudy, but the two along the left side appeared to be intact. Each had a thin sheet of metal hinged above it, a shutter of some sort.

"Well?" Rustle urged.

"It looks like a swordfish. One that has too many eyes. And ran into walls until its nose got blunt. And the nose is a little too round."

"That doesn't help me, Eddy. I don't know what a swordfish looks like. … And from that description, it sounds like it doesn't really look much like one anyway."

"Hmm… What do you know that I know… Oh! You know the eel I offered? The tasty one?"

"Yes."

"It is like the head part of an eel. But too many eyes, no mouth, and too round. And *only* the head part. Because the rest of the thing looks like blocky tuna wearing a skirt made of legs."

"You are very bad at describing things, Eddy."

"Maybe *you* are very bad at *imagining* things! I will push it out until you feel like you can come and look at it, and then you will see."

"Wait! Just be sure it isn't *moving* or alive or anything first. If it's just sleeping, I don't want you to wake it up. We've woken up *enough* dangerous, magical things already."

"It does not *seem* like it is moving, but that is good thinking, Rustle. I will listen close."

He set his pick down and pressed his hands and ear to the warm surface of the mechanism.

"I do not hear anything. Nothing like a heart. But I do not know what the inside of a big mechanical thing would sound like. … Wait… I do hear something…"

It was subtle, but something was rattling.

"I hear it, too," Rustle said. "It's not coming from inside the creature, it's coming from under it. Get out of there!"

"Good thinking!"

Eddy gripped the mechanism and hauled himself forward. It was a tight space to navigate and trying to do so swiftly didn't make it any easier. He'd barely gotten his shoulders free when the rattling revealed itself to be just the first audible indication of a growing rumble that shook the entire tunnel. This wasn't the same thunder that had drawn them here. This was something far more substantial. This was the same sort of earth-shaking that so frequently spoiled the routine and damaged the walls back in Barnacle. But this was more powerful… and much, *much* closer to the source.

The merman eased his chest through and was on the cusp of slipping entirely free when the heavy mechanism shifted. With a metallic clank it rocked to the side, pinning Eddy to the wall. He cried out.

"Eddy!" Rustle yelped.

He darted forward and tugged at the merman as he struggled against the machine. Despite his exceptional strength, Eddy didn't have the leverage to shift it aside.

The rumbling was getting worse. The water transferred the motion with destructive efficiency, rattling their bones and threatening to deafen them. Fractures split the wall of the tunnel behind them. Fragments of razor sharp stone pelted fairy and Merman alike.

"Go! Rustle! Go!" Eddy called, waving the fairy away.

"What about you!?" Rustle cried.

"Don't worry!" Eddy smiled through the fear. "I bounce good, remember? Better I get buried than you!"

Two cracks racing across the ceiling met. A slab of stone dropped down and shattered behind them. Pulverized stone began to pour through behind it.

"I can't just leave you!"

Eddy didn't waste time arguing. Instead, he snatched Rustle firmly in his grasp. Trapped as he was, he had precious little range of motion, but he didn't need much of a windup for what he had in mind. A snap of the wrist hurled the fairy's streamlined form like a dart.

#

Against his will, Rustle cut through the water, as more of the ceiling tumbled down around him. He buzzed his wings and flailed his limbs, trying to bring himself to a stop. The terror that seized his brain was almost maddening. His fairy instincts screamed at him to take this precious head start and swim for all he was worth away from the collapse. His concern overruled them. Eddy was his friend, they were in this together, and he was in danger.

He brought himself to a stop and turned. Bravery, alas, wasn't always enough. He'd barely managed to begin his heroic flit back toward the merman when the roof of the tunnel completely let loose. Stone collapsed, forcing the water aside. A wall of water and debris struck him, forcing him backward faster than he could ever hope to fly. He and Eddy's bag, the only loose things in the tunnel, launched, slid, and bounced along its length until they were both ejected ahead of a plum of waterborne dust.

Rustle coughed and shook dust from his hair, trying to get his bearings. He was drifting in the center of a cloud of silt. He could scarcely tell up from down. His meager natural glow barely illuminated more than an arm's length around him. He held still and clutched his hands as the rumbling continued. There was a very real threat that the whole cavern would collapse, but the concern that pierced his chest and burned his mind was all for his friend.

After what seemed like an eternity, the earth calmed again. Rustle waited and watched as the dust settled and his vision cut farther into the water around him. When he could finally see the floor of the cavern, his heart dropped.

"No…"

The whole of the floor had slumped downward. Riddled as it was with these bizarre, unnatural tunnels, it completely gave way. Where once had been the entrance to the tunnel that held his friend now was nothing but a field of jagged stone.

Rustle buzzed about, tugging at this stone and heaving at that. He would have to move half a mountain if he hoped to find Eddy, but right now his mind refused to even entertain the possibility that his friend was lost. He spotted a distinctive form among the rubble and cleared away a layer of silt to reveal Eddy's bag. He plunged inside and emerged with the digging gauntlet, then ducked inside again and found the single claw he'd dislodged earlier.

Properly equipped he went to work, digging and chipping at the broken ground.

#

In Barnacle, Mira held tight to the wall as the last of the earthquake subsided. It was the worst the city had endured in many months. When the danger was gone, she surveyed the damage. Her own home had only one fresh crack in the wall, but from the sound of it, others nearby weren't as lucky. She swam to the exit. There were at least two homes she could see that had taken considerable damage, and one had partially collapsed.

"Does anyone need help?" she called.

The community had sprung to action more quickly than she had. Injuries seemed to be minor, and at least one of the damaged homes was mercifully empty when it had succumbed to the quake. Any other time, she would have rushed to help regardless of the fact matters were well in hand. Not right now. She knew in her present state of mind, she would be of little use.

For the last hour she had been drifting about in her home, casting frequent glances to the west, in the direction of their farm and mines. Eddy wasn't late yet. The return tide was only just starting, and thus on a normal day he would only have just been leaving for home. That hadn't steadied her nerves. Ever since her chat with Disaahna she'd had the worst feeling. When the earthquake came, it was almost as though she'd been waiting for it.

She surveyed the lesser consequences of the tremor. Things were in terrible disarray around her. Displays of bones had toppled to the ground. Eddy's spare tools had tumbled from their hooks. She reached down and gathered the worn, crooked pick he kept for light work. It, like most of their tools, had belonged to their father. She gripped it tight, then swam for her room. She rummaged about in the mounds of clutter that had once been her personal library and wardrobe.

"Where is it?" she muttered, thumping books into rough piles.

She'd not looked into her old spell book in years. In truth, there were only a handful of spells she really made use of. A bit of language, the indispensable water-for-air, and a handful of warding and defensive spells to protect herself were enough to allow her to survive and thrive. She'd memorized the rest of them—it was part of her education--but as with any spell it was usually best to refresh oneself rather than risk miscasting. But her most basic spell book was nowhere to be found. Without it, she couldn't be certain she would have proper protection from depths much further down than Barnacle itself.

There was no telling what had happened to her spell book. In another state of mind, she might have suspected her brother, but at the moment she was too busy feeling anxious about him to feel suspicious of him. So she abandoned the search.

The book she'd misplaced was anything but rare. There were probably three more similar books to be found within Barnacle. But her fellow residents were busy picking up the pieces. What's more, the more her mind swirled and churned through the terrible things that might have happened at the farm, the more she feared she might need help. And if Barnacle was busy recovering, her next best bet for help was the nomads. They were never far from Barnacle this time of year.

Mira grabbed a large conch shell. She cleared away some of her fallen belongings until she uncovered a small chest set into the floor. Among the charms on a chain tucked within her bodice was a small silver key. She clicked the chest open and revealed a satchel of hand-picked gems and pearls. She hoped she wouldn't need them all, but for what she had in mind, she'd need *something*. Those people didn't work for free…

# Chapter 9

Eddy stirred weakly and tried to focus his eyes. He was in a great deal of pain, but in his slowly clearing mind, that was good news. If he hurt, it meant he was alive. His natural glow fell upon a claustrophobic chamber mounded with shattered rock. Little patches of glass-smooth stone here and there suggested the collapse had sent him down into a similar tunnel that had been bored beneath the one he'd been exploring. Some larger slabs of stone were propped up by the metal hulk he'd been investigating. Those slabs had in turn sheltered him from the debris above.

He flopped some stone from his tail and winced in pain. He was covered with lacerations, but none were deep enough to be the source of this pain. He'd at least strained a muscle, at worst torn it. Again, as injuries went, it could have been worse. A shake of his head made the world around him swirl sickeningly. He must have taken a terrible blow. That was worrisome, but still ranked among the least of his problems. Far more pressing was the grind and clatter of still-settling stone. The void that had sheltered him was terribly small. As he pulled himself entirely free of the stone that had mounded atop him, there wasn't even room enough for him to stretch himself out to his full length.

A bit of sifting, taking great care to avoid completely shredding his hands, turned up his pick, which he carefully freed. He gave one experimental jab to what he deemed to be the weakest—and therefore hopefully the thinnest—spot in the layer debris beyond the sheltered area. A stone shook free and the entirety of his shelter trembled. It was clear, one wrong move and the roof would come down upon him.

"When the only actions available lead to disaster, think instead. Contrary to my usual methods, but desperate times call for it, I suppose." He felt his head and checked for blood. "Ah, well. At least I don't have to filter my thoughts through that broken translation spell."

He cupped his head and weighed his options.

"I cannot rely upon Rustle for rescue. There is just no telling how far I am. … Or if he's even survived. And digging myself out is plainly out of the question."

Eddy looked to the mechanism beside him. He painfully pulled himself closer to the device.

"But what about you? As far as I can tell, you were *making* that tunnel. And I would wager if we searched to the end of each of those tunnels we would find another one of you. … Unless the *others* got to wherever they were going. Which introduces the question of *where* you were all going. Another fine mystery that Rustle and I could solve." He shook his head again, quickly regretting it. "No, Eddy. Not right now. Like Rustle insists. *Focus* is important. Doing something is what will get you out of this, but *learning* is what will reveal what needs to be done."

He investigated the details of the device that he'd only gotten a glimpse at prior to the collapse. The thing was by any measure a work of art. He'd never seen metal plates joined with such skill, hammered with such precision. There was considerable wear—this thing had visibly done a great deal of hard work in the past—but for the life of him he couldn't see any damage that might have stopped it from functioning.

"I am no mechanist, but the only bit of you that seems truly *broken* is a few of your eyes."

He leaned low. Some of the glass orbs were shattered. Most had large dents and scars on the shutters that covered them. Two, however, were fully intact. To his frustration they were currently the two half-buried in debris. He dusted them off with the care of a historian. Some of wafted water cleared them without threat of scratching them. As the water cleared, he noticed another detail.

Until now, what little they'd found that wasn't simply volcanic rock, air, and water was *covered* with runes and carvings. Here, they were remarkably absent. The only obvious blemishes on the surface were the pebbled marks of hammers on some of the rare curved sections of the device. But on the flat section of the ring where the eyes had been mounted, there was a slight recess. In that recess was a stamped emblem, like a maker's mark. It was two tools crossed. One was a round-headed hammer. The other was a rather cruel-looking spear with two uneven length prongs.

"That's curious…" he said, blinking to be sure he wasn't seeing things. "That is surely Tria's hammer. But that spear…"

He rubbed the maker's mark with his thumb.

"It looks like the Spear of Tren. Why would anything bear the marks of both The Maker Goddess and The Breaker God together?"

A trickle of fine dust and a sprinkle of pulverized stone rained down from above him amid the worrying sound of settling debris.

"Less time wondering, more time learning," Eddy said.

One of the mechanism's limbs—whether they should be called legs or arms was of little concern—was entirely free of debris. He lifted it and found, despite some patina fouling some of the joints, it still moved quite freely. In trying to clear away enough stone to reveal the base of another of the arms, he found more markings. These were far less mysterious, just a few symbols of ancient script.

"Let us see here… it looks like… It looks like it says *Borgle*. Is that your operator? Or is that *you*? Come to think of it… I haven't found any controls yet. No holes for cranks… No *handles*… No wheels for water to turn… What made you function, my mysterious friend?"

A hunk of black stone slipped free from the roof of his slowly failing shelter, narrowly missing his tail.

"If I do not learn the answer soon, I may never learn." He said, his seemingly impenetrable air of optimism finally showing the cracks of panic. "Think, Eddy. Focus. Focus…"

He ran his hands over the surface. The metal wasn't *so* different from the bars of the gate to the chamber they'd found. That was a place all about magic and focus. And while the carving depicted Tria, central to the room was an altar, which only Tren required of his followers.

"The old tales tell of all sorts of mechanical marvels crafted by Tria. That could mean this is the work of the divine… Or at least work in the *name* of the divine. But if it bears Tren's influence, that would make it *unholy*. As unholy, perhaps, as the altar… And maybe fueled by the same thing."

Another stone shifted, this time bashing him in the shoulder. The flow of black sand that followed was steady and didn't seem to be slowing.

"Out of time. Nothing to do but try it. It can't make my situation any worse."

He smeared his thumb against one of his many injuries to gather some blood, then wiped it across the beak of the device. Nothing happened. Next, he applied blood to the nameplate. Again, nothing. The flow of sand had been joined by fragments of sharp, broken stone. The last thing that seemed distinctive was the maker's mark. He brushed a thick smudge of blood across it.

The result was immediate, a pulse of light from the mark itself, then the slow smolder of amber light behind the device's "eyes." The shutters around them twitched. The free arm shifted. Its pincer dropped down and embedded in the loose debris.

Eddy backed away as best he could, huddling in the far corner of the rapidly diminishing shelter, and pulled his pick to hand. Sounds clicked and sprung from within the heavy metallic body. Things whirred and resonated. He heard it ticking and clacking in a rhythmic, oddly musical way. One by one the eyes flared and dimmed until only the two relatively intact ones retained their glow. The glow resolved to a roughly defined point in the center of each eye and dimmed toward the edges. The shutters above each functional eye flipped up, then dropped down, shielding them.

It drew one arm effortlessly from the debris. The sudden motion caused the slab of stone propped atop it to shudder and rumble.

"No! Stop!" Eddy called.

To his surprise… it did. The mechanism came to a complete, statue-like stop. The shutters above each eye raised and the points of light shifted about in their orbs, sweeping the chamber until they locked in his direction.

"You actually listen?" he said, squinting through the raining dust.

The machine did not reply beyond the syncopated rhythm of its operation. Its eyes, however, began to scan around the void. The points of light stopped again and sharpened. A grinding sound roared from within the mechanism. Limbs stiffened and curled from where they were trapped.

"Stop, stop, stop!" Eddy cried.

This time it refused to heed his orders. One of its segmented limbs speared toward him. He raised his pick to deflect, but the pincer easily wrenched it aside, bending it like a pin and sending a second pincer inches above his head. He huddled down and closed his eyes, with nowhere to run and no way to defend himself against the device.

He trembled, ready for the blow that would end him, but as the heartbeats stretched into seconds, the killing blow didn't come. The rumbling grind subsided to a gentle tick tock again. Eddy opened one glowing eye.

The mechanism's illuminated pupils were staring at him. Its arms had woven themselves into a complex arrangement, each supporting a slab of stone or a section of the ceiling. Notably, one of them was directly above Eddy's head. Had it not acted, the stone would have delivered the very killing blow he'd feared the machine would.

"Good work, Borgle…" Eddy said shakily.

A bright chiming sound rang from within the mechanism and the shutters raised slightly. When a fresh stream of dislodged stone began to cascade, it looked to the source, then lowered its shutters and sharpened its gaze. A swelling pulse of light sparked from the base of the nearest arm, traveling along the arm in accelerating waves. When they reached the pincer, short, astoundingly potent bursts of heat were the result. A handful of pulses brought a hissing boil and briefly rendered the black stone to a molten glob. It cooled quickly—more quickly than Eddy imagined was possible—into a glassy shell that sealed the weak point in the shelter. A sequence of other pulses secured the bits of stone the arms were holding in place. When it was through, the repeated rapid heating had raised the temperature to an uncomfortable but not dangerous level. More importantly, the little void was quite solid and stable, no longer in risk of collapse.

"… Good *work,* Borgle!" he repeated.

He reached out and patted the mechanism on the 'nose'. The shutters rose, and again there was a bright chime. Eddy picked up the bent pick.

"Can you help with this?"

Borgle released an inquisitive whir.

"You bent it. See? Bent. It needs to be straight."

Another whir. Evidently its capacity for understanding was limited. Eddy beckoned with an exaggerated gesture. The machine leaned lower. It shifted one of the broken eyes toward him. A moment later it raised one of its pincers to the fractured orb of that eye. After a plink of disappointment and a slump of its form, it rotated to bring the functional eyes to bear.

"The pick here. See? It's bent like this."

He crooked a finger.

"It should be straight like this."

He straightened the finger.

"Can you fix it? Since you broke it."

Borgle shifted backward and swung two pincers around. A bit of tension and a groan of metal returned the tool to his hands, straighter than it had been in years.

"Good work, Borgle!"

Eddy patted Borgle's nose again and was rewarded with two quick chimes.

"Now I imagine you are very good at digging, Borgle. I need to—"

At the sound of the word "digging," the machine set its eyes on the floor of the chamber. All six arms jabbed effortlessly into the floor in sequence, and Borgle began rattling its beak against the stone, turning it to powder.

"No, no! Not down! Not down, Borgle!" Eddy called.

It did no good. The machine either didn't hear him or no longer wished to obey him. The rhythm slowly increased, and gradually the pincers gathered up and cleared away the pulverized stone into whatever space was available around it. The fish-like tail slid bit by bit from where it had been buried, and Borgle plunged down into the hole it was creating. Here and there, sparking bits of heat melted and smoothed the walls.

Eddy watched helplessly as his helper bored in entirely the wrong direction. He held his ground, careful not to get too close as the machine flash-melted stone. It was cooling with the same supernatural speed as the first few repairs, but there was a considerable difference between stone that was no-longer molten and stone cool enough to risk touching.

Borgle's cacophonous boring reduced to a muffled rumble before Eddy was willing to venture into the fresh tunnel. Down was certainly not the direction he'd wanted to go. At this point, though, any motion was good motion. With any luck, the tunnel would join with one of the others and he would be able to find his way out. If not? Borgle *must* have been heading somewhere.

#

Rustle's stomach was rumbling and his body was aching. Twice he'd made a pit several feet deep, and twice secondary tremors caused it to collapse, the second time nearly trapping him. Now a combination of fatigue, frustration, and anxiety had brought his progress to a crawl. Nevertheless, he refused to stop. Not for a moment had it entered his mind that Eddy might be dead. He'd never met a creature made of sturdier stuff than the merman. He doubted there was anything in the whole of the sea that could knock him down and keep him down. And if he was alive, Rustle would find him. He needed him, and even if he didn't, Eddy was his friend and he needed help.

The fairy huffed and puffed. He'd been having difficulty catching his breath for the last few minutes, and it was only getting worse. He'd tried to shrug it aside and keep working, but when his hands started shaking and his head began to spin, he realized this was not simple fatigue. He wasn't just out of breath. He couldn't *breathe*.

Rustle buzzed his wings and kicked his legs, rocketing toward the surface. He burst out of the water like an arrow from a longbow, coughing out his latest lungful of water and gasping at the dank air of the cavern.

"The water-for-air spell," he coughed. "It wore off…"

This wasn't a complete disaster. He was still a fairy, and a *water* fairy at that. If he poured a bit of his burgeoning mystic skill into it, he could hold his breath for well over an hour. Even working hard at digging, he'd probably only have to return to the surface for a breath every half-hour or so. But the water-for-air spell wasn't the only one Eddy had cast. There were also spells to cope with the depth and perhaps others he'd not even mentioned. If any of those failed, there was no telling what would happen. There were so many tunnels, too. What if he dug far enough down that he couldn't return to the surface in time?

The spell book was still in the bag, but he couldn't read it. He needed someone who knew merfolk magic. And he needed them *quickly*. To his dismay, he realized there were only two people who *might* be able to help him. The dead wizard they had left behind, and the one they were searching for.

It felt terrible to even consider it, but if he was going to be able to help Eddy at all, he was going to have to leave him for now. Worse, he had been frightened to face these wizards even when the strong and brave merman was by his side. Now he would have to face them *alone*. It was something no fairy was ever supposed to do. Fairies did *not* act alone. But fairies didn't abandon their friends either…

"There is no other way," he said.

With resolve he wasn't sure he'd ever felt, Rustle took a deep breath and plunged into the water. He dove toward the floor of the cavern and pulled at Eddy's bag. One of the fronds of seaweed Eddy had been harvesting had survived. He sliced a bit of it with the digging claw and fashioned it into a sling. He packed away two of the sweets. As he pushed the plug back into the jar containing the last one, he noticed something with an odd sheen near the bottom of the bag. It was the strange-shaped pearl Eddy had gifted to Rustle. Though it wasn't clear even to him why he felt compelled to do so, he fashioned a pouch from another bit of frond and hung the pearl around his neck.

A few minutes later, he burst from the surface of the water again. The sling with his supplies hung on one shoulder. The digging claw was strapped to the other arm. He shut his eyes and listened to the wind as it whispered its foreign message. He let the instincts of his race fall into place. The motion of the wind wove into the back of his mind. When he opened his eyes again, he knew that so long as any air remained in the cave, he could follow it back to this place, to the place where his friend was waiting for him.

He buzzed his wings a little harder to sling the last of the water from them then shut his eyes again, this time feeling for the other sensations. Like the wind, these were things he'd never imagined other creatures didn't feel. It was subtle, not so easily defined as the motion of the wind and the stories it told. It was the warmth and glow of anything with a mind. Perhaps others felt it as that strange sensation, that instinctive knowledge of being watched. He had to quiet his mind greatly in order to detect it with any degree of reliability. At a time like this, when desperation, fear, and anxiety drenched his mind, it should have been impossible. But at this moment there was something else. Duty.

He'd always felt an obligation to his pond, and to the fairies who lived there. But it had never been so sharp, so focused. Many hands making light work was a fundamental tenet of fairies. No task had ever been wholly upon his shoulders. No fairy, not even the eldest and most powerful, was ever expected to take on a task alone. The very thought of it had always terrified him. But now that it had happened, the raw terror had begun to give way to something different. It felt like he'd been sharpened to a point. Forged into something harder, stronger.

His mind cut through the doubt and dismay and settled onto a dim collection of points of focus. One was Stuartia, far behind. Another was the weak sensation of Eddy himself. The merman was not much of a mystical force, his spirit was almost too weak to feel, but it was undeniable. He was alive down there, somewhere.

The last point was different. Unfamiliar. Like the chamber that held Stuartia, it felt like focus in the absence of will. It had to be the second chamber. The prison of the wizard Merantia. If Stuartia was to be believed, Merantia was evil. But then, Stuartia herself was imprisoned. *Could* she be believed? Should they be helping her at all?

He opened his eyes and set them on the inky void, windward. Right now, what mattered most was that Merantia's prison was closer. He darted forward, ready to face him, her, or it in exchange for the spells necessary to save his friend.

# Chapter 10

Myra swam through the cool darkness of the sea, heading out for the open water. Merfolk were as varied in their culture and behavior as any of the surface creatures, a fact that was not only unavoidable, it was essential. The sea was a vast place, but the places a merfolk village like Barnacle could be founded were comparatively rare. A proper village was one resting on a stable stretch of the sea floor. It should be deep enough in the sea for the mermen to be comfortable, but not so deep that the mermaids wouldn't be comfortable there. That described a wide range of depths, but only a tiny slice of the sea floor. Few places, mostly clustered along shorelines, actually remained within that range of throughout the day and throughout the year. What of the rest of the sea? And how did cities trade with one another over distances far larger and with far fewer stops than trade routes across land?

With any luck, Mira was within earshot of the answer.

Mira raised her conch shell to her lips and blew through it. She had never quite gotten the knack of producing the proper note. The sound was a ragged squeal rather than the sonorous wail of a well-executed call. She hoped it would still do the job.

Nearly a minute later, she heard exactly the sort of sound she'd been trying to produce. Two long, low blasts on a similar shell. She immediately darted in the direction of the source. In no time at all, forms began to emerge from the murky water. There were dozens of smaller shapes and one enormous one. Little points of light, various illuminated shells and jellies, traced out interesting patterns. The water out here was much cloudier than back home, so she was practically on top of them before any real details emerged.

The group of nomads were thirty members strong. By far the most notable aspect of their group was the creature at its center. A whale, larger than the cluster of homes where Mira lived, swam smoothly along between them. Large bundles had been affixed along its sleek, rubbery body. They were skillfully attached with wide straps of woven fronds. Faintly glowing streaks of fluid traced out shapes in smoldering orange and cool green. They were artful and specific markings, the symbols of this particular band of nomads.

"Hak, hak," called one of the merfolk, lightly tapping the whale just above its eye.

It obediently allowed itself to drift to a stop. Mira looked over the nomads, more than a bit uncertain of how to proceed.

The Adventures of Rustle and Eddy

At birth, nomads were physically identical to Mira and the others who had more permanent homes, but one would never know that by looking. A life of endless travel had forged them into something very different. Most wore much more clothing, essentially carrying their every possession on their person. Males and females alike wore snug, sleeved tunics littered with shallow pouches that could seal tight against the body to keep them streamlined. They also wore long garments wrapped tight against their tails, something between a skirt and an apron. Everything had a handmade look, a good deal closer to the original sea creatures that had given their hides to make them than the sort of outfits the people of Barnacle wore. Patches were so common one would be hard-pressed to know what the color of any garment was when it started. The one exception to the obvious care in keeping their bodies streamlined for travel was jewelry.

The mermaids wore rings on every finger. Their hair was braided, long strings of beads woven into it. Earrings abounded. The mermen wore everything the mermaids did, but added piercings to both their fin-like ears and the ends of the tail fins.

They were a formidable bunch, hardened by their endless travels into lean, muscular physiques that were evident even hidden beneath their garments. An older mermaid, the matriarch of the group if the sheer quantity and quality of her jewelry was any indication, swam up to Mira and gave her a measuring look. She had much darker skin than Mira and carried a short spear strapped to her back with a length of rope coiled at its end. A shorter, blunt-ended scepter hung at her side, also tethered to a cord.

The matriarch sniffed. "You want to do business? Not much business to be done with just one shore-lover."

Her accent was as patchwork as her clothes. The rest of the nomads rumbled with something between laugher and agreement. Mira crossed her arms. This much she'd anticipated.

"Seems to me like a bunch of flotsam like you should be happy to get what you can get," she said.

They murmured and chattered more loudly. Rather than malice, they seemed pleased. Mira breathed a sigh of relief. Doing business with nomads was always a gamble. One band of them could be as different from another as one nation was from another. But they all seemed to enjoy testing each other with a bit of verbal sparring before getting down to business.

"You hear this? Stuff like this is why we skip Barnacle," the matriarch jabbed. "You *are* from Barnacle, right. I can hear it in your accent."

"I am."

The matriarch nodded, then furrowed her brow. "Felt like quite a tremor not so long ago. You folk get hit bad?"

"We did, but no one was hurt. Not in the city proper, at least."

"That why you're so far out here? Someone outside the city get hurt?"

"I don't know, and I want to find out. I wonder if I could hire some of your men. I need to check my brother's farm, down in a rift, and I've misplaced my spell book."

"Bah. Spell book. You spit in the eye of Mer when you use that stuff. She gave us the boys for heading to the floor and the ladies for heading to the surface. Floor work is men's work. Leave it to them. … If we like what you've got."

Mira pulled out her satchel.

"I'd like two… no, three men. I'll take you near to the farm. Just go down and tell me if there is any damage."

"That's it?"

"That's it. Unless there *is* damage."

"What then?"

"Then I'll need you to help find and rescue my brother."

The matriarch nodded. "That'll cost you more. Not *much* more. Hard to charge for saving someone trapped, but we'll expect gratitude."

"Of course."

"We prefer to take our gratitude in the form of precious stones."

"You'll have all I can spare."

"How far from here is this place?"

"A few hours."

"A few for you? Or a few for people who know how to swim properly?"

"It's at the far end of Droomla's Rift."

"Droomla's Rift…" She turned her head. "Frish. Droomla's Rift."

One of the comparatively brawny mermen swam up and tugged a folded roll of cloth from one of his many pockets. After a moment, he handed it to her. She shook her head.

"A few hours? I thought I was joking about you not knowing how to swim properly. This time of day, that's against the current. No sense heading there now."

"Please. I can make it worth your while," Mira said, holding up the satchel of gems.

"We're due for a meet-up with Casta's Drift. We don't get to meet with her but twice a year. *Big* trades happen. That bag isn't big enough to make it worth our while if we miss out on that."

"I don't need all of you! Just three strong men."

"We do our own trading. No one bargains as hard for her friend as she does for herself. And we've all got our deals and bargains set up from last time. The wrong person shows up, they don't get what they bargained for."

"Please! It's my brother! I've got a terrible feeling. It's probably nothing. Just help me to be *sure* it was nothing."

The matriarch looked Mira in the eyes. If she was moved by Mira's plea, it certainly didn't show in her expression. When she spoke, it was with a raised voice, addressing those lingering around her.

"Bult! Sitz! Cul! Up front!"

Three mermen emerged from the crowd of nomads. They were substantial specimens, to be sure, and they looked to have seen their share of rough times. The first, Cul, was missing an eye, or at the very least had chosen to cover one with a scallop shell. He was also as dark of skin as the matriarch, and had a bulkier build than most merfolk could boast. Sitz's hair was trimmed short along one side. The roughness of his scalp and the sorry state of his ear suggested it was a consequence rather than a choice. Bult smiled, revealing broken, serrated teeth. Again, they weren't menacing, but something about their demeanor didn't give Mira the warmest of sensations.

"What's your name?" the matriarch asked.

"Mira."

"Mira, I'm Trendana. These boys are the fastest we've got. If anyone's going to check on your boy and catch up in time to earn their living, it's them. I feel for you. Had a brother of my own. Made some bad choices, that one. Ended up on the wrong end of a spear. But I don't feel for you so much that I'm going to order these boys to risk missing Casta's Drift. So, it's up to them."

The three mermen looked to each other, then to Mira, then to her sack of valuables.

"What's in the sack, eh?" Cul asked.

"Yeah. You got something I want, I'll take a look for your boy," Bult said.

"Gotta be some good stuff, though. I missed Casta two years back. Still haven't made back what I'd have made if I'd been there."

Mira tugged open the sack and poked about for some careful selections. Cul snatched the whole bag from her and rummaged through himself. Trendana swam up and thumped him on the back of the head with her scepter.

"Who raised you? Snatching the young thing's goods. Each of you are doing this job for one gem or pearl or what have you. Just one. Until we find out if she's going to need more than a look around."

"Worth more than one pearl," Cul said. "Pearls are barely worth the trouble. Gotta make a deal with one of the ladies, get her to go up top and sell it to one of the sailors. And then you lose whatever she decides her cut should be."

"Then pick something that isn't a pearl. But be quick. Now it's *you* that's wasting our time, not her," said Trendana.

They passed the bag between them and, with the eye of a jeweler, plucked out the three most precious gems Mira had. Cul handed the bag back.

"That'll do for a quick look, I think," Cul said.

"Fine. Get what you need. We'll be listening for you once the tides are right for you to be swinging back," Trendana said. "If we don't hear from you by the time we're swinging back after doing our trade with Casta, we'll ride the current along Droomla's Rift and see what's become of you."

"Thank you. You don't know what this means to me," Mira said.

"Best not to talk it up too much, girl," Trendana said. "Otherwise these boys are liable to expect a little more gratitude when the time comes."

Mira felt a twinge of concern at the advice. Something about the phrasing suggested that gems might not be the only form of gratitude favored among the nomads.

"Hold on," called a reedy voice from among the nomads.

An equally reedy figure darted out from among the others. She was a younger mermaid, barely out of her adolescence. Everything about her suggested she was just beginning her life as a nomad in earnest. She had relatively little jewelry. Her outfit was light on patches and seemed to boast more empty pouches than full ones. But she had a fiery, feisty look to her, and made up for her lack of gold with three large knives with sharpened onyx blades hanging at her sides. Her skin was just one of many ways in which she bore a resemblance to Cul.

"I'll tag along," she said.

"You and your sister," muttered Bult to Cul.

"Cora, she needs boys. The problem's at the sea floor, and Droomla's Rift is *well* down below where the ladies can go without getting hurt.

"Sure, but what'll Mira do while you're down there? Just float in the sea waiting? Big fish out there. Nasty things. And her with just the one blade."

"It isn't the number of blades, it's how you use them," Cul said. "You having three of them isn't going to do much if you don't know where to stick a shark if it comes along and doesn't decide to mind its business."

Cora put her hands on her hips. "Well you're my brother, Cul. Maybe you should have been *teaching* me. And two is better than one, besides."

She turned to Mira. "Let me see the bag."

"I'm not sure I need you Cora," Mira said.

"There's a lot of dangerous things out there in the open sea," Cora said. "Looks like you get a lot of sun. Probably you spend most of your time going in toward the shore rather than out. I hear that surface folk can be a handful."

"They can be. If you find the wrong ones."

"But if they start making trouble, you can just head down and they can't follow."

"That's true."

"The same can't be said of some of the wrong sort out here. Sometimes you have to head up. Sometimes they'll be faster than you."

Mira considered her words, then held out the satchel. Cora picked a small, rough garnet.

"Come on. Quickly," Mira said.

She darted off toward where she knew the rift to be. Behind her, the nomads went on their way. Those she'd hired to help her followed. For all she'd heard of their fabled prowess at traveling from here to there, they quickly fell behind.

"Come on! Quickly!"

"You go just as fast as you want, lady," Cul called after her. "We'll see you soon enough. Well before you get to anything you'd need *our* help with."

Mira gritted her teeth and worked her tail. She didn't know precisely what she would do when she reached the spot above the rift without them. But it burned at her that they didn't seem to have the urgency she had. She redoubled her efforts and rushed into the murkiness ahead.

#

Rustle had been flying with his eyes shut for almost an hour. He was just above the surface of the water, navigating by the flow of the wind and the distant point of focus that he hoped was the spirit he was seeking. Shutting his eyes was partially to help filter out the distractions, but it was the lesser of two reasons. Now that he was beyond the portion of the cavern that was riddled with tunnels, there was little but black stone and rippling water, neither of which were terribly distracting. What *was* distracting, and what his shut eyes helped keep at bay, was the terrible realization that the water level was getting *awfully* high. Once it reached the roof, there was likely to be plenty of pockets of trapped air, but his movement would be much slower, and the risk of being caught somewhere without a way to breathe would be *much* greater.

Such precious ignorance cannot last forever, alas. He reached a point where, no matter which direction he went, the distant point of focus only seemed more distant. This was the place, or as near to it as he could get without dipping below the surface of the water again.

He opened his eyes. The tunnel itself didn't seem much different. It was a bit deeper here than elsewhere, perhaps. Otherwise, if he hadn't been keeping careful track of his movement against the gradually more familiar curls and sweeps of the wind, he would have imagined he'd barely moved at all. He flared his personal glow as bright as he could manage. It penetrated *just* deep enough to reveal the mouth of a narrow tunnel. It was the only tunnel in sight. It could only be the one leading where he needed to go.

Rustle thought back to their time dealing with the other prison chamber and weighed the risk. If it was a similar distance to the chamber itself, he would probably be able to reach it by taking a deep breath and relying upon his fairy nature to make the very best use of the air in his tiny lungs. But if he was wrong, it would be the last mistake he made. If he was going to hedge his

85

bets, he was going to need enough air with him to sustain him through whatever unforeseen trials lay ahead.

"If I was a better water fairy, this wouldn't be a problem," he moped. "Great-Grandmother can stay under the water for as long as she pleases. And if I was a better *air* fairy I could probably conjure my *own* air wherever I please." He crossed his arms and indulged himself in a bit of feeling sorry for himself. "It isn't *fair* that I need to *be* better at *everything* in order to *get* better at *anything.*"

He huffed a breath.

"Enough. I am what I am. Eddy's somewhere down there, and he needs my help. I… I don't know if this is the right thing to do, but it's the only thing I can think of."

Rustle clenched his mind around the air around him. The natural affinities all fairies had to air came without any training. His watery nature was more of a choice made by the tribe. All of the mysticism of *that* element was learned. It was something like learning a second language, though. Until he became fluent, he always fell back the familiarity of his mother tongue.

He buzzed his wings and felt the wind gradually acclimate to his will, like a cool suit of clothes warming once slipped onto the body. He was anything but a skilled practitioner, so the amount of wind he could force to yield to his will was very limited. He held it tight and fluttered his wings, dipping downward. The surface of the water dented beneath him for a moment before he sprang back. Another quick dive caused a hemisphere of water to displace around him before ejecting him again. He buzzed his wings even more powerfully and thrust himself downward. The water spread, arched, and finally collapsed over him, held at bay on all sides by the air he'd dragged with him. In essence, he was at the center of a bubble. Keeping it with him was difficult, but if the contents of his lungs could be made to last an hour, the contents of the bubble would last him *ages*.

Rustle plunged downward and began to navigate the tunnel. The air wanted very much to force him to the surface. He let it, floating up to the roof of the tunnel. The bubble flattened into a dome and rolled along with him until, to his combined relief and anxiety, he came to a grating precisely the same as the one outside Stuartia's prison. He didn't bother wrestling with the lock. The gap in the grating was quite large enough for him to slip through. The hard part was coaxing the wobbly orb of air to squeeze through with him.

He finally got it to slurp through the grating with him and ended up bouncing up to the roof of the prison chamber. It was different than the other chamber. For one, the ominous glow of the crystals in the roof of the chamber was entirely absent. There were still gems, and there was still a carving, but aside from his own glow there wasn't a flicker of light. That should have worried Rustle. There was reason to believe that a place so devoid of any sign of magic would also lack the sort of help he required. For better or worse, he was far too terrified of the evidence to the contrary.

In Stuartia's chamber, he'd felt the presence of focus without will. Here, it was almost the opposite. There was a will, a mind. It was dagger-sharp and tightly coiled. He could almost hear its voice in the back of his mind, muttering to itself. It was rumbling with anger. But for all of its intensity, it seemed unaware of him, and unable to reach out.

He forced the bubble down with him as he quested toward the floor of the chamber. There he found the shallow dish of an altar, just the same as in Stuartia's prison. He tried to steady himself with a deep breath. It did no good. No amount of slow, calm breathing was going to wipe away the fact that he was about to perform a blood ritual to a foreign god, to awaken the trapped spirit of a powerful wizard. There was nothing to it but to do it.

Rustle ran his finger along the edge of the digging claw until he drew a drop of blood, then crouched and smeared it against the surface of the bowl. Power welled and surged, though not to the degree it had for Eddy. Perhaps, like the magic, this place was only *really* meant for merfolk. But a blue glow pulsed and breathed in the gems around him. They illuminated, gradually offering a better glimpse of the carving on the domed ceiling.

If Eddy were here, he would have been fascinated. The mural was very much like the one in Stuartia's chamber, though rather than the massive behemoth lurking behind the other shapes, there was the same insect-like shape repeated in an interlocking pattern. It repeated thousands of times, and even those spaces between individual insects appeared to simply be another insect in another position.

He'd only started to make sense of it when a radiant form finally resolved in the center of the chamber, directly above him. As before, the shape was indistinct aside from the broad strokes of arms, head, fins, and eyes. It was a merperson. If he were pressed, Rustle would guess it was another mermaid. The will sharpened only slightly as it wavered into view, but it was enough, at least, for the voice to finally form words.

It was different than with Stuartia. The words didn't come as simple understanding. This was language. It was as though he could hear her smoldering, rage-filled voice in his ears. Certainly female. Certainly intelligent. And completely incomprehensible. It was the language of the merfolk.

He floated up to eye level and drifted back until he was beyond the perimeter of her prison. She looked at him through narrow eyes.

"M-Merantia?" he asked. "I'm sorry, but I need your help."

The voice lashed out in his mind again, but he couldn't make sense of it. From the tone, he suspected she couldn't understand him either.

"Of course," he said. "If the water-for-air spell has failed, why wouldn't the language spell?"

The glowing eyes narrowed further and the voice made a demand. Rustle's mind raced. It was bad enough he didn't know how he would ask her for help. The last thing he needed was to have awakened a wizard only to infuriate it with his inability to communicate.

"Uh… Uh… My friend! He… He looks like this!"

Rustle coaxed the bubble around him to pinch and tug, to elongate around him until it formed a passable approximation of Eddy's form.

The eyes looked with a degree more interest. He heard a single word in his mind now. He imagined he was being asked to continue.

"He's trapped! Trapped at the bottom of a tunnel…"

Rustle continued telling his tale, shaping the bubble of air around him into forms that he hoped would make his point clear. A falling stone, a mound of rubble. He pantomimed his inability to breathe, this inability to understand. He even attempted to produce Stuartia's form and explain that he'd been told the story.

That last bit may have been a mistake, because the semblance of Stuartia caused the feeling of rage to surge around him, and a flurry of words that had the edge of profanity, even if he didn't understand them.

"I just need help," he urged. "The spells he cast are failing. The breathing spell stopped working. I need to help my friend. I…"

His voice trailed off as a dull but very real sensation of pain began in his ears. It was the same pain he'd felt periodically when he and Eddy were traveling down toward the sea floor. The bubble around him seemed like it was squeezing tighter, succumbing to the pressure that a now failing spell had been holding at bay. His time was running out.

"Please! *Please*! You've got to do something. I can't help him. I can't help you. I can't help *anyone* if you don't help me! *Please!*"

With this final plea, he darted past the perimeter of the spell that imprisoned her. The pain was growing more intense. Soon it was difficult for him to think. The glowing form before him looked at him curiously. His vision began to dim. She placed her glowing hands on either side of the bubble and gradually the pain eased.

The voice in the back of his mind took on a different tone now. It was lilting, almost like it was murmuring a lullaby. With each cycle of its lyrical chant, he felt it probing deeper into his mind. Word by word, the song began to make sense to him. And as each word became clear, his own thoughts became murkier.

"Listen, listen. Hear and know. Think only of what I say…" she crooned.

Soon, these words dominated his thoughts. They crowded out logic, dedication, and fear. If not for the upwelling of magic around him, he likely would have lost control of the bubble of air he held in place.

"Good… Good… That is better isn't it?" Merantia said as Rustle wavered before her.

He was transfixed. The voice of the mermaid was the most soothing sound he could imagine. All he wanted was to hear her speak, to luxuriate in her words. He drifted close to her.

"It was good of you to awaken me. I am so very grateful to you."

"You are welcome, Merantia…" he said, his lips curled in a vacant grin.

"But you have no place down here, do you? The water is trying to squeeze and bruise my precious little helper. Let me see to that…"

She stirred the water around him with her glowing fingers, causing the bubble to flutter and wobble. Instantly the pain of the pressure dropped away.

"Thank you, Merantia…"

"You are a surface creature. Such a good and clever helper to bring your own air…"

She poked at the bubble. It wavered and rippled.

"Tell me. The air is a long way away. How did you bring it so far?"

"It isn't far… Just beyond the tunnel…"

The glow of her eyes became more piercing.

"I see… so that is how they hoped to keep them captive…"

Rustle squeezed his eyes shut and tried to remember what had brought him here.

"My… My friend Eddy. I need to help him."

"Oh, my dear little helper. You needn't worry about your friend. Wouldn't you rather help your dear Merantia?"

She ran her hand around the edge of the bubble. He could feel little sparks of power filter through to him.

"… I would do anything to help you, Merantia."

"Just as a little helper should." Her glowing lips curved into a smile. "And *why* do you want to help me?"

"Because you are power and beauty. Because you are wisdom and grace…"

The words barely seemed to be his own. With each passing moment Rustle felt his own thoughts floundering beneath a sea of devotion.

"What would you have me do, dear Merantia…"

"You have spoken to Stuartia. I can feel her influence upon you…"

"We did, dear and wonderful Merantia…"

"And I imagine she sent you here to destroy me."

"I would never dream of hurting you. You who are as sweet as the wind that carries the scent of honeysuckle…"

"Wind? Honeysuckle?" She seemed displeased. "Oh, cruel fate to send me a know-nothing creature of the surface as my first follower in death…

You don't know how to worship me *properly*. No matter. I have made more from less. Have you encountered the Thieves?"

"I don't know. I have encountered Stuartia, and I have encountered a thing with a face like the head of a round eel with no mouth attached to the back half of a tuna with a skirt made of legs."

"… I believe my helper may be broken… Listen, helper. Here is what I wish you to do. First, you must find where they have hidden the thieves and release them. Then you must find a way to get rid of all that nasty air that you say is so near. Then you must banish Stuartia."

"The water in the cave is already rising, oh magnificent and majestic Merantia."

"Splendid work! Then you have just two tasks remaining."

"How shall I perform the other tasks?"

She sneered. "I don't know… If they have been able to lock me away, and Stuartia as well, then they have used enchantments unknown to us."

Merantia reached out and ran her fingers along the edge of the prison. A red gleam followed her finger as she tested the edge of the barrier.

"This feels like it has holy magic. The work of both Tria and Tren." Her smile widened. "Ah, yes… I remember now… Surely Stuartia spoke of this."

"Please tell me in your own words, my beauteous and merciful Merantia…"

He had been drifting steadily closer, his eyes locked upon hers and unblinking. Now he was nearly face to face with her. His expression was that of someone hoping for the chance to steal a kiss.

"Ugh. Back," she said.

A motion of her hand thrust him away, bouncing him and his bubble off the far wall like a flicked insect.

"As even the simplest mind should understand, the gods are forbidden from clashing with one another. They are simply too powerful. The world would not survive." She smiled broadly. "It seems when Stuartia and I tested our skills against one another, we approached the same level of destruction, at least in the eyes of the other gods. We are, thus, very nearly gods ourselves. Not that, of course, I was not already fully aware of my might."

"You are a goddess to *me,* Merantia."

"And you are delightfully susceptible to my mystic wiles, little helper. But please, I am speaking. The same rules that prevent the gods from clashing with one another prevent them from imposing their will entirely upon the mortals below. There must *always* be a way for us to undo their workings. Anything less would be to rob us of our will, and then what purpose would we have to exist? More to the point, what purpose would *they* have to create us?"

"Tell me, oh brilliant goddess Merantia."

She looked sharply at him. "There *wouldn't* be a reason. The question was rhetorical. All you need to know is that *everything* the gods have inflicted upon us *must* be reversible *by* us. Us, in this case, indicates the merfolk, though I will include strange, simple-minded surface creatures as well. And most importantly of all, they will have left the knowledge of how to undo their work. You shall search until you find the proper incantations. They will be inscribed in tablets or upon the walls themselves, in places of great importance."

"But I cannot read, dear Merantia."

She glared at him.

"… I would be hard-pressed to find a more useless pawn to serve me. Try to clear your mind. It seems that is a task to which you are very well suited." She shut her eyes. "*Listen, listen. Hear and know. The language of the sea…*"

Rustle felt his thoughts stir. Symbols and shapes flooded into his mind. They came in pairs, first a symbol, then a thought. They layered atop each other, flashing with dizzying speed. Some twist of magic or flex of will kept the images from slipping away. In the space of a minute, the entirety of Merantia's knowledge of her written language found its way into his mind. His head ached terribly when she was through.

"Now go. Search. Find a way to free me, destroy Stuartia, and unleash my precious beast. And do not return until you have succeeded."

He buzzed rigidly before her and all but saluted, filled with the bone-deep *need* to satisfy her orders. He ushered his bubble back to the gate, squeezed through and began to navigate through the tunnel. As his distance from her grew, the edges of her influence frayed. It was slight, but enough for him to realize a few key things.

"Wait…" he said. "I went to her to try to get her to fix me, so I could find Eddy. She fixed the pain from being so deep, but I still have the water for air problem."

He turned, preparing to go back and request to receive that blessing as well, but he hadn't drifted more than a few inches when he was stricken with doubt.

"Oh… but if I go back to her so soon, she will be disappointed. I cannot disappoint my dear and wonderful Merantia. She who is like the sun in the sky!"

He reached out and dabbed his finger at the water held at bay by his magic.

"I suppose this is working well enough… I just need to be mindful. That is all. I need to refresh it at every opportunity. You can do this, Rustle. This is your time. This is your time!"

He buzzed off down the tunnel, infused with the sort of confidence and dedication that only an enchantress can inspire.

# Chapter 11

Eddy flicked his tail a bit and gazed at the cooling walls around him. This adventure had taken a rather tedious turn. Things had been going so well. Hidden caverns, mysterious spirits, dangerous collapses, living machines. Now he'd been reduced to slowly following said machine as it bored through stone. He couldn't even watch it happen up close, because a combination of the lashing mechanical pincers and the intense heat convinced even him that staying back and waiting for the walls to cool was the best option.

Alas, with the thrill of discovery replaced by the monotony of listening to a machine grind through volcanic rock, the nagging pain of his accumulated injuries was beginning to weigh down his normally upbeat demeanor.

"Borgle!" he called to the machine. "Is there maybe a way you can tell me where it is we are going?"

The machine continued to grind onward.

"He cannot hear me..." Eddy muttered. "I miss Rustle. Such an interesting fellow. Even if he *could* barely understand me. Though I'm sure at this point he'd be fretting over the beating I've taken so far."

He touched the sore bit of his tail and winced.

"I *am* going to need some time to rest and something to eat if I'm going to keep exploring... Strange that our adventure would have a part like *this*. Separated in an unknown place is exciting, I suppose. That would be well at home in one of the great epics. But floating along, heading nowhere, and doing it *slowly,* all while nursing an achy tail? What proper adventure has *that*?"

Eddy tapped his pick against the wall, testing its glassy surface. The pick was the only piece of his equipment he still had, so he tried is best to occupy himself.

"Wait... *Of course* they wouldn't write about this part. If it is boring for *me,* it is boring for the people who would be reading or listening! This is just the part between chapters, surely." He grinned. "This is the part where one of the heroes is suffering an unknown fate, and we *all* think he is dead. But really he is getting in place to save the day just when the *other* hero thinks all is lost! Now *that* is a proper part of a story. I should take advantage of this, then! I'll plan what to do next and try to heal up a bit. The *last* thing I want is to be hurt so bad I can't play my part when my big heroic moment comes."

Ahead and below, the crackle and grind of stone took on a distinctive sharpness. A moment later, a calamitous scrabble replaced the regular grinding and Borgle dropped from view. Eddy scarcely had the chance to question what had happened when a strong current drew him forward. Were he healthy, he could have easily outpaced it. Had the walls not been so smooth, he could have jabbed the pick into a crevice to brace himself. In a glassy tunnel, weak with hunger, and injured, Eddy could do nothing but slow himself as he was drawn toward a ruptured bit of tunnel.

"Stay away from it…" Eddy urged himself. "The closer to the hole, the stronger the current. No current stays strong forever…"

He flapped his tail, enduring the jolts of pain, but he was already past the point of no return. Once again, he curled himself into a ball, wrapped around his pick, and hoped the rupture at least lead somewhere without too many jagged edges.

As he launched through the hole, that wish was granted. There was certainly no jagged stone. But he took little relief in the fact, as there was nothing to replace it either. He was plummeting through the air, the column of water turning to a sprinkling waterfall as he dropped. Eddy had lived his life beneath the sea. Until this adventure, he'd never been completely outside of the water, and he'd certainly never fallen. Now, the rare feeling of panic seized his brain for the second time as he helplessly dropped like a stone.

He landed with a wet slap. His body struck a pool deep enough to spare him any broken bones from the landing, but not so deep as to be painless. A blow to the head dizzied him enough to make him briefly forget that his gasping, breathless wheeze was thanks to the fact his head wasn't underwater. He rolled over and stuck his face into the shallow pool, drawing a precious breath of water. When he felt clearheaded enough to utter the words confidently, he recited the air-for-water spell, blinked his eyes open, and tried to work out what had happened. The sight that revealed itself to him offered few answers.

"Wow…" he murmured.

It was bright as a moonlit night in this new cavern, which for Eddy may as well have been a cloudless noon. The glow was warm and yellow, seeming to come from yellow stalks that rose up from the rough stone all around. The stalks were perhaps two feet tall and stood or hung in scattered tufts on the floor and walls of the cave. They traced out a massive cavern, sprawling as far as the eye could see. His brief search turned up no other water, save for the little pool that held him. The ceiling was another thing entirely. It was visible far above him as a dull glow, a bit more orange than the brighter fronds. It looked at this distance to have a spongy texture. He sniffed. It was always somewhat difficult to process what his nose told him when under the influence of the air-for-water spell, but even if it had been in perfect working order he would have been hard pressed to put his finger on the scent. It was fruity and sickly sweet, like sugared melon, two things he'd never encountered.

Wide, smooth paths wove in a serpentine fashion along the floor. They were too meandering to be intended to be footpaths, but they were also far too regular to have been the result of simple erosion. The air echoed with the constant splash of the water showering down from above and the irregular, pathetic clank of metal. He turned to the source.

"Borgle!" he yelped.

The bizarre mechanism had landed nearby. It had survived the fall, but not without consequence. Eddy dragged himself over to the machine, which was sitting in a shallow crater formed by its impact. Three of the arms had hit hard and seemed completely nonfunctional. Its tail fin was bent into an odd position, and two large dents marred its side. A panel had popped open and ejected a handful of gears, chains, and sprockets. The merry clicking and whirring sounds from within its body sounded a bit more labored and dissonant. Eddy pulled himself to the machine's "face" and looked in its eyes, which flickered as they focused on him.

"How badly hurt are you?" he asked. "Can you move at all?"

Its functional pincers scratched at the floor and attempted to heave its massive metallic bulk upward, but a straining groan and a rattling slide were the best it could manage. The motion dislodged another bit of chain from its open panel.

"Stop! Don't move. You are… I suppose this is what it is like to bleed if you are a machine. Stay still and let me see what I can do. I don't know if you *intended* to bring us here. But we aren't getting out without your help."

He gazed into the open panel. A dizzying array of bits and pieces clicked and spun. They were stunning in their complexity, arranged in precise assortments.

"This… will not be easy…"

Eddy gathered the loose pieces. Most looked to be fully intact, dislodged rather than broken free. He fiddled with them a bit, fascinated by their shapes and designs. To his surprise, they clicked into place with little effort, and each seemed to fit *only* in a single position and orientation. It was a puzzle, to be sure. But it at least was a puzzle that had a definite solution and, more importantly, a puzzle that made it clear when something wasn't in its proper place.

One by one he slipped the threaded the pieces together and clicked them into the place where they seemed to fit. Each new piece caused other bits and pieces of Borgle's body to twitch to life. Shutters over his eyes flapped. One of the disabled arms twitched and wriggled. But after two thirds of the pieces were in place, Eddy made a disappointing discovery.

"Oh no…" he said. "Borgle. This piece here… This big wheel… It is badly bent, and even sheared a little. I can't get it to fit anymore, and I can't get any of the other pieces to stay in place without it."

Borgle plinked in disappointment.

"Let me think… Maybe a big rock. If I hammer it flat, it might work still."

Borgle clanked, a sound that struck Eddy's ear as less than confident.

"Don't worry, Borgle. I am good with machines! We don't have anything as fancy as you back in Barnacle, but I've fixed hinges and contraptions that you crank and such. I'll find a way to help you. All I need something smooth and flat. It isn't usually hard to find something like that along the sea floor. Let me just… Do you hear something?"

Eddy had thought the clicking sound he was hearing was just another bit of Borgle's workings falling in and out of rhythm. But as it grew louder than the sprinkling hiss of the falling water, Eddy realized it was coming from behind him.

He turned. The rough floor sloped downward a bit in that direction, giving him a clearer view of the surrounding area. A short distance away, and approaching fast, was a beast the likes of which he'd never seen before. It had hundreds of stubby legs, all working in clacking waves to drag a heavy armored body along the floor with startling speed. Two rounded claws were raised on either side of a tentacled mouth. The beast's body was rocky and blue-gray. If he had to compare it to something he'd encountered before, it would be a huge lobster, but one that someone had grasped it by the head and tail and stretched until it was far, far longer.

Its path swept back and forth, mowing down tufts of glowing fronds as it went. There was no doubt it was heading for Eddy. Another creature would have been terrified. The thing was many times his size and more than formidable. In his current state of mind and body, Eddy had a very different reaction.

"Food!" he cried.

He dragged himself to where he'd left his pick, then took it in hand and painfully pulled himself atop his aching tail. He curled it like a spring and used his pick to balance. His gaze locked on the approaching lobster beast. On his face was an almost demented grin.

It crested the slope and charged toward him. He shoved with his pick and uncoiled his tail, lofting himself into the air. The thing slid to a stop and swiped at him with its claws, but Eddy's lithe frame proved too small and swift a target. He came down hard. With his full weight, strength, and momentum behind the attack, the blunt metal tip of his pick pierced through the armor.

The beast released a whistling squeal and whipped its head side to side. Eddy flopped about and grimaced in pain, but held tight. When the monster foolishly stopped and tried to reach him with its claws, he raised the pick again and hammered it down. Again and again he punctured the beast, holding tight when he needed to and doing more damage the moment it relented.

After a brief, thrashing struggle, the thing succumbed to the crazed attacks of the merman. It fell still. Eddy levered a piece of the shell away. The thing's resemblance to a lobster extended into its innards as well. It had similarly plump and hearty flesh. Eddy gave it a cursory sniff and a tentative dab of his tongue. When it didn't strike him as overtly poisonous, he hungrily dug in.

The flavor was slightly more bitter than lobster, and the texture was a little tougher, but after hours of endless swimming and taking so many bumps and bruises along the way, it was a feast fit for the gods. He ate his fill, and a few mouthful's more for good measure, before pulling himself from the defeated beast and flopping happily to the ground.

"I never had any doubt," he said, wiping his mouth. "The sea provides."

He let the simple pleasure of a full stomach roll over him for a bit, then slowly became aware that he was in complete silence.

"That's… peculiar," he mused. "What happened to the water?"

He gazed up at the faintly glowing roof to find, where once there had been a hole, now there was little more than a bulging bit of fresh, spongy growth. The covering had sealed up the hole through which they had entered. It would have concerned Eddy more if there had been any chance of them using that hole to escape this place, but now that he'd eaten he was keen to explore. One thing that *did* concern him was the fact that Borgle had gone silent. He flopped his way over to the mechanism and checked its face. The glowing eyes had gone dim. None of the bits and pieces he'd replaced had come loose, so he tried the next most obvious solution. He smeared a bit of the blood from his meal over the maker's mark on its forehead. Immediately it flickered and whirred to life again.

"So, you were hungry too," he said. "I can't say I'm surprised, what with all that digging. Come to think of it, there were an awful lot of tunnels up there. I can't imagine someone was swimming about bleeding all over you to keep you going. Sounds like a messy way to fuel a machine."

Borgle released a negative-sounding knock.

"Do you usually run longer with a single, um, *offering?*"

The machine chimed an affirmative.

"Do you know what happened to make you start running down faster?"

The reply was a sequence of rattles and rings that very likely laid out the answer in no uncertain terms. Alas, it was in a language Eddy didn't understand.

"That's another mystery to solve then. Here's a question for you, though. *Can* I fix you?"

A very positive chime was the reply.

"Do you know how? Should I be looking for a rock to beat this flat like I said?"

A negative knock.

"Then what?"

The glowing eyes shifted about and focused on something. Three arms became arrow-straight, indicating a point in the distance. Eddy squinted in the proper direction. Like his nose, his eyes weren't quite as effective in open air as they were underwater—yet another advantage mermaids enjoyed—but with a bit of effort he was able to spot something gleaming in the distance.

"Is that… that's another Borgle!" he said.

A negative knock.

"Another thing that you *are* at least?"

This produced a chime of agreement.

"Of *course*. If you were coming here, it stands to reason all of the *others* were coming here too. And *they* didn't have someone to keep waking them up and fixing them. I'll go see if I can get it to help!"

Eddy flopped painfully along until he came to one of the snaky paths left by either the lobster-thing he'd just killed or another of its kind. He ran his finger across the path. It was quite smooth. Smooth enough it wouldn't rub him raw like the rest of the floor was already beginning to do. He slipped onto it and set about sliding along toward the next adventure.

#

Far above and far away, Mira huffed and puffed, completely spent and still barely half of the way to the rift. She been swimming as fast as she could, but now she could barely keep moving at all.

"Had enough?" called a gruff voice behind her.

She turned. The four nomads she'd hired—and promptly left behind when they refused to match her speed—had caught up. The smallest and youngest of them, Cora, darted forward to catch her by the arm.

"I was getting a bit worried. We didn't expect you to get this far before running out of energy. You almost got yourself far enough along to risk running into the sort of things you wouldn't want to face alone."

"You… hah… You knew you'd catch up?" Mira said.

"Trying to get somewhere as fast as you can is never the fastest way you can get somewhere," Cul said, catching her by the upper arm on the other side.

She tugged briefly against their grip, but having their strong, confident strokes to make up for her own failing stamina was a gift she wasn't willing to completely abandon.

"You go as fast as you're comfortable going. Whatever speed doesn't make you tired. Then you just keep at it. Little by little is how you go from shore to shore. That's what Trendana says."

"No sense explaining it to her. Mermaids like her like to stay put. Gets their heads all clogged up with silt," mocked Bult.

"So?" Cora said. "Still worth knocking some silt free, now and again."

Mira gave a halfhearted smile. "Thank, Cora."

"Don't mention it."

"You know, forgive me, but I never really understood how you could stand to not have home."

"We've got a home. You're in it right now," Cul said.

Cora nodded. "To a nomad, anyplace wet is home enough for us."

"But doesn't that feel… I don't know… aimless?"

"Why would it be aimless?" Cora asked. "We're always heading somewhere. That's about as much of an aim is you can get, isn't it?"

"I suppose. But, how can you ever feel… I don't know… *Safe*? At the end of a long day, when I get back to Barnacle, I can just be at peace."

Cora hiked her thumb at the others.

"That's what these folks are for. Home is the drift. Home is the tribe. If I've had it with swimming for the day, I know one of these folks will grab me just like I grabbed you and give me a tow. And they know that when I'm good and rested I'll do the same for them."

"You've got walls to keep you safe," Cul said. "We've got Bult and Sitz."

Cora leaned close and whispered. "Mind you, some folk make you feel a little safer than others."

"It's folk like *you* that make me wonder," Cul said. "How can you stand waking up in the same place you went to sleep. Sounds like a waste of a nice bit of shut eye."

"Sounds like a *prison*," Sitz remarked from above them.

"Wow… There are some notions I assumed united us all," Mira said.

"There are," Cul said. "But 'home' being a lump of rock on the bottom of the sea isn't one of them."

They were heading a bit deeper now. Farther from the surface, the sea was getting darker. The eyes, fins, and spines of Cul, Sitz, and Bult began to glow, each a subtly different shade of blue or green. Cul, glanced Mira, then squinted at her hair.

"What's that you've got here?" he said, pointing to an ornament she'd woven in.

Mira touched it. "Oh. That's a skull. I get them from a fisher woman."

He blinked at it. "That thing came out of a *creature?*"

"Yes! A *land* creature," Mira said, briefly indulging herself in one of her favorite subjects. "I'm told this is a *rabbit* skull. A little one."

He scratched his head. "They sure do make some strange beasts up there…"

"They really do. Do you do any trade with the surface people?"

"Most of our time is going to and fro between the larger mervillages," Cora said. "If what I've heard is true, it takes a while to find a surface person you can trust to do business without throwing a net over you."

"You do need to be careful."

"We don't have time for that," Cul said.

"We don't have *need* for that," Bult added. "There's more than enough down here. No reason to go up there."

"You're just saying that because only the mer*maids* get to go up there, Bult," Cora said, matter-of-factly. "Bult and Sitz are always sore that most surface folk don't even know mermen *exist*."

"Good riddance…" Sitz muttered under his breath.

"The beginning of the rift shouldn't be much further, I don't think," Cul said. "It's a little tough to tell, swimming against the tide."

Bult made a sound of disgust. "At this rate we'll get there just in time for the tide to turn, and then we'll be swimming against it on the way *back*."

"I'm thinking one gem isn't enough for this sort of trip…" Sitz said.

"A deal is a deal, Sitz," Cul snapped. "Now, Mira, how far along the rift is your brother's farm?"

"A fair way," Mira said.

The mere thought of her brother brought anxiety rushing back. Cul and Cora seemed to notice it.

"Don't worry about it, Mira," Cul said. "We'll get there, and everything will be fine. Now, these land animal bones… How big do they get…"

#

Rustle's body ached and his stomach rumbled. Even before being given his assignment by the beauteous and wise Merantia, he had been flying or working non-stop for some time. The last time he'd had a moment to rest was when he'd been clutched in Eddy's hands as they sought out exquisite being he'd just been blessed with meeting.

He paused, hanging in air over the water, and thought.

"Eddy," he murmured. "This was… I was trying to help Eddy."

Something in his mind tugged him away from that thread.

"Such a quest is not a *divine* quest, handed down by the mighty Merantia. Eddy can wait!"

He buzzed forward again, eyes sweeping the walls of the cave for some semblance of writing.

"There will be a tablet. Something with instructions on how to end the enchantments that imprison dear, kind, gentle, and sweet Merantia. And I can read them now. By her gifts, I can read the words of the merfolk."

His buzzing and searching continued briefly. When he paused, it seemed to take great effort even to remember what he had been thinking about beyond his precious mission from the pristine and perfect Merantia.

99

"Eddy... He could be hurt. Surely anyone as compassionate and knowledgeable as the magnificent Merantia would approve of taking a moment from her indispensable quest to help a merperson in need."

An almost *physical* tug in his thoughts derailed him once more.

"No! Her mission is paramount! She must be freed. The chains of her bondage must be broken, and her opponent must be crushed. It is the only way."

Though his words were spirited, Rustle hung in air, grappling with his own thoughts. It was as though he was literally of two minds. Both were his own, but one was utterly devoted to the tasks set forth by his lovely and all-knowing patron, and the other wished only to help his inconsequential merman friend. No matter how hard he foolishly attempted to divert himself from the crucial mission, that second part of him could not help but be countered by the far more measured and virtuous instructions of the majestic and mighty Merantia.

"The task must be done. It must be done, there is no question. ... But two sets of eyes searching are better than one," he reasoned. "Eddy can already read his own language. He can breathe water already, and he can move far more quickly underwater than I. If I find him, I can honor the wishes of my delightful and radiant Merantia far more effectively."

Suddenly the tension was gone. Both halves of his mind still existed, and still disagreed on the motivation for his action, but they agreed on the action itself. Eddy would be found. He would be rescued. And he would be put to work in service of Merantia.

He squeezed every ounce of remaining strength out of his body, hungrily devouring one of his two sweets along the way. He couldn't remember having ever worked so hard on anything in his life. He'd been making almost constant use of his limited mystic knowledge and driving his body for all it was worth. Though it was wearing terribly on his body, with each flex of his magical abilities, the spells and techniques became easier.

"Is that the secret?" he wondered, wiping a purple smear of gooey sweet from his mouth. "I always thought magic came with time. That you would be strong or you wouldn't. Merantia, may her musical name ring through the halls of history from the world's birth to its demise, has existed for years beyond number and she is more powerful than any other. I thought... I thought one either *was* strong or one wasn't, that the strong *uncovered* their strength by working their magic. Can strength be *created*?"

He munched a bit more, easing at least the ache in his belly. When the sweet was gone, and his tummy was packed with the much-needed meal, his mind turned to the burning fatigue in his wings. If he didn't rest soon, he wouldn't be any good to Eddy *or* Merantia.

Rustle dropped to the warm surface of the water and was swiftly dragged beneath by the weight of his equipment. Some buzzing and kicking brought him to the surface, but it took just as much effort to remain afloat as it did to fly.

"Maybe… Maybe if I can just remember the proper spell…"

He dug through his mind to the icy spell he had cast, very nearly with tragic results. It had been difficult to remember its details before, as they were effectively nonsense sounds to him. But now that the whole of the merfolk language had been wedged unwillingly into his head, his memories of the spell seemed to have a flow and lilt, like an ancient rhyme. All he needed to do was churn up the first few words and the rest of the spell emerged from the murky depths.

An idea formed. He flitted up and shook the water free from his body, then carefully spoke the words of the merfolk spell. The air crackled around him as the final words rang out. This casting wasn't nearly as potent as the one in the chamber of the wretched and evil Stuartia, but it was enough to crystallize a sizable slice of the water beneath him. He dropped down on to the makeshift raft and quickly flitted up again. It would serve as a way to rest himself, but freezing himself to the bone in the process was hardly an improvement. He set down his digging claw and perched atop it. *That*, at least, was tolerable.

Now there was the issue of continuing his quest. He could rest for a minute or two and then continue on his way, but the current was flowing opposite the direction he wanted to go. He would be losing time and distance for every moment he wasn't in the air.

If magic could solve the first problem, it could solve the second. He flapped his wings once or twice, just to get the air around him moving, then shut his eyes and set his mind upon the wind.

Wind was life. Wind was an extension of a fairy. It was one of the fairy's senses. Part of a fairy's body. It was a vessel for a fairy's will. He stirred the air with his wings a bit more, then let his thoughts weave into the air, coaxing it forward in much the same way he had dragged it down to form a precious breathable bubble when under the surface. The wind around him began to shift direction. It caught his wings and started to grow in strength. Soon it was enough to threaten to heave him from his perch atop the digging claw. He flipped the claw over, so its curved bite dug into the ice. He curled his fingers around the blunt end of the claw and leaned into the wind, is filmy wings spread like a sail.

Gradually the ice slowed and reversed direction. Starting the wind had been difficult, but keeping it going required little of his mind. Keeping his wings spread and firm wasn't quite as restful as he'd hoped, but it was still somewhat less exhausting than flight.

"I can't believe it!" he exclaimed. "I've never been able to conjure a wind this strong in my life! I really *am* getting stronger! I might actually be able to find Eddy! And save him! And serve the wondrous and elegant Merantia! *Adventure!"*

# Chapter 12

Eddy slid to a stop at the bottom of a slope. The long smooth paths ground into the surface by the mysterious and tasty creature he'd grappled with weren't the best way to get around. He tended to build up a bit more speed than he could handle and ended up pitching off into tufts of sticky golden stalks, but it was better than dragging himself. And the good news was he'd reached his destination.

He turned and peered up the slope he'd traveled down, spying Borgle's distant form. When he turned back and spread the stalks ahead of him to investigate the similar machine he was heading for, he'd expected to find an exact duplicate. Perhaps at one time that might have been the case, but no longer. This mechanism had plainly been here for ages. Tufts of the stalks grew up through it, and the plummet through from the ceiling, whenever it had broken through, had been far more destructive. The thing lay smashed apart. Its delicate internal mechanisms had spilled out on the ground.

"Oh… Dear… You will not be waking up to help us, will you?" he mused.

Eddy slid forward and painfully curled his tail. His injuries were *really* starting to accumulate, another thing that didn't seem to be in keeping with the narrative of any adventure *he'd* ever heard. But this could simply be the bit between chapters.

"Let me see now," he said, sifting through the spilled remains. "If you can't help us, perhaps you can donate a part or two. Hopefully whoever made you did so with great precision, because it seems whenever *I* find myself trying to replace this or that, I've always got to make adjustments to make it fit."

None of the sprockets and gears on the ground were the right size, but there were plenty more where they came from. He tugged at shafts and chains, gently disengaging them as best he could without doing too much damage.

"Ah! A-*ha!*" he proclaimed. "This looks just about perfect. And if not this one, then this, or this! Three gears, just the same. And so well made."

He cupped a handful of smaller sprockets and held them up to glitter in the light of the stalks and his own eyes.

"The sea has barely *touched* them. And they are so intricate. I wonder what sort of things Mira could do with these. No sense leaving them here to go to waste!"

He threaded one of the smaller drive chains through the gaps and holes in a dozen or so small gears—as well as the three he hoped to use. Raising his arms to hang the makeshift necklace about his neck revealed at least five other aches and pains he'd not noticed.

"Oh…" he murmured, looking at the hill between him and Borgle. "This will *not* be a pleasant climb. How do land creatures do this? I can't imagine legs are *that* helpful. What if they hurt one of them, like my tail is hurt? Didn't Mira say something about how people move faster on land? What is the name of it… A carriage! Yes. That's the thing. I remember it now. Those round things for rolling… wheels."

He reached into what remained intact inside the mechanism and gave one of the larger free gears a spin.

"Gears are like wheels. And there's plenty of rods for them to spin on… I wonder…"

#

"So, they have *music* too?" Cul said. "How does anyone *hear* it? Trendana says you have to shout for anyone to hear up there."

"You don't have to shout. You just have to get close. I've heard Disaahna play something she called a lute once. It was quite lovely."

Mira found herself almost at ease for the first time since her thoughts had turned to Eddy's potential fate. It wasn't that she was no longer concerned for him. But Cul had proved to have an unquenchable curiosity for the details of the surface dwellers and their ways. Mira half suspected he was just trying to distract her, but she couldn't fault him for it. She needed a good distraction, or the worry would have eaten her alive by now.

"We're right near the end of the rift now," Cora said. "We should be near your farm, right?"

"Yes. Yes, I believe it is below us. Eddy has been growing seaweed, and we've got a very nice bed for farming pearls. It should be easy enough to find the place."

"And what exactly do you want done once we find it?" Bult asked.

"First, just go and see if anything has happened. Any collapses, fresh breaks in stone, anything like that. If something *has* happened, come back up and let me know," Mira said. "If nothing has happened, then you've done all you need to do, and I thank you. If it looks like something may have happened, and there isn't any sign of Eddy, come back and tell me and I'll tell you how to find the mine."

"Why waste our precious time?" Sitz asked. "Just tell us where the mine is now so we can check it all at once."

"It is a very deep, very complex mine, I wouldn't—"

"She doesn't trust us," Bult said.

Cora darted up and poked Bult in the chest. "The way you two have been acting, *I* don't trust you."

"Come on. We've been paid. We do the job as ordered. Just like when we do labor back in Deep Swell during our swings up that way," Cul said.

"If I wanted to keep doing labor, I'd *stay* in Deep Swell," Sitz muttered. "But fine. Let's go."

The three mermen thrust their tails and swam downward, quickly moving beyond the depth Mira could comfortably travel without magic. Cora remained behind with her.

Mira turned to the nomad mermaid. Even if she'd not been dressed differently, Mira would have known Cora was a nomad. There was something about how they moved, even when idle. Her head had a slow, casual pivot, perpetually scanning the area. It stood to reason. In a life of constant motion with no comfortable, familiar surroundings, knowing precisely what was around you was probably essential for survival.

"I really do want to thank all you for your help. It is probably nothing. But I worry."

"You paid. No thanks necessary. And of course you worry. You'd be a lousy sister if you didn't. Your brother's family. Family's just the word we use for 'people who we worry about and who worry about us.' It's why we're all here."

Mira smiled weakly. "I am not certain if that is a wonderful or terrible sentiment."

Cora shrugged. "Just the truth."

"Your brother is very curious and interested."

"Nope."

Mira was taken aback by the blunt denial. "He plainly is."

"Nope. Not until you came around. That's the most I heard him talk all at once in a *year*. But then, you're the first person with the stink of the surface on her he's got a good whiff of in a while." Cora grinned. "Just a turn of phrase by the way. You don't stink."

"I'd assumed. Or at least I'd hoped." She reached up and touched the skull in her hair. "Tell me. You say you don't do much trade with the surface."

"We don't do *any* trade with the surface. Nothing directly. But we have plenty of third and fourth-hand contact. Not much value in it for us, though. Once a thing has passed through that many hands, the price gets so high we're not likely to find someone willing or able to pay for it."

"How often do you and the others pass by Barnacle?"

"Three or four times a year, depending on who we're set to meet with. Why?"

"As I've said, even if I *am* paying you, you didn't have to do this. And if it turns out you'll miss that meeting with... with..."

"Casta's Drift."

"Yes. I wonder if trimming down the chain to simply *secondhand* goods from the surface could help you at all."

Cora grinned. "Now you're talking a language a nomad can understand."

#

Rustle gazed into the blackness, shivering a bit. His icy raft was doing its job, but it wasn't the most comfortable way to travel. As the ice melted—which it was doing quite rapidly—less wind was necessary to keep him moving. But it also made for an unstable vessel. Worse, eventually the cold migrated up through the shield-size digging claw that had been the closest he could come to an insulated perch. He was just about recovered enough from the long flight, and energized enough from the big meal, to take to the air again, but it was difficult to pull himself from his reverie.

Images had been flitting through his mind. The most frequent was the stunning face of the marvelous and magnificent Merantia. She was a creature with a severe beauty, a perfect balance of power, authority, grace, and elegance. These reminiscences of her wondrous visage were periodically tempered by the reminder from another part of his mind that he'd never once actually *seen* her face. This image in his mind was either imagined or inserted. Both possibilities were equally unreliable.

A second focus for his daydreaming was of the escalation of power he'd noticed. He found himself hungering for further strength and growth. That much was a staple of his longing and dreams for as long as he could remember. But now there was more. He saw that power being used for glory. For domination. And for attaining *further* power. No other fairies had a place in these dreams of aspiration. It was all about individual achievement and gratification. It was all very unfairylike.

The lowest, weakest layer of his stack of daydreams was the longing for the thrills of what would come next. He'd always wanted to discover things, but not until he'd met Eddy did he realize that he had wanted no part of the excitement that so often accompanied discovery. Now, as he thought of how he would find Eddy, how Eddy would help with Merantia and Stuartia, and how they would eventually escape, a tiny part of him was quite enthusiastic for the dangers they would surely overcome.

For the dreams of devotion and empowerment, he worried that these thoughts were not his own. For the dreams of excitement, he worried they *were* his own.

What finally shook him from the near fugue of layered daydreams was the gleam of something other than water and volcanic rock in the distance. He only saw it for a moment, lit by a reflection from the water's surface, but it was certainly not the same field of black.

He blinked. "How… How could I have missed something? I flew this way to *find* my beloved and adored Merantia. … Oh, that's right. I had my eyes shut, as I'd yet to awaken her, and thus her incomparably powerful spirit was too weak for me to feel otherwise. If only I had known the wisdom of her

106

desires, I might have come to her with the full knowledge of the things she'd sought. How proud she would have been for me to have foreseen and fulfilled her demands before I'd even met her!"

Rustle tugged the digging claw. The ride thus far had caused it to sink somewhat into the ice, so yanking it free took some effort. When it finally broke away he buzzed toward the source of the unexplained glimmer. It was a large rectangular tablet, similar to the one he'd fetched for Eddy before they'd become trapped here, but much more substantial, and more firmly affixed to a smoothed section of the wall now half-submerged in the water. He swept his eyes over the tablet and felt oddly terrified. It wasn't *what* the tablet said, but that he *knew* what the tablet said.

His people had no written language. Not only did he not know how to read, he'd never even understood how reading could function. It just seemed like another form of magic. The larger creatures, like humans and elves, etched special shapes onto pages and bits of wood, and those shapes could conjure the message they were thinking of at the time in the other person's head. What could that be *except* magic. But now, as he looked upon innocuous loops and points, it was as if a voice in his head was speaking the words to him. Astounding, and unsettling. Just to make it more like the speech that had until that moment been the source of everything he'd ever learned, he decided to read the message aloud.

"Woe be to the merfolk unfortunate enough to read this message," he said. "If the divine are true to their covenant and the fates are kind, this tablet will not exist long enough to be read. By the joint workings of Tria and Tren, and under the observation of Tria's Left and Right Hands, the diggers have been sent forth, to reach through the earth and bring forth the cleansing burn of the glowing heart. If the children or children's children of those who witnessed the formation of the Broken Fields look upon this tablet now, fear the stirring of the Great Ancient and the Thieves. Should they rise again, when they fall, they will take the very sea with them."

He stared for a moment, blinking in silence.

"*It was supposed to have instructions!*" he snapped. "Merantia *said!* I don't need a *warning*. I *know* this is all horribly dangerous. The moment I felt the water close over my *head* when Eddy *grabbed* me I knew it was dangerous. It being dangerous and uncertain is why Eddy *likes* it so much. *Being dangerous is what makes it an adventure!*"

He buzzed up to the tablet and kicked it. Though he immediately regretted the decision, while flitting about in pain, his flaring glow cast on another fleck of white further below the half-submerged table. He took a breath and darted below the water. With breath held, he couldn't read aloud, so he was forced to deal with the unsettling experience of having words form in his head simply by looking at the strange shapes.

*This point lies between the cages crafted to hold the lingering spirits of the mages foolhardy enough to threaten the sea in their efforts to prove once and for all which was the mightiest. Like the Great Ancient, and like the Thieves, they could not be extinguished. In death, they remain dedicated to their endless aspirations. The strength of the spirit of Stuartia empowers the chains that bind the Great Ancient. The Spirit of Merantia seals the crypts of the Thieves. The struggling of the Great Ancient seals the cell of Merantia. The flails of the Thieves seal the cell of Stuartia. So long as the creation of one exists, the other shall remain focused upon its defeat. So long as the spirit exists, the beasts of the other cannot escape. So long as the beasts exist, the spirits cannot escape. Pay heed to this. Any who would free the world of their torment must take all in a single stroke, lest the others escape.*

Rustle darted for the surface and spun the droplets of water from his body. He tried to fit the pieces together aloud.

"The Great Ancient and the Thieves. They are dangerous monsters. Merantia and Stuartia *created* them, I suppose? One each. And they hate each other's monsters, and keep them at bay. My magnificent and wise Merantia wants me to destroy Stuartia, free her, and release her beast. … It doesn't say how to destroy Stuartia, but Merantia's beasts somehow fuel the spell that binds her… I would have to destroy her beast to free her… I don't think she wants that. If I destroy *Stuartia's beast*, that would free Stuartia… This is a terrible knot to untie. And I don't know where either beast is anyway, and I don't know how to destroy them. Except, maybe… that bit about 'the cleansing burn of the glowing heart,' and I don't know where *that* is either." His shoulders slumped. "I am going to have to find a lot more tablets…"

A quiet but insistent part of his mind spoke up.

"And *that* is why I need to find Eddy first!"

He darted off toward where his friend had been buried. Now more than ever he needed the merman. There was too much to do for one little fairy.

#

Eddy took a break from hammering two pieces of metal with a rock to catch his breath. This was by a *large* margin the longest he'd ever breathed air, and by an even *larger* margin the longest he'd been entirely out of the water. He did *not* like it. His skin felt awful, like he had been rolling in sand. The worst of his injuries had swollen a bit, and supporting his weight on his folded over tail was easily the most uncomfortable thing he'd ever had to do. He turned aside and flopped onto his back.

"I don't know why surface folk always seem to *build* things. It is terribly unpleasant to work without being able to move freely in all directions."

Now that he'd settled back to rest, he slowly became aware of some fresh aches and pains. His hands felt strangely numb, a consequence of striking great big gears and feeling the shock rebound clear up to his elbow. He may as well have been bashing gongs as well. Each fresh blow brought a mighty clang that left him half deafened and with a throbbing headache. Now that there was relative silence and his hearing was gradually returning, something seemed… off.

Here and there while he'd been working, he'd heard the clacking footsteps of one of those long lobster creatures, but it was always far enough away that he wasn't concerned. Now he was hearing something else. It was far too small to be another such beast. And it was far too close for comfort. He glanced aside. His pick was well out of reach. Quietly he worked himself toward it, wriggling on his back rather than taking his eyes off the stalks around him long enough to flip himself over.

He heard the rustle of stalks and saw a subtle swaying motion.

"Hello?" he called, eyes locked on the source of the motion.

No answer.

He stretched and scrabbled with his fingers until he caught the edge of his pick. When he tried to pull it closer, the long metallic grind shattered the silence.

"*Ha!*" cried a raspy voice from the thicket.

Eddy pulled the pick in front of him as a flurry of motion swept the golden fronds aside. Something stout and frenzied launched toward him and pounced on him. The attacker was a blur of maddened motion, barely discernable. Whatever it was, it was roughly human-shaped. The thing was short and stocky, and from the weight as it grappled with him, it was of a very sturdy build. The assailant was covered head to toe in strange, overlapping plates of chitinous material, bound with twisted golden fronds and accented with sparkling gears and levers. The thing's head was hidden behind a mask of sorts, a rather ornate one with care taken to craft it into a fearsome, angular visage with matted white hair poking out the bottom. It carried two hatchets, one in each hand. They had clearly been fashioned from parts harvested from diggers like Borgle. The heads of the axes were wedges of gear with sharpened teeth. The one thing Eddy had in his favor was a significant size difference. It was very squat, and only a bit over half his height.

"Stop! Stop! Wait!" Eddy grunted.

He curved his tail and flopped to the side, spilling the attacker off him and rolling atop it. Slamming to the ground caused the attacker to lose its grip on its hatchets. They clattered to the ground and the gauntleted hands instead wrapped around the shaft of Eddy's pick. They wrestled over the rusted bit of metal. It was a test of strength. If not for the beating he'd been taking, Eddy would have been able to overcome his opponent, but whatever this thing was, it was stronger than it looked, and his own arms were knotted with fatigue and pain.

"Listen!" Eddy grunted, putting his full weight on the pick and pinning the attacker to the ground. "I don't know who you are, but we can *talk* about this! I don't mean you any harm!"

The struggling attacker responded with a boot to his midsection. Eddy grunted, and grimaced.

"*Fine!*" he barked.

He heaved himself aside. The attacker held tight to the pick until the force of the roll launched it into a tuft of fronds. As it scrabbled to get back on its feet, Eddy jabbed the pick down in to the stone beneath him, embedding its tip and giving him something to anchor himself with. He rolled to his back and held tight to the pick. The squat little attacker recovered and rushed him once more. It made an ill-advised dive. Eddy flexed his entire body, putting his well-developed swimming muscles to work to swing his mighty tail upward. The tail struck the attacker and turned its dive into an arching, out-of-control arc. The hostile creature flew like a batted ball into the half-gutted hulk of the digger Eddy had been scavenging. The hollowed-out shell rang like a bell and rolled over backward, sending sprockets and chains scattering in all directions.

Eddy clenched his teeth tight. His muscles tightened in pain. The attack had further aggravated whatever injury had already been ailing his tail. On the other side of the upended digger, he heard the attacker groan.

"The first thing I see in who knows how long, and it fights dirty..." the thing muttered.

Clattering and clanging signaled the attacker's attempt to haul itself back to its feet. Eddy wrestled with his pick until it finally slid from the ground.

"I didn't want to hurt you, but you attacked me," Eddy said, clutching his pick warily and looking in the direction of the voice.

The attacker limped out from behind the digger hull. The mask was askew. Rather than fight it back into proper alignment, the stranger simply removed it. The face beneath was barely visible, hidden as it was behind dense white hair. Every place hair could find purchase was thick with the stuff. Beard and mustache hid the lower half of the face. Eyebrows so long they curled at the tips reduced the eyes to little more than a twinkle beneath. The hair atop the thing's head was wiry and barely tamed by a sloppy braid that disappeared down the back of its armored suit. Only the forehead and nose were clearly visible, pocked and creased with age.

"Look, I don't understand that garbled nonsense you're spouting, so you can just shut that mouth for all the good it's doing."

Eddy slumped a bit. It seemed he would have to rely upon the spell again.

"If you come and do a hit as your first thing, I do a hit back," he said, struggling to resume use of the badly cast enchantment.

"Ah. So you *can* talk. In a fashion," the creature said.

"Who are you?" Eddy asked.

The stranger pulled a hunk of dislodged digger from the wreck and propped it up as a makeshift seat.

"Mab Mill-Mason," it said.

"I am Eddy. I am a merman."

"Are you? You look a bit more fishy than I thought they looked. I have it in my head that mermaids are half and half."

"Mermaids are. Mermen are different. Are you a very small human, or a normal-size dwarf, Mab?"

"I'm a dwarf. Isn't it obvious?"

"I have seen as many dwarves as you have seen mermen."

"Mmm… I suppose that stands to reason."

"It does stand very much to reason. But now we each have seen one of the other type of thing. Eddy the merman and Mab the dwarfman."

Mab's hirsute brow furrowed. "For someone who can barely talk, you can certainly fit a lot of mistakes into a single word. No one says 'dwarfman.' I'm just a dwarf."

"Oh? But mermaids and mermen are how we say it."

"That's fine. You talk about yourselves however you want. But no one else sees the need for that. And even if we did, you got it wrong."

"Did I?" Eddy leaned forward and squinted. "Are you a dwarfmaid?"

"*It's just dwarf!* Not dwarfman, not dwarfmaid!" Mab snapped. "… But yes."

Eddy pointed. "You have hair on your face."

"Very observant."

"I did not know anything that wasn't a man could have face hair."

"And I didn't know a merman looked like a monster. Nice of fate to give us both a chance to be ignorant."

Eddy smiled. "Yes! It is very nice, and a fair thing. But I still wonder, why did you attack me, Mab the dwarf who has hair on her face."

Mab shut her eyes and shook her head.

"How long have you been here?" she asked.

"A few hours."

"I've been here years. Most everything I've run into has tried to kill me. When sort of thing happens enough times in a row, you make it a habit of making sure you strike first."

"Well I am very much *not* trying to kill you."

Mab removed a gauntlet and rubbed her neck. "You could have fooled me."

"I was trying to be not killed by you. It is very much the same as attacking you, but different, too."

"Fine."

"Is this your home?"

"It is now," she muttered.

"You have a very strange home. I am sorry I smashed through the top of it."

"I'm sorry I did, too."

"Are these diggers *your* diggers?"

"These hunks of slag?" She kicked a gear. "Nothing but spare parts. They don't work, and there's no way *for* them to work. A bunch of moving parts with nothing to move them."

Eddy shook his head. "Not so. A digger brought me here."

Mab creakily stood. "It's been ages since I've had someone to talk to, but if you're going to lie to me, I may as well be alone."

"I tell the truth. Look! It is at the top of the hill there, waiting."

The merman pointed and Mab turned her head. After a bit of squinting, she fetched a cobbled-together contraption that looked to be three eyes harvested from diggers fastened together in a row. She gazed through one end and pointed the other toward Borgle.

"How… By the mountains themselves, how did you get one working."

"I smeared blood on it."

"What has that got to do with getting a clockwork contraption running?"

Eddy pulled himself over to the "head" of the dismantled digger and pointed to the mark. "That thing with the two points. That is the symbol for one of the gods of bad things. Tren. To please Tren you need blood."

"Magic…" Mab muttered. "Of course it was magic."

She kicked the hulk angrily.

"*Who ever heard of magic and clockwork being used together!?* You *stupid, worthless* machine. All of that time wasted patching them up, swapping parts, collecting parts, and it was *magic*. And *you* figured it out when I couldn't? A fish who can barely *talk!*"

"I can talk very much. It is just that I am not so good with the casting of the spell for talking to people who do not talk the talk that I talk when I'm not talking with magic."

Mab shut her eyes angrily and quietly worked through the sentence. "Are you saying you're using magic to speak to me, and that you cast it poorly?"

Eddy nodded.

"Do you think that's supposed to make me feel *better?* That you're bad at magic and you still figured it out when I didn't?" She turned back to the broken digger and thumped it repeatedly with her boot. "Stupid, stupid, stupid machine!"

"Why are you so very much angry now?"

"Do you know how many years I've been here?"

"No."

"Neither do I!"

"I see. No sun and no tides, time can be not easy to count."

"I'm a dwarf. We go months without seeing the sun. Marking the hours as they pass is something we all learn to do intuitively. But I've lost count a hundred times now. I may have been here five years. I may have been here *twenty*. The best guess is keeping track of how long it takes for the Skitter-Clamps to grow."

"Skitter-Clamps?"

"That's what I call the big things that grind these paths into the ground here."

"Oh, yes. Very tasty!"

"You'll change your tune after you've been eating them day in, day out for a few years."

"I will not, because I will be leaving soon. Borgle will help me."

"Borgle?"

"That's the digger I am making work better with these parts! Or I hope I will."

"Right, right. The digger. Wait. I thought you said it was working fine. I can see it moving."

"It is awake, but it is hurt. From the fall from the sea up above."

Mab clapped some dust from her hands and fetched a hammer and pliers from her belt with all of the flair of someone drawing a dagger. "If you need help fixing one, I'm your dwarf. Let's get out of this place."

"Hah! You see! The sea and adventure are the same. They provide a way, no matter how bad things get."

The dwarf glanced about, eying the distance between herself and the functional digger.

"How did you get this far from that thing if you're a fish out of water?"

"Much sliding and much crawling."

"Ah. Well I hope you don't expect me to carry you. That little tussle has got my joints complaining already. I'm not a youngster anymore."

"No, no. I had a thought. I was working on this for helping to move better when you came and tried to kill me with axes."

He painfully slid himself to the project he'd been hammering on before he was assaulted. Two of the larger gears had been roughly affixed to a curved shaft between them. A bit of digger-carcass was attached to the inside of the curve, producing a sling of sorts.

"What is it?" Mab said, scratching her head.

"Wheels! For land moving!" Eddy said proudly.

"You're trying to make a cart?"

"Or something. Anything for land moving. But it isn't a good moving thing yet. More hammering is needed, I think."

Mab marched up and gave it a rattle.

"Wobbly. You'll need to shore this up with a brace. And here you'll want a counter balance. This needs to be straightened. That should be peened over… Give me a few moments. I think I can get you rolling."

"Yes, please!" Eddy said. "Very, *very* please! But let me watch. I want to know the way to build a thing like this. I think people at home will use them."

Mab fished around in the scattered mound of parts and made a few selections, then went to work with speed and skill while Eddy watched with rapt enthusiasm. And to think, he was beginning to wonder if this adventure had taken a turn for the worse!

# Chapter 13

Rustle buzzed about in the wobbling bubble of air he'd dragged down with him. For a last-ditch effort to solve the issue of not being able to breathe water, the bubble was proving to be quite a workable solution. It took concentration to keep it in place around him, but beyond that, if he was focused on his work, he could almost forget he was even underwater.

He'd found his way back to the jagged ground where he'd lost Eddy and was scanning through the wavy surface of his bubble for the lost merman's bag. He grinned as he spotted it, not a dozen yards from where he expected it to be.

"At least I'm still good at navigating by the wind," he murmured to himself, flitting to touch down on the shattered black stone and silt of the cavern floor.

He tugged open the flap.

"The spell book…" he said, almost reverently.

In his journey back to this place, he'd been wracking his brain for what he could or should do to find and rescue his lost friend. An idea had come to him, but before he could even attempt it, he would have to liberate the spell book from the bag. The task was more easily said than done. The book was many times his size, and though fairies were stronger than they looked, he was by no means the strongest fairy he knew. He wriggled into the bag. His improvised air supply caused it to bulge and billow. No matter how he heaved, pushed, buzzed, or shoved, he couldn't get the tome to shift.

"All of the magic I could ever want to learn, and I can't get to it!" he cried in frustration.

He took a moment to rest and think about a solution. All of this traveling, and all of the magic he had been using, had him utterly exhausted. His tiny body burned with fatigue. Now that he'd taken a moment of respite, he discovered just how much of a fight it was to keep his eyes open. He laid back and gazed up at the bag above him. Inflated as it was with the air he'd dragged down with him, he could almost imagine it as a little home. It was cramped enough to make him uncomfortable—small spaces were not a fairy's favorite—but the open end was enough to mitigate those feelings. He fluttered his wings a bit to get them to lay flat beneath him, then put his aching mind to work solving his problem.

Rustle's imagination offered up meager, ill-conceived solutions. He could try wedging the spell book open while it was still inside the bag. … No, there wasn't room. He could cut the bag open. … No, it was rubbery and tough. Being tossed about as much as it was hadn't so much as torn or punctured it. Even with the digging claw, he didn't imagine he would be able to get through it.

Bit by bit, his imagination shifted to other, more enjoyable tasks. He found himself reminiscing about his home. So bright during the day. Nice and cool a night. Predators never came very near. The flowers were heavy with nectar. Oh… Nectar. The sweets Eddy provided were passable, but nothing compared to a sweet, sticky draught of honeysuckle. He could feel it trickling down his throat and spilling over his chin. He could hear the language of his people, complex and musical, not filtered through a spell. It was such a wonderful place, he wondered why he'd ever gotten it in his head that he needed to leave its borders to explore. The image of it dancing in his head was enticing enough to push even the magnificent and compassionate Merantia from his thoughts.

The reverie shattered when he felt himself tipping upward.

"What?" he snorted in a daze.

The book he was laying atop flipped up on end, dumping him out into the warm water. He flailed about and tried to get his bearings as the former contents of the bag plunked down around him and the bag streaked toward the surface. He swam after it and splashed into the air to take a breath, then gazed down. The bag was floating on the surface.

It took him a second or two to realize what had happened. He must have dozed off. Without his mind focused upon it, the bubble he'd dragged down with him bobbed back to the surface, ripping the bag along with it and tipping its contents out. He may not have had the strength to lift it by himself, but his inborn affinity for manipulating air meant the bubble he'd formed was more than a match for it.

"Wow…" he said. "I wish I'd done that on purpose."

He prodded at the bulging bag until it upended. The trapped air spilled out and it drifted back toward the floor of the cavern. The half-second of sleep and the rude awakening had done little to restore his strength, but now that the book was free the promise of its contents was enough to spur him downward, once more with a fresh bubble of air in tow. He lifted the cover of the book. Words formed in his mind as he swept his eyes across the shapes. It was different this time. The words didn't have a precise meaning. They were incantations, not meant to be understood. They were meant to sculpt mystic forces. It wasn't as simple as knowing how the words sounded, he needed to be able to recite them properly. Failure to do so correctly could produce a malfunctioning spell like the one that Eddy had muddled through to enable them to communicate. Doing so with a less innocuous spell could have far more troubling results.

"I can't try 'water-for-air.' For all I know if I botch it I could end up unable to breath *either*. But there must be *something* that can help me, and that won't *hurt* me if I cast it wrong…"

He leafed through the pages. Slowly, as though the thoughts themselves had become jealous for being ignored, he felt his adoration and devotion to the exquisite and infallible Merantia weave back into his mind.

"I should learn something *impressive*…" he mused. "Just think how proud my dear Merantia will be when she discovers I've learned the magic of her people…"

#

Bult, Sitz, and Cul swam along the rift, gazing at the sea floor lit by their combined glow.

"You ever seen a farm, Sitz?" Bult asked.

"Nope," Sitz said.

"How are we supposed to find one if we don't know what it looks like?"

"We know what the rift looks like, right?"

"Sure."

"So we swim until we see a part of it that looks like someone's been digging around in it. Simple."

Bult nodded. "That's good thinking."

"No. That's just ordinary thinking. How long have we been swimming and you didn't speak up to ask that question until now? What were you doing if not watching for something out of the ordinary?"

"I don't know. I was just sort of following. I figured one of you knew."

"Lucky we did," Sitz said.

He turned to Cul.

"Or at least, lucky *I* did. Because Cul here's clammed up again."

"Hmm?" Cul said, looking up at the sound of his name.

"You heard me. You were sure chatty with that shore-lover. And now that you're back among your own you're quiet as a jellyfish," Sitz said. "I never knew you had a taste for the shore."

"It's interesting, that's all."

"Plenty more to see down here than there is up there," Bult said. "The three of us have seen more of the world than any shore-lover *or* surface-dweller ever will."

"I know that. But the thing is, I've *seen* what I've seen. And I haven't seen what she's seen. New is new, even if there's not much of it."

"So it's just novelty then," Sitz said doubtfully.

"I don't like your tone, Sitz," Cul said.

117

"You were making eyes at her. Which is fine. Nothing wrong with having a maid here and there, so long as they don't meet. But those weren't the eyes you were making. Nomads and shore-lovers don't work together in the long haul."

"You don't know what you're talking about, Sitz."

"He thinks you're falling in love with her," Bult said.

"*I* know what he's talking about," Cul snapped. "I'm saying *he* doesn't know what he's talking about. I just met her today! How fast do you think a merman can fall in love?"

"Not that fast, but you've had plenty of time to *think* you're falling in love. Plenty of time to get dragged by the current far enough along to find yourself in a bad place when it finally lets you go."

"What do you care about it anyway? Since when do you have an opinion about who I talk to?"

"Since I'm the one who'll have to drag your mopey tail around behind me when we head on our way and you're left pining for her."

"Has that ever happened?"

"Not to you maybe, but to plenty of others. Remember Hadge? Tried to take a shore-lover with him. The shore-lover couldn't keep up, ended up costing us four whole tides and a rendezvous before they finally cut it off."

Bult nodded. "And then we had to deal with him and his heartache."

"That was after we did business with that same mermaid for over a year," Cul said. "You're seeing things that aren't there, Sitz."

"Care for a wager?"

"On what?"

"If it turns out you're falling for this… What's her name?"

"Mira."

"If it turns out you're falling for Mira, I get the gem she paid you. If we leave her behind and you don't drag the floor like a bottom feeder, I'll give you mine."

"Deal. Easiest gem I ever made. And look. There's the farm. Let's go."

The three came upon the orderly, well-maintained rows of fronds and swam down among them.

"Say… Whoever this missing brother is, he does good work," Bult said.

"So now we found the place, what are we looking for?" Sitz said.

"You know what the sea floor looks like after a bad trembler. Anything that looks like it happened recently and might have hurt someone. Simple," Cul said.

They drifted down and began their investigation. Bult, in particular, was intrigued by the bed of bivalves that made up the pearl farm.

"Pearls... They're precious and all, but it never made sense to me that of *all* the things you find down here, it's the *pearls* that surface folk like most."

"I blame it on the shore-lovers," Sitz said. "It's the same as when you sold those blue snail shells to that couple in Deep Swell and then when we swung around for the next trip everyone wanted one. Nothing special about blue snail shells, except that you can't get them around Deep Swell. But the right person comes along and offers the right thing for sale, and suddenly everyone wants it. Good riddance. It's hard enough getting the good stuff for ourselves. Those crystals from the bottom of the Trensgate? Can you imagine if the surface folk started trying to buy them, too? And then they'd just hang them from the prow of their boats or whatever it is they do with precious things..."

Bult knocked on the shell of one of the larger clams. "How often do you think he checks these? ..."

"Bult, we're here to find Mira's brother, not to steal things," Cul snapped.

"If her brother's dead, by the time someone comes to see to this, it'll have grown back, right?"

Sitz slapped Bult on the back of the head. "You idiot. They'd still know, because it would have been *bigger* if it wasn't taken. ... Now these fronds. No one will miss a few of these."

He tugged a few of the seaweed fronds from the ground and coiled them up.

"Sitz!" Cul growled.

"What's done is done. Not like I can put them back," he said, grinning greasily as he slipped the purloined goods into one of his many pockets.

"What difference does it make? We already don't do business with Barnacle," Bult said. "So what if they think we steal? Shore-lovers barely move around anyway."

"If someone robbed me when they'd been hired to help me, even if I was a shore-lover, I'd make certain I spread the word. Now let's split up. And no one steal anything else," Cul said. "We'll meet back here once we've checked enough of the rift to be certain nothing might have happened near enough to the farm for someone working here to be hurt."

Cul swam forward, taking the center of the rift. Sitz and Bult looked to each other knowingly before taking the north and south walls respectively.

#

Mab hammered at an axle and stepped back. It had only been a few minutes since she'd started working on it, less than half the time Eddy had spent, but that was evidently plenty. She'd completely transformed a rickety assembly of cobbled-together gears and struts into something that Eddy would have believed had been forged specifically for this purpose. A two-wheeled cart of sorts, with its seat slung between the wheels and low to the ground.

"Let's see how that works for you," she said, stowing her tools and slipping her gauntlets back on.

Eddy slid himself up to it and dragged himself into the sling. It was a tricky bit of maneuvering. The cart was eager to roll away from him as he tried to mount it. After a painful flop forward, he managed to slap his tail in place on the sling. He dug his claws into the ground and pulled forward. Sure enough, hand over hand, he was able to "walk" along in much the same position he normally swam, and all without scraping his already somewhat-raw tail along the stone.

"It works! A land roller! I can go on land as easy as you, and without magic!" He paused. "I need magic for the breathing, and for now the talking. Also, it would hurt me very much to go on land high up without magic. But now it would take *less* magic!"

"Enough tinkering," Mab said. "I want to see one of these diggers finally *working* after wasting so much time trying to fix them."

"Yes! We go! Take with you that pile of gears, please. Those are the parts that I think are missing."

Mab gathered the indicated parts and they went on their way. While it was certainly faster and easier to wheel along with the cart, it was also a great deal louder, but Eddy didn't seem to mind. He pulled himself forward with a broad, toothy grin.

"How did you get here, Mab?" he said.

"Long story."

"I *like* long stories. We are *living* in a long story right now! Your story can be part of the story when I tell it to the people back home."

"So, you think you're getting back home, do you?"

"Why would fate send us on a fun adventure to learn all new things, and then not let us get back to *tell* about the adventure. Every adventure ends with *someone* going home again."

"That's not how *my* 'adventure' ended…"

"That's because your adventure isn't *over* yet. But tell me the first part, please!"

She sighed. "I thought I *missed* having someone to talk to… Fine. But listen close. This isn't the sort of story I'm liable to tell twice."

She cleared her throat.

"What do you know about mining?"

"Very much! I have a mine. I got here *from* my mine."

"Good. I had a mine, too. My family did. It ran dry long before *I* was born." She tipped her head. "Poor choice of words. It was never *dry*. We were close to the sea, and water was always finding its way in."

"I can see that would be a problem for a bad swimmer."

"What I meant when I said it ran dry was that we'd mined out everything we could make use of, in the tunnels and caverns that wouldn't flood. The copper was gone in my grandfather's time. We found some good flint, not worth much but always worth *something*. That was gone by my father's time. Now even the strongest and most beautiful *stone* was mostly gone. When you're a dwarf, if you can't find what you need, as often as not, the solution is to go *deeper*. So we dug and dug, and dug and dug and dug. Finally, I found this vast cavern. No telling where it connected to the surface, but the air was fresh, so I climbed down. It went on forever, or so it seemed. Down and out. I didn't know the surface as well as my brother, who had been working another branch of the mine, so I didn't realize that all that digging and exploring had taken me out below the sea."

She shut her eyes.

"Old adage. A dwarf has no place above the trees or below the waves. Put your pick through a wall and flood out a perfectly good shaft and you'll soon understand just how much we *hate* water. But I *didn't* know how far I'd gone. And I was too busy dreaming about just what we could *do* with a cavern so large. If I could prove I was the first to find it, it would belong to the Masonmill family. This place was large enough to found a *city*. So I did what any good dwarf would do. I started sampling the stone. Stupid. Should have waited."

"Why?"

"Because I've got a terrible sense of smell."

Eddy looked up, puzzled. "Why is smell a thing for mining?"

Mab scratched her neck. "Sometimes we strike firedamp without knowing. I suppose it wouldn't be a problem for *you*. You'd just see the bubbles rising."

"Firedamp?"

"It's like bad air that explodes if it touches flame."

"Flame!" Eddy said brightly. "I have just seen flame for the first time. It is hot. Very much of it, and very fast, would be very bad."

"I know…" she said. "It's got a very distinctive smell, but I can't smell it. At some point while I was digging I must have found some of it. If the cavern wasn't so big, I probably would have died. You can't breathe the stuff, you see. Instead, it found one of my lanterns back near the entrance before it found me. Big explosion. Big cave-in. Water started rushing in from everywhere. By the time it had settled enough that I could think, the way back was blocked. I could only follow every fresh path I found to try to stay ahead of the water. My food ran out, my water ran out. Eventually I found this strange, spongy substance growing through the stone. I tried to take a sample and the whole wall gave out. I tumbled down into this place."

She shook her head.

"I really ought to learn not to take samples anymore. Anyway, I'd ended up here. That stuff grew over the hole, and any new holes I dig either get grown over as well or spew water. So I've been living off these fronds and those skitter-clamps for longer than I care to think about. How did you get here?"

"My friend felt air in my mine, and when we went there, I cast a spell I shouldn't have cast and ended up in a place with lots of tunnels. One had Borgle. Then the earth shook and I got buried, but I woke Borgle up and he dug me to here."

Mab shut her eyes.

"The quakes... They've been getting worse, haven't they? Lately they've been bad enough to shake more diggers loose. That's what I thought sent *this* one down here," Mab said, pointing to Borgle, now just a short distance away. "If that stuff wasn't growing on the ceiling, holding it all together, I think this cavern would have collapsed ages ago."

Eddy excitedly rattled up to the top of the hill.

"Borgle! Look, I found a friend who can help make you not broken!" he said.

Borgle released an enthusiastic chime. The points of light in its functional eyes shifted to follow Mab as she walked a slow circle around Borgle. She looked like she was appraising the digger for sale.

"Borgle is a very good digger. Maybe we cannot dig out of here, but if we *can* dig out of here, I'm sure Borgle can dig us out of here. As long as we can figure out how to ask nicely enough," Eddy said.

"You are talking to it," Mab said flatly.

"Yes! How else would he know what it is I am trying to say?"

"This is a mechanism. You wouldn't talk to your pick."

"Sometimes I talk to my pick," Eddy defended. "Mining is long and lonely and talking makes the time pass. When my pick does not cut the rock very much and I *need* it to cut the rock very much, I yell at the pick."

Mab paused. "Granted. It can do a bit of good to shout at a recalcitrant bit of apparatus. But you don't very well expect it to *listen.*"

"Borgle, make some noises!"

The digger produced three deliberate grinding whirs. Mab's jaw dropped.

"So it *thinks* then."

"Yes! It is very good. Very much a wonderful, new thing."

"New isn't always good, Eddy." Mab said. "If a thing can think, it can disagree. Fine for a friend. Lousy for a hammer."

"Good that Borgle is a friend, then," Eddy said.

Mab looked doubtfully between them.

"It doesn't much matter. There's no two ways about this. If we want a way out, this is the thing to do it. Let me see what sort of damage you've done to it."

Mab peered into the open hatch and pawed at the loosened parts and unpopulated slots and holes. Eddy rattled forward to give Borgle a reassuring pat on the "nose."

"Mab is very good with hammering and things, Borgle. You see? She made me this thing for rolling! We'll have you fixed soon, and then, you can dig us to a better place!"

# Chapter 14

Reading a book that is many times larger than one's body is a slow and challenging endeavor. Rustle learned this in no uncertain terms as he flitted to the corner of a page and peeled it back to begin another spell. All of the incantations he'd encountered in Eddy's spell book thus far had been far too dangerous for him to risk miscasting. Aside from refreshing his memory of the ice spell, his perusal had done little to reveal any tools that might help him find Eddy. It was profoundly discouraging.

"There must be *something,*" he murmured, unwilling to give up.

The shapes on the latest page formed words in his mind. This spell was a short one. Its title was simple, if a bit ambiguous.

"Stir the currents… Utter the following words with light focus while gesturing one's hands in the desired direction." He paused. "This might be safe to cast. Even if it isn't, I am wasting time here if I don't try *something.*"

He buzzed upward, dragging his bubble with him, and glanced down at the shifting shapes below. His lips formed the awkward, unfamiliar wording, and he thrust his arms forward. The effect was subtle, and not immediate. At first, he thought the spell had failed entirely. But then he saw that the bubble was rippling forward.

Rustle allowed himself to drop down until all but his head was dipped into the warm water, then repeated the spell. There was no doubt. The water around him moved in the direction he'd waved his arms. It was a tiny motion, barely enough to disturb the bubble or jostle his wings. The size didn't matter, though. What it helped him realize was the *real* prize.

The water moved *just* like the wind did. He wasn't the *best* manipulator of wind by any stretch—though he'd improved markedly over the course of the day through sheer necessity. But until this moment he'd never truly been able to link the motion of water to the same flexing of will that allowed him to stir the breeze. Now he had. It was as though someone had lit a candle in a darkened room, and now he could see what had always been there.

He cast it again and felt its motion. This was *so* like the magics that were a part of him from birth. It was just a matter of *this* twist of the mind instead of *that.* And he *knew* he could navigate by the breeze. He knew he could follow it to the outside, no matter where it led, and feel its presence, even when it was far from him. He cast the spell yet again. In a half-heard whisper, he heard the water begin to tell the same tales.

Again and again he cast the spell. Each time he learned a bit more of how the water differed from air, how to adapt what he knew to what he *needed* to know. Finally, he set the spell aside and instead attempted to sculpt the water around him not with words, but with the same innate magic that was as natural to him as flying.

It took more will than he imagined should ever be necessary for a spell, but finally he felt a sluggish imitation of the spell's effects without the spell. The amount of strength he poured into moving the water would have been enough to cause a veritable *gale* if he'd been directing it to the air, but that didn't matter in the slightest. What mattered was that, just as Merantia had done with her written language, the sea had just made its own voice known to him.

He took a deep breath and let the bubble drift away. His mind became still as he listened to what the currents could tell him. From the wind, he'd already cobbled together an image of much of the cavern, and he knew that there was no connection to the surface. Now a similar, complementary image of the flooded cavern came to mind. It wasn't yet enough for him to navigate by. He could feel that there was, for now at least, no direct connection between this place and the rest of the sea. And he could feel which of the tunnels around him dug deepest into the earth. He could feel chambers, vast and unexplored, that had been just beyond the reach of his glow as he'd flown about.

There was no clear path to the dull flicker of Eddy's spirit in the depths beneath, but there *were* chambers that seemed closer to it. That was enough for him. He launched to the surface and darted toward the largest and deepest of them. It was his best chance to find Eddy.

#

Cul swam along, sweeping his sensitive eyes left and right. The rift that held Eddy's farm wasn't very wide, but it was deep enough to be almost devoid of light, even in the middle of the day. He was limited to what light his own personal glow could provide, and thus could only search a small patch of the rift at a time.

He tried to keep himself from being distracted, but the words of his teammates refused to leave his thoughts. They thought he was falling in love with Mira. Absurd! She simply knew more about the surface than anyone she'd met in ages. Why *wouldn't* he talk to her? She spoke quite intelligently as well, and seemed to be quite the trader. Weren't those worthwhile reasons to have a chat? She was quite lovely, too. A strapping young merman like him would have been a *fool* to pass up a chance to spend some time with her just because she was a shore-lover.

His argument was absolutely solid. He knew he was right. He also knew the only things doing a better job at keeping his mind spinning than the *implications* of his burgeoning feelings for her were his thoughts of her specifically. Her face, her voice.

He shut his eyes for a moment. Infatuation. That's all this was. Again, entirely natural. She was lovely and interesting. It was infatuation. Entirely different from love. Those two didn't know what they were talking about.

The circles of distraction shattered as he heard two high-pitched chirps of a horn. He shifted his direction toward one of the rift walls. Bult had found something.

Though it took scarcely a minute to reach the source of the trumpet toot, Sitz was already there when Cul arrived. The merman had been busy. The pouches of his outfit were notably more tightly packed than they had been when they'd parted ways. Bult's own harvest was even less subtle, with the feathery tips of some stolen fronds sticking out of a pouch on his side. He'd also taken the liberty of snatching a few snails to munch on.

"You two are going to get a thump from Trendana when we get back. We weren't supposed to be robbing this place," Cul said.

"How is she going to find out unless you snitch?" Bult said.

"Yes. Or if she has *eyes*." Cul batted the bit of improperly stowed frond.

Bult tucked the evidence out of sight. "It's just a few fronds… Hardly anything…"

"Did you just call us over here to let us know what a lousy thief you are? Or was there more to it?" Sitz asked.

"Just follow me," Bult muttered.

He swam down to the floor and along the base of the rift. The others stayed close behind. It took a trained eye to see what had convinced him to summon the others. The entire base of the rift was made up of stones that had broken free and tumbled down over the untold centuries. A quick glance would have suggested this stretch of the rift was just more of the same. But the fractures here were fresher, free of the thick growth that clung to everything else. And there were caves as well. Plenty of little shallow caves, some still visible above the mounds of stone. Others were half-obscured by fresh debris. One could only imagine how many others were entirely hidden.

"You called us over here for *this?*" Sitz said.

"A merman could fit in one of these caves. If he'd been in one when the trembler hit, he might have been trapped."

"Why would he be in one of those caves?"

Bult shrugged. "He's a shore-lover. They like little places, right? And look here. This one's got empty shells in it. Maybe he eats lunch in one of these caves. And he's got a mine, right? If these things can get buried, a mine can."

"We've got to tell Mira," Cul said.

"She's going to make us search all of this and we're going to end up missing our first shot at a proper chance to trade in *weeks,*" Sitz objected.

"Someone could be hurt, Sitz," Cul said sharply.

Bult nodded. "We took her gems. A deal's a deal. And I'd want someone looking for me if I got trapped."

"You wouldn't have *got* trapped because you're sensible enough to live your life in the open sea, not cramming yourself into little hollows like an eel…"

"Sitz…" Cul rumbled.

"*Fine.* But if we miss Casta's Drift, remember who just *had* to look around for *nothing.*"

#

"What do dwarves *eat?*" Eddy asked, rocking his improvised cart up and down as he watched Mab work.

Eddy had *thought* it would take only a few replacement gears and a few minutes of work to get Borgle up and running again, but Mab had been working for far longer than it would have taken to install them. Considering her evident skill with machinery, he trusted she knew what she was doing. As a bonus, this gave him the opportunity to indulge his curiosity about this fresh resource on the nature of things beyond the sea.

"Mira says people from the surface eat things that grow in the sun and things that eat the things that grow in the sun. We do the same, except also we eat things that grow in the warmth down below where the sun isn't. You live in caves. Caves are places where the sun *isn't.* So what is there to eat?"

Mab looked wearily to him, then leaned back into the open hatch of the digger. When she replied, her voice had the tinny resonance of Borgle's insides.

"We eat plenty. Mushrooms grow in the mountain. Bats and lizards live in the mountain. We trade for wheat and cabbage and potatoes. And we brew ale."

She paused and pulled herself from her work for a moment. Her eyes were shut. She seemed lost in a lovely memory.

"Oh… the ale. The mead. Even the rotgut. I can feel it on my lips now. I can feel the nourishing *burn* as it trickles down my throat…"

"What are these things you are remembering?" Eddy asked.

"You don't know ale?"

"No."

"It's booze."

Eddy blinked expectantly.

"Don't you drink? … No, I suppose you don't." Mab scratched her head. "How *do* you drink?"

"Fresh water? It comes from the food we eat… What is booze?"

"It is a beverage. A whole *type* of beverage. The *finest* type of beverage. Great, brimming tankards of foamy golden delight. The perfect balance of bitter. Or the harder stuff. Like drinking fire."

"That sounds like it would be not very much fun."

"You only think that because you haven't done it. A little bit of booze eases away the day's troubles. A little bit more hides the woes of life in a pleasant fog. And a *lot* more makes it so hard to think you just give up on it and enjoy the night."

"Oh… *oh*… This is like pannet."

"Which is what?"

"Pannet is like a dough. It is made by the mermaids up at the surface. They leave things in the sun to… turn… not good."

"Ferment."

"Yes. The spell for talking is weak. But they leave it in the sun for that, and then mix it into dough for serving at festivals. Very pleasant. Except if you eat too much. Then, headaches the day after."

Mab nodded. "Yes. That's booze."

"I would like to try some."

"I've made some from these stalks, but it is barely worth drinking. And if you've never had liquor, best not to start with the stuff the dwarfs drink. Talk to some elves. Their stuff is fit for infants."

"I would very much like to meet an elf! Only I have met merfolk and a fairy and now a dwarf and one time a human very far in a boat who didn't see me."

Mab shook her head. "You don't want to meet elves. I don't even think *elves* want to meet elves. I never met an elf who liked anyone else half as much as he liked himself."

"Always some are bad of a type of person. But always some are good as well," Eddy said sagely.

"You find me an elf worth *half* what the worst dwarf is worth and I'll give you a barrel of the finest ale."

"I will do this!"

Again she shook her head. "No, you won't."

She clicked a final cogwheel into place. Eddy didn't need to ask if Mab was through. Borgle made it clear. The mechanism rattled and chimed ecstatically, then raised itself up on its many legs. At first it wobbled and teetered with its blunt nose pointing straight up, then it rearranged and curved a few legs to angle itself to face the others.

"You did it, Mab! You are very much good at fixing!" Eddy crowed.

Mab mopped some sweat from her forehead. "Now to see what good it will do. Can we use this thing to get out of here?"

"We can! Borgle will help us because he is a helper in our adventure! All we need to do is know what it is Borgle should help us by doing. When I ask him to dig, he digs down, and down is not where we need to go."

"This is why you don't use magic to give a machine a mind. A hammer doesn't disobey."

As they spoke, Borgle rolled itself from leg to leg until its two operational eyes were on the bottom of the ring, putting it in a much better position to look Mab over. The merry ticking melody of its workings gradually became harsher. The points of light in its eyes darted about, focusing on various bits Mab's equipment. One of its pincer-tipped legs curved forward and poked at the gearhead hatchet on Mab's belt. Borgle gave an accusing whir and gestured with the same pointer to the open hatch on its side.

"What's this about?" Mab asked irritably.

"I think… Oh, I see. If I may speak to Borgle in my native tongue? It is the language Borgle knows. I *think.* "

"Do what you must. But I don't like how that thing is looking at me."

Eddy cleared his throat and looked to the mechanism.

"Do you think she stole some of your parts?"

Borgle chimed an affirmative.

"It is not so. Do not worry. There are other diggers all about. They fell in here like we did, and all are very broken. Much more broken than you. These parts she has utilized as part of her equipment are from other diggers, not you. Mab is a friend. She is here to help us, and we are here to help her."

Borgle looked doubtfully to Mab. It reached down with a claw and shut its open panel with a slow, deliberate click. The distrustful look lingered for a few moments more before Borgle turned and looked to Eddy, awaiting orders.

"We will tell you what to do as soon as we determine just what it *is* we should do. But listen to me very carefully. Do *not* dig down."

Borgle chimed happily and drove all of his legs deep into the stone angling himself downward.

"No, no, no!" Eddy scolded.

He flopped from his cart and slid between Borgle and the ground. The mechanism came to an abrupt stop rather than bash into Eddy. It gave an inquisitive whir and backed away.

"You can do that *later*. But right now, *down* is not where we need to go. At least, I don't *believe* so. Can you wait? Can you dig downward later? After we get out?"

Borgle chimed and settled down. It kept its eyes focused on Eddy.

"Is that thing through trying to escape then?" Mab asked.

"I think it is," Eddy said, slipping back into his broken enchantment. "I wonder why it is that Borgle wants always to dig *down*."

"Plenty of reasons to dig down. Deeper down is harder to reach, so fewer people have been there. Fewer people having been there means if there's anything good, it's *still* there. Some things you don't even find unless you dig down good and far. I wouldn't advise digging down too much further *here* though."

"Why?"

"Those quakes feel like they are coming from somewhere close." Mab ground at the stone beneath them with her boot. "And this stone doesn't show up unless there is lava nearby."

"What is this, lava?"

"It is stone so hot it is molten."

Eddy's eyes widened. "Glowing pools… I *knew* it! There are glowing pools near here. I have said, many times, the good hot water *must* come from something like glowing pools. And there is a *lot* of good hot water in the rift. So that means there must be glowing pools somewhere."

"I wouldn't be excited. We've got plenty of stories back in the mountains where I grew up about dwarves who dug too deep. Once lava starts flowing it is hard to stop. A few hundred too many pick-blows near molten stone leads to a few million to chisel out what's left of a mine after the lava flows through."

"But glowing pools are important for us! There are only a few, and that is where the *metal* is made."

Mab scratched her head. "You mean you use lava for smelting?"

"Maybe this is what we do? I do not know the words, it is not a thing I do. But tools, things made of metal and not stone, come from people with glowing pools near. And there are *no* glowing pools near Barnacle. We could use some." He scratched his head. "But I should not be talking about things like that. First, we leave this place, then we talk about the exciting parts."

"Agreed."

"Borgle, perhaps you can answer this. Are you *heading* for the glowing pools? The lava?" Eddy asked.

Borgle paused, then released first a knock, then a chime.

Eddy frowned. "I know the knock means no. And the chime means yes. So… No and yes?"

Borgle chimed.

"First you aren't, and then you are?"

The digger chimed much more enthusiastically.

"Splendid!"

"What's all this gibberish?" Mab asked.

"Borgle was digging for the glowing pools."

"Then… maybe we shouldn't have fixed it up. Things are bad enough here already without a harebrained thinking-machine trying to dig a lava well."

"No, it is good. It is a thing we learned. Always it is better to know than to not know. And we know that it is heading somewhere else first! Maybe we can learn that. Maybe *that* is a thing that will help us. Let me talk some more."

"I have a better idea. Why don't you get it to do what we *say* so we can get out of here regardless of what it wants to do. It shouldn't *want* to do anything."

"Do we know what we can do to escape?"

"Do we… what do you think I've been working on since I got here!?"

"You have a way out?"

"I have a *plan* for a way out. I just haven't been able to do anything about it because I'm too *old* and *used up* to do it myself."

"What do you want to do?"

Mab revealed her spyglass and held it up.

"Look, there. Near the edge of that crust of growth on the ceiling."

Eddy turned the looking glass about in his hands, then held it up to his eye.

"This… This is for seeing *far!*" he said excitedly. "Mira says there are things like this that the sailors have!"

"Try to focus, Eddy," Mab said. "It's not the spyglass I'm trying to show you. Do you see that dim spot?"

"Where it does not glow much?"

"Yes. That's what dim means."

"I do."

"I've paid attention to the way that stuff acts. Where there's water, it glows bright. Where there's stone, it has sort of a medium glow. When it's dim like that? That's when it's got *air* behind it. There's a tunnel behind there. And it's the same direction I came from. All we need to do is dig through it and we're out of here. I guarantee you, with a machine that can dig, I can find my way back to dwarf tunnels. I would have been through it *years* ago, but the stuff grows so fast I can't dig through it."

"That is very good for you. Not good for me. I do not need to get to dwarf tunnels. I need to get to the sea."

"Not everything is about you. But if you'd been listening to how I got here, you'd know that most of those tunnels are flooded. The water had to come from *somewhere*."

Eddy considered this.

"It is still not good. My friend Rustle is looking for me. If I go to the tunnels and then to the sea, how will he find me? How will I find him?"

"I couldn't care less. I've been trapped here for longer than I can count. I just want to get out!"

"Yes… maybe this is the part of the adventure where I help the one who helped me…" Eddy nodded. "We go. But when you are on your way, I come back. There is more to explore here, and this is where Rustle will find me."

"I've been all around this place. There's nothing worth seeing except…"

Mab flinched, evidently realizing a word too late that it might not be the best course of action to suggest there is something interesting in the cavern.

"Is there something amazing here? More amazing than the glowing and the stalks and the lobstery tasty things?"

"No. Nothing. Forget I said anything."

"Show me to this interesting place, Mab! Show me and I will ask Borgle to dig you to wherever you want to dig!"

"It is nothing! Just a statue of a mermaid holding a hammer."

"*A statue of one of the right hands of Tria!*" Eddy cried. "You show me! You show me now! Please, please!"

"It's a long way from here, and my legs aren't what they were."

"Borgle, please give our dwarf friend a lift and go where he leads. There is something interesting to see."

Borgle chimed happily and grasped Mab with one pincer, hefting her up and dropping her astride its back.

"What is this! Get me down, you foolish contraption!"

"Now you don't have to walk, Mab! Show us to the statue please, and then we dig where you want to dig!"

Mab made some faces and furious gestures, but ultimately sagged in defeat.

"Very well. This way. At least we can make it quick… It will take us past my home. I could use a drink."

"Forward, Borgle!" Eddy proclaimed. "To the next discovery!"

The digger, moving rather gracelessly along on its many tentacle-like legs, thumped along the ground with a dwarf atop it and a merman in tow.

# Chapter 15

As Borgle, Mab, and Eddy clattered along, the landscape of the cave steadily changed. The sweeping, irregular paths ground into the floor by the skitter-clamps became less common, and those that remained seemed far more deliberate. They were less trails and more roads, carefully maintained and even marked with stones. Signs had been erected, each fashioned from bits of shell and marked with a what may have been charcoal, though the writing was indecipherable to Eddy.

"Did you put these signs?" Eddy called to Mab.

"Who else? I'm the only one here."

"Why did you leave signs if you are the only one here?"

"Have you ever been left alone in a cave for ages?"

"No."

"The mind does strange things. The signs are there half for those days when I can't seem to focus well enough to find my way home, and half so I can pretend I am still in some sort of society."

As they continued, more attempts to civilize the cave came into view. The haphazard, natural layout of the stalks gave way to orderly grids. Shallow rectangular pools were carved into the level parts of the ground and filled with water.

"Those are the farms. The stalks grow better with some irrigation," Mab explained.

"Irrigation?"

"Water. And back there is where I do my cooking."

"Oh, yes. Yes. Cooking. That is heat and food. I cook sometimes as well. With the good hot water. Very nice sometimes. But raw is also nice."

"Animal…" Mab muttered. "The meat of those skitter-clamps doesn't keep very well on its own. But smoked over some burnt stalks it'll last for ages, and it's got a better flavor, too."

"Smoke?"

"Black stuff. Stings the lungs. Goes with fire. How do you not know this?"

"In the very far north and south, where it is coldest, very cold, salty water pushes down from the ice above and freezes when the salt goes. It makes a long hollow tube from the ice above to the sea floor below. Also, the puffy spiny fish make big complicated circles on the ground when they look for mates. The circles are large and if you didn't see them being made, you would never think that something as simple as a puffy spiny fish could make one.”

“What does that have to do with anything?”

“Did you know those things?”

“No.”

“Then we both don’t know about things we’ve never seen before.”

“… Fair enough. Watch yourself. We’re coming to the trench.”

Ahead, a wide, shallow trough had been dug into the ground. It was perfectly angular, with sharp edges and a smooth bottom. The trench traced out a wide circle. It was miles long, at least.

“You did this all yourself?” Eddy said in amazement.

“I’m a dwarf. We dig.”

“But that’s very much digging!”

“I’ve been here for a long time, Eddy.”

“What is the trench for?”

“Skitter clamps won’t cross it. Note how much nicer the stalk fields are on the other side. Though, those things aren’t completely mindless. After hunting them for as long as I have, most of them stay far away. A nuisance, really. Takes ages to track one down and kill it. But it means I can have a few more fields and not worry too much about them getting wrecked.”

“Do you need all of this to stay alive?”

“No. Don’t need half of it. But you give a dwarf time and tools, she’ll get something done or go mad.”

Borgle easily straddled the trench. Even with his cart, Eddy wasn’t going to be able to cross it.

“Borgle, a little help?” Eddy said.

The mechanism turned and looked between Eddy and the trench for a few moments. It lifted one pincer toward the edge of the trench and sparked it.

“Don’t you dare touch that trench!” Mab snapped.

“Stop!” Eddy said quickly. “Just lift me over.”

Borgle chimed happily and used two pincers to grab Eddy’s cart by the wheels and somewhat clumsily heave him to the other side.

“Rotten machine, trying to chip away at what I made…” Mab said.

“Borgle is a digger. Diggers dig, too. Like dwarves. You should be friends!”

“You don’t make friends with tools. And you shouldn’t have to argue with tools and babysit tools lest they ruin what you’ve made.”

“Then Borgle isn’t a tool.”

“I suppose not. More of a pet.”

“Then you can be friends with it!”

“I don’t have much use for pets either. This thing here is a pile of parts. Pretty useful in the shape it’s in. But I’m not so sure it wouldn’t be *more* useful in a different shape entirely.”

"Like what?"

"Like that."

Mab pointed to what was slowly becoming visible behind a jagged berm ahead. As they drew closer and more of the structure revealed itself, Eddy found it progressively more confounding. In its general shape, he supposed it must have been a house. He'd seen a few drawings of what made for shelter on the surface, and this was similar. It had shutters over windows, shingles on the roof. But for everything that was reminiscent of a house, there were three things that Eddy had never seen and couldn't imagine the purpose for. Everything had gears and struts attached. Springs, wheels, and pipes abounded. At one edge, a fire burned underneath a cauldron or kettle. Everything had the same shimmering, shiny look of the metal that composed Borgle's body.

"Is that… your home?" Eddy said in a less than confident tone.

"Such as it is…" Mab muttered.

"You built it out of diggers?"

"There's not much to use around here aside from stone, shell, stalks, and diggers. Diggers have the best material. I don't know what they're made out of, but with nothing but stalks to burn, even with the best bellows I could manage, I couldn't melt them down. It's all I can do to soften them enough to work them."

"It isn't… I do not very much like the thought that you have been using things built by my gods to make a house."

"Well *they* weren't using them anymore."

The trio approached the house.

"How many diggers did you use?"

"Who counts such things? Maybe six. Maybe ten."

Eddy craned his neck. The place was a good deal larger than his own home. If he were to hazard an estimate, he would have placed it at near the size of one of the huge fishing trawlers he'd seen from below when accompanying his sister on trips to nearby villages for trade.

"It seems large for even just ten diggers."

"Those things are packed with useful parts. Hook them together right and they stretch quite a ways."

Borgle stopped at the front door of the gleaming, vaguely clockwork manor. As it had been approaching, Borgle's merry little rhythm of ticking, whirring, and clacking had been getting rougher. Now, as its two functional eyes swept over the structure, its hull was grinding and vibrating. It was almost like a beast's growl.

A pincer curled around and grasped Mab by the collar. It plucked the dwarf from its back and unceremoniously dropped her.

"What has gotten into you, you daft machine?" Mab fumed, pulling herself to her feet and dusting herself off.

Borgle pointed with two pincers at the assortment of gears surrounding the door, then pointed at its own body. It produced a rather aggressive thunk.

"I think Borgle does not very much like you using pieces of its fellow diggers for making things either," Eddy said.

"I don't think Borgle gets to have an opinion. Egad. I didn't think if I ever met another person again I'd find myself longing for solitude so soon."

The doorway wasn't quite large enough for Eddy to easily navigate it in his cart, but that didn't stop him from indulging his curiosity. He flopped from the contraption and slid himself in behind Mab as she trudged inside.

If the outside of the house had been a dizzying and complex bit of ingenuity, the inside was at a whole other level. It was dark, what little light was visible came from bouquets of the golden stalks. Eddy leaned close to scrutinize the walls, which were hung over every available bit of surface with tools of various descriptions. Hammers and picks were most common, but there were also pliers and grippers, knives and tongs, and things he knew neither the name nor the purpose of. Like the building itself, each was fashioned of bits of digger and lashed with twisted stalks.

The ceilings were low, barely tall enough to prevent Mab from bumping her head, but that was hardly a problem for someone who had been reduced to dragging himself along the ground. What *was* a problem was the mounds of scattered parts and debris all over the floor.

"You are not as tidy as you could be, Mab," Eddy said.

The dwarf rattled at some metallic cups and flasks, shaking them to find one that was full.

"I wasn't expecting company. And I don't remember inviting you in," she muttered.

There was more muttering, mostly under her breath, as she leaned over a pile of neatly crafted stone blocks to twirl a handle. Chains and gears squeaked and jingled, causing struts to shift and shutters to rise. The light from the outside bounced off the polished surface of several walls, suddenly bathing the interior of the place with more than adequate light.

Mab pulled a lever and weights dropped, clicking some mechanism or another and yanking open a door that lead further into the home.

"Does everything in this place have a switch or something or other for doing things?"

"When you've got gears and chains, you use them."

He squinted at what little of the bare walls he could see behind the mechanisms. There was etched writing, the kind of spider web-thin lines one gets by scribing with a needle. At first, he supposed it was left over from some sort of mystic writing that had been on the original bits of digger, but the shapes seemed wrong for something of merfolk origin, even the truly ancient stuff he'd been encountering.

"Did you write these things?" he asked.

Mab glanced in his direction, then at the mostly hidden writing.

"Oh. Yes. Ages ago. Just after I built this place."

"What does it say?"

"You wouldn't understand."

"I *don't* understand. That is why I am asking what it says."

"It had to do with dwarfs."

Eddy blinked, patiently waiting for further explanation. Mab sighed.

"I was taught that we only get what we earn in life, and you only earn something by working. Your pay for a job? You earned that. Your good fortune? You earned that. Your bad fortune. You earned that. So, when I got myself trapped here, I knew that it was because I earned it. Did the wrong sort of work. Got the gods mad at me. If you want forgiveness, and the good fortune that comes with it, you've got to earn it. There's more to it than just working, though. You need to let the gods *know* that the work you do today is for them. So, I kept track. Every day, every job. I marked it down. This is a tribute to you. Please see your way fit guiding me home."

Eddy gazed about. The messages peeked out from nearly every bit of wall and support. Even some of the older looking struts had messages scrawled along them. But the newest things lacked them.

"Why did you stop?"

Mab sighed again.

"There is an old saying among the dwarfs. It is a bit too appropriate these days. You can't dig a mine in water."

"You can if it is ice," Eddy said.

"That's why I said *water*, not *ice*. Look, it doesn't matter. What it means is, if you keep working and when you're through you find yourself right where you started, day after day, week after week, then you are doing something wrong. No sense working at it if you'll never succeed."

"So, you gave up. You believed you would never leave this place?"

"I'm still not convinced I ever will. If the gods saw fit to send me a fish out of water and a pile of disobedient scrap, something tells me they weren't too pleased with the work I was doing."

Eddy smiled. "We will show you that you are *wrong*. We are the things you need. Because we are on an adventure, and the hero of an adventure always helps his friends."

The merman seemed as though he had more to say, but he was silenced when the walls around him began to shake. Slowly, one wall lifted and tilted.

"Your house is *moving*, Mab! I did not know houses *did* that," Eddy said, fascinated.

Things started to tumble from the shelf on the offending wall. "It *doesn't* move on its *own.*"

She hustled outside.

"You cut that out!" she snapped.

Borgle, either bored or curious, had found a large handwheel fashioned from the same sort of gear that formed the wheels on Eddy's cart. Spinning the wheel cranked in this chain and spun that strut, causing one corner of the house to shift.

The machine, upon seeing Mab and Eddy emerge from the house, backed away, awaiting new orders. Mab muttered under her breath and spun the wheel in the opposite direction, restoring the house to its proper angle.

"What is that for?" Eddy asked.

"When the earth shakes, sometimes it settles differently. I designed this place so I can level it. Now come on. I need to stock the still."

She stomped irritably around to the rear of the house, where a small hallway from the inside ended at a large, simmering kettle. The sides of the hallway were strapped with bundles of stalks, some still plump with their sweet liquid, some dried husks. She grabbed a few of each and approached a potbellied monstrosity that rattled and rumbled almost as aggressively as Borgle had.

Eddy dragged himself up and practically pushed Mab aside to investigate it.

"What is *this*?" he said, eyes wide and face enthusiastic.

"I said. It's a still. It's for making booze."

"Why does it bubble and hum?"

"Because you need heat the… Look, I'm not here to educate you. And even if I was, I wouldn't educate you about *this*. This is just about the worst made still, which makes the worst made booze, that you've ever seen."

He nodded. "This is very much so. But also, it is the best. Because it is the only."

"If we make it out of here, maybe you could cart yourself down to Smeltersons Distillery. The stills are bigger than this house, and there are dozens of them. Some of the best brew and booze to be had, and enough of it to keep a whole mountainside of dwarves from getting thirsty."

"Maybe I will!" Eddy said. "With this cart, I do not even need land swimmers. And I can…"

Eddy trailed off when Mab kicked open the door to the fire box.

"Wow…"

Mab raised an eyebrow. "What?"

"Look at the glowing…" Eddy said, approaching the dusty, smoldering embers. "And the heat. I can feel the heat."

"You are easily amused."

"It is like... little fragments of a glowing pool…"

"There plenty of things down here that glow."

"But not that color. That red color. I've only ever seen fire once. I didn't know it could be so still…"

"Between your lackluster language and how easily amazed you are, I'm beginning to think you aren't the most brilliant specimen of mermen."

Mab loaded up the firebox, sprinkled a bit of this and that into the assorted compartments and canisters of the still, and decanted some sort of liquid.

"Is that the booze?" Eddy asked eagerly.

"It is…" Mab rumbled.

She was clearly running short of patience. Eddy remained oblivious to that fact.

"I would very much like to taste some please! I am a little thirsty and you make me want to know what booze is like."

"I said it before. This isn't for you. Badly made dwarfen rotgut is no way to introduce yourself to the world of spirits. That you think this is the sort of thing you drink when you are thirsty is sign enough that you're not savvy enough to be drinking it."

Eddy rolled to his back so he could cross his arms. "I am an adult. I am savvy. More savvy about the sea than you, and that's where we are."

"But we *aren't* in the sea, we're in a cave *under* the sea."

"Mab, if you do not want to share with me because you want more for yourself, that is your decision. But if you do not want to share with me because you are afraid I do not know how to *drink.* That is *my* decision. I would like very much to try some."

Mab shook her head. "It's your funeral."

She fetched a hammered metal cup and decanted some of the liquor from the bottle she had just filled. Eddy sat up and propped himself against a wall in a sitting position. He held out his hands like a child receiving candy and accepted the cup.

To his credit, Eddy didn't immediately gulp it down. While Mab jingled and sloshed other nearby bottles, he tipped the cup back and forth and considered the contents. It was almost perfectly clear, though to his eye there might have been a slight amber tint. It was a bit thinner than water. Even to his untrained and stunted sense of smell it was powerful in its scent, similar to but significantly more substantial than the more delicate aroma of pannet. He dipped his finger into the stuff. It felt warm from the still, yet strangely cold at the same time as he pulled his finger away.

Once he'd tested it with all other senses, *then* he gulped it down.

His large eyes opened wide. Catlike slits of his eyes opened round and large as saucers. The glow of his fins surged extra bright. He gaped his mouth open and tilted his head back, silently panting.

"A bit much, yes?" Mab said, handing him a second cup.

Eddy waved it off as though he were being offered a vial of poison.

"It's fresh water," she said, pushing it back in his face.

He snatched it and drained the cup in one grateful swallow.

"I warned you," Mab said.

"Not enough," Eddy wheezed. "It does not even have a flavor. It is just pain on my tongue. You drink that?"

"Every day."

"Are you hollow inside? It feels like it is eating a hole through my belly. Is that because it is my first drink?"

"Nope." She tipped back a swig from the bottle. "You just start to look forward to the fire in your belly."

Eddy tipped his head back again and resumed his baby bird position, tongue lolled out and eyes slowly easing back to normal. Mab chuckled at the bizarre sight. Her jovial attitude faltered when she heard a sudden and vigorous cranking noise and one corner of her home started to raise up.

"Again!?" Mab growled, thundering off toward Borgle.

#

Mira gazed down at the inky depths below.

"They've been down there a long time…" she said, anxiety in her tone.

"That's good news!" Cora said. "Seems to me if there was something that *definitely* meant bad things for your brother, they'd have spotted it really quick. That they're taking their time probably means there's not much damage to see."

"I hope you're right…"

Cora fished out the gem she'd taken as payment and twisted it in her fingers.

"I don't know much about mining. Do you get all sorts of gems out of just the one hole? Or is it one type of gem per mine?"

"Mostly you are lucky if you find any gems or precious materials at all, let alone more than one type. We have been very lucky that our mine has had a great deal of variety, if not a great deal of quantity."

"That's nice. Shows Mer is smiling upon you. That's what father used to say. … *There*! Is that them?"

Cora squinted downward.

"Oh, sure. That's Cul alright. Easy to spot him. There aren't too many mermen with just the one eye."

"What happened to the other eye?"

"He had a belly full of pannet and thought he'd show a guard at Deep Swell who was boss."

"I haven't been to Deep Swell, but I've heard the mer*maids* are as formidable as mermen, and the mermen are absolute beasts."

"Cul can attest. They hit harder than they have any right to."

Sitz, Bult, and Cul approached from below.

"Did you find anything?"

"Mira, it is probably nothing but—" Cul began.

"A bunch of rocks fell along the edge of the rift. Could have crushed someone if he wasn't paying attention," Bult said.

"Bult!" Cul scolded, slapping him in the head.

"What? It isn't a lie," Bult said. "We've got to set her expectations."

"We didn't find any sign of him," Cul said. "But there was definitely some damage near the seaward side of the farm. The rest of the farm held up well."

"The seaward side is where the entrance to the mine is…" Mira said shakily.

"Tell us where it is and we'll take a look."

"It isn't as easy as that," Mira said. "There's vents. Scalding water. Eddy needs to wear a special outfit to get past it."

"So you pulling us way out here out of our way was just a waste of everyone's time, then," Sitz muttered.

Cul slapped him in the head as well.

"I thought it was best to… I thought if it all happened quickly… This is terrible…"

"Do you have more of the equipment?"

"His spare is in for repair. The material is hard to get, and he's the only one who needs to go to the mine. I'll get it. I'll go get it and I'll see if any of the others have suits they can spare. By now surely the commotion has died down back in Barnacle. I can get the others back home to help me."

"Good. Then we'll be on our way then," Sitz said.

"You go. I'm helping her," Cul growled.

"Yeah. You can't just tell a girl her brother might be hurt and then go on your way. Where's your heart?" Cora said.

"Right near my stomach, which'll be growling if I don't get the money it takes to keep me fed, and that won't happen if—" Sitz began.

"*Then go*. No sense wasting everyone's time arguing," Cul said.

He thrust his tail and headed shoreward with Mira. Cora lingered long enough to glare at Sitz and Bult.

"You're why shore-lovers look at us like we're nothing but flotsam, Sitz."

"Call me names if you want. No one else can watch ol' Sitz's back better than Sitz. I owe it to me keep my best interests in mind. Bult knows, right, Bult?"

Bult glanced between Sitz and Cora.

"I think I'll head back down and see if I can't find someone pinned under something," Bult said.

Bult drifted downward, leaving Cora to offer one last judgmental glance at Sitz.

"Fine. You can all waste your time! More for me when we meet with Casta's Drift!"

He darted off to the south. Cora shook her head.

"The things you learn about your friends when things get tough…"

# Chapter 16

Rustle, once again enclosed in a bubble thanks to his lack of the proper enchantment to breathe water, navigated a wide tunnel that had branched from the main one. His slowly improving skills at navigating by the currents the same way he navigated by the breeze had led forward quite reliably. What was failing him, as was so often the case, was his nerve.

"I've got to do it for Eddy. And I've got to do it for Merantia. I've got to do it for Eddy. And I've got to do it for Merantia…"

He muttered the phrases over and over again, hoping to drown out the darker thoughts flitting through his brain. Of course he would rather *die* than fail the magnificent and wise Merantia, but that didn't change the fact that if he *did* die he would *still* fail Merantia. And right now, death was becoming more and more likely, if his intuition had anything to say about it.

Nothing in particular stood out to suggest he was walking into the jaws of danger, but there was something in the air—or rather, in the water—that didn't feel right. It was… dead here. He couldn't quite put the feeling to words, but if the lifelessness that seemed so out of place to Eddy back in the main cavern were to be treated as just another current, then it felt like this tunnel was its source. The farther he traveled, the more thoroughly he became convinced that the vibrant, vital nature of the sea was somehow draining in this direction. His magic, which by sheer duration of usage was beginning to make him weary again, seemed to require incrementally more effort to keep in place the farther he went.

Then came the first physical evidence that what he was feeling was not all in his mind. It was a gate, the same sort that blocked off the chambers of Stuartia and Merantia, but large enough to span the whole of a tunnel easily five times the size of theirs. He squeezed himself and the bubble thorough the grating and, shortly thereafter, he found another, and another.

"Three gates…" he muttered. "The wizards who almost destroyed the sea got one gate each. Whatever is in the chamber has three… What am I getting myself into?" he murmured.

His wavering glow barely cut into the blackness ahead. New sensations filled his mind. For a moment, he thought back to how Eddy didn't seem to be sensitive to such things. He envied that sort of spiritual blindness now. Stuartia's chamber had felt like a will without a mind. Merantia's chamber felt like a mind without a will. This was… something else. It felt like a hole into which both mind and will fell. Rustle believed, at the very least, he'd known what 'nothing' was. Now he realized he had been wrong. This, what he was feeling here, was so much less than what he would have called nothingness before. This was a gnawing hunger, something that drew at even the darkness in search of some sort of nourishment. It made him feel cold and hollow inside, and it was only getting worse.

Light finally glimmered upon something below. He swallowed hard and flitted downward. Gradually, an array of what could only be described as crypts spread out beneath him. They stretched endlessly in all directions, ancient stone boxes etched with symbols. The stone had flaked and pitted. If such a thing were possible, he would have believed the rock itself had somehow rotted away. So great was the damage to each crypt that he had difficulty finding one with all of its symbols fully intact. When he found one, the shapes sluggishly brought thoughts to mind. Elsewhere, simply seeing the symbols the merfolk called a language had been enough for him to understand their meaning ever since the wondrous Merantia had provided him with the proper knowledge. He wondered if the slow, incomplete understanding he felt now was because these symbols were beyond even Merantia's understanding, or because the spell itself was being weakened by the withering influence of the chamber.

"Within this box…" he uttered, drifting as close as he dared, "there lies entombed a Thief of Stuartia's creation. Its mind is empty. Its heart is stone. The being knows only hunger and the will of its creator. A single thief is a foe fit for the greatest of warriors. Here rests an army. Destroy them utterly, as we have sought to do, or leave them undisturbed. Do not risk the release of a single thief, or the others will soon rise, and only the edge of the sea shall contain their wrath."

Rustle blinked and tried to come to terms with the words. Like all matters of ancient history and magic, there was a riddle-like quality to them, though far less so than many such warnings. Destroy them all or leave them be. That was simple enough to understand. He should continue along, to find what corner of this massive cavern took him nearest to the glimmering glow of Eddy's spirit… But these were the creations of Stuartia.

He felt anger and hate smolder inside him. It was an anger fueled by an ancient rivalry, a hatred spurred on by events that happened ages before Rustle or anyone he'd ever known was even born. The tiny part of him that had not fallen wholly under Merantia's influence bucked and struggled under the weight of it. Little sparks of logic and wisdom flickered feebly under Merantia's thrall. This was not his fight. What did he care about these 'thieves,' whatever they were? He should heed the warnings. He should search for Eddy and leave this terrible place behind.

It wasn't enough. His desire to make the stunning and majestic Merantia proud, and the smoldering hate that she had thrust upon him for all things with Stuartia's influence, were too great. He raised his digging claw and brought it down. It bit easily into the stone, like he was chipping away at stale bread. Whatever had weakened the stone had done so thorough a job that large chunks of the dusty stuff sloughed away at the pecking of his tiny weapon. He hammered and slammed the point of the claw against the stone with the intensity of a woodpecker, chiseling a line across the center and tracing back across it. The pulverized stone, already barely strong enough to hold up its own weight, slumped down and crumbled atop whatever the crypt held. He darted down to rummage through the rubble in search of something his claw could slice into. The moment his tiny feet touched the dark, scale-like hide of what lie within, he felt an icy shock of pain. It was like even *touching* the thing had practically torn his soul from his body. In spite of Merantia's influence, in spite of the externally imposed hatred, his body decided of its own accord that he would not remain anywhere near something that could injure him so. He darted up and away, until his glow barely traced out the edge of the still crumbling crypt, then watched wide-eyed as the thing he'd been determined to destroy emerged.

It was large, easily the size of a bear—which was the largest beast he'd ever had the poor fortune of encountering back in the woods. But it didn't look like any bear he'd ever seen. The thing was angular, sharp. And it was familiar. It didn't take long for him to realize this was one of the strange interlocking beasts that served as the backdrop for the carving in Merantia's cavern. Six legs, scythe-like pincers. He would have compared it to an insect, but at this size it was difficult to even imagine such a thing. It was more like one of a dozen creatures he'd seen skittering along the sea floor while Eddy had been bringing him to the farm. And there was more. The chitinous hide had regular grooves coiling into complex whorls. They seemed far too consistent to be anything devised by nature, but they had no meaning that he could determine.

Though the thing had drifted up, shedding the remnants of the shattered stone slab, its tangle of limbs remained limp, motionless. It was floating, not swimming.

"I… I can see why the divine and infallible Merantia wishes these things to be destroyed…" he muttered, the tiniest feeling of relief settling over him as he realized it was not poised to attack. "They are horrible. But perhaps I am lucky. Perhaps *time* has done the job for us. I do not know of anything that can live for so long locked in a box."

A brittle smile crossed his lips and he flitted closer.

"Yes… yes, that must be it. The people who locked them up engraved them with a message that claimed they'd intended to kill them all. Locking them up must have been how they were going to do it. And it worked! Merantia will be very pleased with me for discovering this."

He paused.

"But it did hurt my foot in a very strange way when I landed on it. Perhaps, like the wretched and profane Stuartia, it remains dangerous even in death?"

He buzzed closer and gazed at it.

"Dead things rot, don't they? This did not rot. And it is not a machine like the thing Eddy found. … Eddy… I need to find Eddy, and I can't until I *know* that I can destroy one of these creatures. If I can destroy one, then I can destroy the rest."

Rustle rubbed his hands together.

"It is the only strong spell I know, and it was very dangerous to Eddy. I owe it to the glorious and resplendent Merantia to give it a try."

He shut his eyes and forced away as much of the buzzing doubt, fear, and concern as he could manage. With each casting, the spell was becoming easier to remember. He held his hands out past the edge of his bubble and spoke the words quickly and clearly. Curling lances of mystic light sprung from his hands, but they slowed as they sliced toward the creature. Filaments of ice formed behind them. When the spell struck the inert being it splashed against the thing and caused a thick layer of ice to encase it. The ice froze tight around its head, or at least the part of the creature that held its mandibles.

Rustle heaved a breath of relief and flitted back to the center of the bubble. He shook frost from his fingers.

"There," he said. "Right in the face. If the thing has to breathe, that will end it."

He allowed a feeling of pride and self-satisfaction roll over him. The feeling, alas, was brief. A tiny crack in the ice shattered his confidence in the efficacy of his attack. The thin crack formed at the base of one of the pincers. Then another wove toward it. Though the ice was not visibly melting, somehow Rustle could *feel* it weakening, as though the supernatural freezing of the water was being undone somehow.

The water split with the sound of cracking ice as the pincers spread. Fragments of ice crystal burst toward him, peppering the surface of the bubble. One of the creature's legs twitched.

"No! No, no, no, no, no!" Rustle cried.

He darted in panicked circles. Not even Merantia's powerful enchantment was strong enough to overcome the instinct that had served Rustle's people so faithfully over the generations. If something was scary, flee.

Rustle squealed in a decidedly unheroic manner and buzzed in a random direction. He didn't care where he was going, just that he was getting away from whatever that thing was before it realized where *he* was.

#

"You were not lying, Mab. This statue *is* far," Eddy remarked.

It was telling that his endless enthusiasm for all things was far less prevalent in his voice than usual.

"I told you," Mab said, holding tight to Borgle as the thing tirelessly thumped along.

Eddy stopped and flexed his clawed fingers. Borgle, quickly determining that his merman companion had chosen to take a break, stopped and turned to him.

"Something wrong?" Mab asked. "Getting tired, or hungry?"

"I am not very much tired, and I am not very much hungry. But I am very much… dry. And my hands hurt."

"Dry? I'd wondered about that. I don't remember any stories of mermen crawling along on the land. Seems like you folk would spend most of your time in the water for a reason."

"No, no. That is not what I mean." Eddy looked over his hand and rubbed at the skin somewhat. "Perhaps that is *part* of what I mean. I do very much want to be swimming again. But I mean… I am having trouble with the word. When you need to have water inside you."

"Thirsty?"

"Yes! That is the word. The air-for-water spell does very much to make it so I do not have to be in water to live, but it is not perfect. Or maybe I did not cast it perfect. And I get most of my water from my food, and that lobster thing was not very wet."

"So drink something."

"What is there to drink?" Eddy shut his eyes and shook his head. "Except booze. No booze."

"I have a canteen of water, but I don't want your fishy lips all over it."

"Where did you get water?"

"You can wring some sticky, sweet stuff out of these stalks. Refreshing the first few dozen times I drank it, but after that I had to gather the parts to build my still so I could render it down to fresh water."

"I will try some!"

He flopped from his cart and tugged one of the stalks from a nearby tuft. A sniff or two convinced him it probably wasn't poisonous, so he stuffed one end in his mouth and sliced through it with his serrated teeth. A rush of thin, slightly syrupy liquid filled his mouth. It wasn't the cool, quenching sensation he would have liked, but it was certainly better than nothing. After sucking and chewing upon the mouthful of stalk for a moment he was left with nothing but fibrous remnants. He spat them free and took another bite.

"I usually wring it out into my mouth," Mab said.

"It is good to chew," Eddy said, the faintly glowing nectar slopping out juicily. "All the best things need to be chewed. It is why we have teeth."

He finished chewing up and spitting out one whole stalk and grabbed another to dangle from his mouth as they continued on. Borgle happily clanked its way up a smooth slope.

"It isn't much farther now," Mab said, sipping from her canteen.

"How did you find this place?"

"When I first got here, I was looking for *anyone* else. Any*thing* else, even. I like a bit of solitude, but when days and months go by without another voice besides the ones in your head, you start to worry you won't be able to tell what's real from what isn't."

Mab paused and glanced down.

"You… *are* really here, aren't you?"

"I am as here as you are," Eddy said with a smile.

"But how do I *know*? Not so long ago, I found myself arguing with my sister-in-law for the better part of a day before I realized I was just shouting at my own echo."

Eddy paused long enough to spit out his current mouthful and take another bite.

"That is a very interesting thing to ask me, Mab. How do I prove I am not imaginary? How do I prove *you* are not imaginary? … How about this?"

He picked up a stone and threw it at Mab. It bounced harmlessly off her makeshift armor.

"What was *that* for?"

"Imagined things do not throw stones," Eddy suggested.

"But I could have just *imagined* you threw a stone."

"Mmm… Yes. This is very tricky… Maybe this is the question you should ask. What does it matter?"

"What do you *mean* what does it matter? There is a difference between reality and fantasy. It is an important difference!"

"Not for you and me right now it is not. Maybe there is a place where you are not real. Maybe there is a place where I am not real. Many people do not know about mermen, and I did not know about dwarfmaids. So until we *did* know about each other, it didn't matter if we were real. So we *weren't* real. Not to each other. But at the same time, we were always real. Something can be real and not real at the same time. If it helps you, and it does not hurt someone else, then what does it matter if it is real or not?"

"… Are you certain you aren't a booze drinker, because right now it sounds as though you've had a bit too much."

"One taste of booze was too much. And I have not had pannet since the Neap Tide Festival." He rubbed his head. "I had too much, then. Pannet is *very* strong."

Mab looked at her canteen. "Well if you're real, and we *do* get out of here, I'll have to try it. I could use some. What does it taste—"

"I see the statue!" Eddy blurted, pointing excitedly as they crested the slope.

A much, *much* thicker field of stalks covered the gentle slope on the far side of the peak they'd just reached. Their glow was brighter as well. Unlike in the rest of this strange cavern, the stalks were entirely undisturbed. No sweeping paths where the skitter-clamps may have mowed them down. At the bottom of the slope there was a small pool. Its surface was glassy smooth, utterly motionless. Beneath the surface, clearly illuminated by the surrounding glow, was a gray form grasping a round-headed hammer.

Eddy heaved the wheels of his cart over the peak and scrambled with his hands to pull himself toward the mysterious statue. Stalks split and tore free as he plowed through them, spilling their sticky contents all over him. Soon the momentum was such that the cart wanted to move more quickly than his hands could oblige. Very shortly after that, he hit a stone that overturned the cart. He flopped and rolled through the remaining stalks until he splashed into the deep, clear pool.

It took him a second or two to recover from the tumble. He likely should have taken a few more seconds, because his first action upon landing in the pool was to take a deep, refreshing breath of water. Having not yet banished the effects of the air-for-water spell, this did not produce the desired effect.

He burst to the surface, hacked up the breath of water, and blinked at Mab and Borgle, who had taken a more leisurely pace to the edge of the pool.

"You're about as graceful on land as I'd *expect* a fish to be," Mab said.

"All of this moving between water and air is very confusing," Eddy said. "I wonder if the maids have trouble keeping things straight."

"Don't know, don't care. This is the statue. I think you'll agree, it wasn't worth the trip."

"Wasn't worth the trip!? Are you mad, Mab?"

Eddy took a deep breath. It was something he was quite unaccustomed to doing before a swim, but it was easier than casting the water-for-air spell and the air-for-water spell over and over whenever he needed to talk to Mab. He dunked below the water.

The statue was exquisite. Eddy did not have an eye for stone, but if he were to venture a guess he would suppose it was some manner of marble. It glimmered in the light of his eyes and the glow of the stalks with a pearl-like sheen. The figure was certainly a mermaid, and certainly beautiful, but not in the way most mermaids were. Her hair was short, her arms and tail hardened by travel and toil. One hand held the handle of a metal hammer that must have weighed twice what Eddy did. The other held a heavy chisel. He turned and glanced about. The floor was strange, perfectly flat, and with seams, as though it had been not just carved, but constructed from slabs of stone. Then he looked to the walls. His eyes widened.

Eddy burst to the surface and took a breath.

"There is writing! Writing all around. You didn't mention that."

"I didn't know that," Mab said. "Dwarfs don't do well in water. Didn't even think to check. What does it say?"

"I don't know, there's a lot of it. I will take another look."

He dove again and turned his eyes to the walls.

The words were chiseled in a precise, steady hand. They wove a tale, one Eddy had never heard before. He found the start and eagerly began reading…

*Whomsoever may read this, I apologize for the sorrow and tragedy that brought you here. The fault can only be my own, for mine was the task left unfinished…*

#

Whomsoever may read this, I apologize for the sorrow and tragedy that brought you here. The fault can only be my own, for mine was the task left unfinished. May Tria forgive me, and take as my replacement someone worthy of her trust, as I certainly was not. All that remains for me is to record for you how this terrible misfortune came to be, and she who should be cursed by those who have suffered for it.

My name is Dua. For a time, I was the second of Tria's three right hands. I still remember the day I was selected by her. I was one of the builders of her great temple, a place now shattered and broken. Tria smiles upon the crafters, the makers. I had devoted my life to honing my craft, and to honoring her name. Mine was the first chisel to meet stone when her temple's construction began, and mine was the last hammer to fall when it was completed. I gained her favor, and so she took me as her apprentice.

The tasks of the hands of Tria are not for mortals to know, but if the sea functions, know that it functions in part by her machinations. She is divine, a being slow to anger and quick to forgive. Even her own brother, Tren the Breaker, was dear to her heart. But there was one thing she could not abide.

Just as a single clumsy blow from an unskilled sculptor can ruin the work of master, so can the fumbling of lesser beings threaten the workings of the mighty. Tria wished for all to know the joy and value of building, but mortals were to keep to the things of mortals, and gods to keep to the things of gods. Two mortals had taken up the forces of the sea and turned them upon each other. They were not divine, but swam closer than any before had come, and they knew not how to wield such raw power with discretion and reason.

I shall not sully these walls with their names. Better they should be forgotten. They deserve no place within our history. But in their thirst for that most worthless of things—glory—they unleashed terrible horrors upon the sea. It was a dark day, the day the walls were raised. The day the sea boiled. The temple I helped to build fell that day. Many places fell. And had Tria not sought the help of her brother Tren, what was made would have been the end of sea.

It was a terrible battle, the nearest since the dawn of time that the gods themselves had come to intervening. Let us all be thankful they did not. Just as a flake of ice melts in the warmth of the southern currents, so would the world be snuffed out should the gods ever show their true power. I swung my hammer. All the hands of Tria did. The followers of Tren jabbed their spears. The beasts and their creators were broken.

Alas, for things of such power, it is not enough that they be broken. They must be unmade, lest they rise again. We pleaded with the vile summoners of the horrible beasts, in their fading moments, to unravel the spells that bound their creations to this world. They refused, blinded as they were by hate. Tren assured us that it was within his power, and the power of his avatars to strike them down again and again, should the need arise. But each battle would be more potent than the last. Soon the clash to strike them down would be as dangerous as the one we had worked to stop. So Tria sought another way.

Though the sea is mighty, it still is but a blanket thrown about the shoulders of the land below. The beating of the waves may wear down the tallest of mountains, but the forge and crucible that lays at the heart of the land shall always build them anew. Such is the balance. And if these terrible creations are the work of the sea and its children, then it was the throbbing heart of the land which must be called upon to wipe them from this world. It fell upon our shoulders to prick the finger of the earth, such that its blood might mix with the sea and wipe away this terrible mistake once and for all.

We all had a task. Mine was in most ways the simplest. I was to plot the path, to be the first to find the route to the heart of the earth. As ever, I swung my hammer fast and true. I bored through the sea floor while the others worked to craft machines that could do the same. And in time, I came to this place. We had selected this patch of the sea because the ground was nearly as firm a prison for the forces of magic as the caverns to the west. It had shielded this place for untold ages. I do not know how or when the strange plants and creatures I found here came to be, but they fascinated me. When I finally found the molten earth we sought, I instructed the others and the diggers were given their destinations. It would take them many years to burrow through and reach the cleansing blood of the earth, and it would do little good if only one or two of them reached it. A trickle would not perform the task we sought. We would need a flood.

Left and Right hands, under the guidance of Tria and Tren, had done fine work on the diggers, but we couldn't trust that they would function perfectly for as long as was required. Someone needed to stay behind, to repair those that failed, to awaken those that slept. I volunteered.

The task should have gone to someone stronger, wiser.

While I waited for them to make their way, I returned to this place. I studied the creatures. I tinkered and crafted. My focus wavered. I was a fool.

The thieves and the Great Ancient both slept. The Great Ancient was a threat only when it stirred, and my fellow hands forged the chains strong enough to hold for a hundred lifetimes. We believed that at rest, the thieves would be harmless. We were wrong. Too late I learned even while they slumbered, even while locked away in their crypts, their hunger was not slaked. They sipped at the strength of the sea. They drew away the power from anything within the cavern. And what they fed upon grew weaker. The growth in the cave. The diggers. Even myself.

By the time I realized what was happening, it was too late for me. I lacked the strength to leave this place. In time, some of the diggers found their way here, but only a few. They all should have. They should have bored tunnels to the chambers of the thieves and the Great Ancient, then tunneled to this place and beyond, to unleash the molten blood of the earth to end the monstrous creations once and for all. But they were weak, they ran down, and without me to tend to them, they would never awake.

I do not know what became of the others. I do not know why no help ever came for me. Perhaps even the eyes of the divine cannot pierce the stone of this prison. Perhaps this was a test, and I have failed. No matter. I abandoned my task long enough for it to become impossible to complete. I am undeserving of my place as one of the hands of Tria. As I record this, the stalks and creatures that once thrived in this place are withering, succumbing to the same terrible thirst that weakened me and the diggers. If they vanish entirely, I shall wither and die without them to sustain me.

There has been little for me to work with here, but I have done my best to craft a mechanism which might complete the task of which I have been so poor a shepherd. It is complete, but just as I lack the strength to leave this place, I lack the strength to awaken it. It rests beneath me, as useless as I. All is lost for me.

I have resolved to sacrifice myself. I give up my vitality, my immortality. May its power push back the terrible hunger of the thieves and allow this place and the sea around it to recover. Perhaps it will allow the diggers to awaken again. Perhaps it will merely delay the inevitable awakening of our slumbering foes. It does not matter. It is the last act available to me. May Tria and Mer have mercy upon me and forgive my failure.

#

Eddy surfaced for the tenth time and recounted the last of the tale. He huffed and puffed.

"Holding breath very much is not fun at all. Now I know why surface people do not swim very deep…"

"So that thing down there is a demigod?" Mab said.

"Yes! She is an almost god. I am not a worshiper of Tria, I worship Mer, but the hands of Tria are still very important almost gods. I did not know of Dua's story. It seems a strange end for someone so important."

Mab peered down into the water. "We don't all get the end we think we deserve. Wasn't there something about *building* something in that story of hers?"

"Yes! She said she was trying to build something that could help, but she could not awaken it."

"You've been waking up these diggers. Seems like you should be able to wake this thing up, if it was anywhere."

"Yes… It is a curious thing that I do not see it. It says that it rests beneath her, but I see nothing but stone."

"And the demigod *turned* to stone." Mab scratched her head. "Is that what you things do when you die?"

"No."

"So why did she?"

"I do not know. I think it was magic. Magic is always the way in these stories."

"So, coming here has earned us nothing."

"It earned us a story and I got to see the stone remains of the divine! That is very much!"

"We are still trapped in a cave."

"But we are trapped in a cave with a divine being."

"A *dead* divine being."

"A dead divine being is more alive than most things that are *not* dead. Probably."

"If she can get us out, I'll bow down to her. If not, she's a landmark."

Eddy's expression hardened. "A very *important* landmark."

"Not to me. To me she marks the spot where I got my hopes up for the last time. Now let's go. The sooner we get to that weak spot and start digging, the sooner I'm back in the tunnels and hopefully headed home. I don't like this end of the cave. Something about the way the stone feels beneath my feet. Wetter. Riddled with little tunnels. Doesn't feel stable to me."

Eddy crossed his arms. "There is a machine, somewhere below her. That is hidden treasure. A *very* important part of any adventure. Borgle, dig down, but carefully. We want to find this machine, but not break it. And stop when I say so."

"No, no! What did I just tell you, it isn't stable enough—"

Borgle eagerly chimed. It removed Mab from its back, dug its claws into the stone, and began hammering.

"This is a dangerous waste of time!" Mab called over the pounding impacts.

"What did you do yesterday?"

"I hunted."

"And the day before?"

"Nothing."

"And before?"

"Hunted."

"So you were due for nothing today. This is *much* better."

"But the stability!"

Borgle threw chips and pebbles aside as it thundered deeper. Mab crossed her arms and muttered under her breath, no longer willing to strain her voice trying to shout her warnings over the din. As the digger sunk into the stone, flash-melting the sides of the fresh tunnel, the dwarf gazed at it with curiosity. Out of the water, Borgle didn't dig nearly as quickly, but it was still clearly enough for Mab to be impressed, even if it was in spite of herself.

She picked up a cooling bit of stone with her gloved hand, then tossed it into the pool to whistle and spit against the water.

"Digging machines… Round holes…" she grumbled. "They'll be the end of all of us."

# Chapter 17

Rustle darted through an ever-narrowing sequence of passages. He'd ceased thinking about where to go several minutes ago. The passages he chose were more about how to get farther from the mess he'd inadvertently left behind him. Finally, he wedged the bubble that served as his air supply into a narrow enough crevasse for his discomfort with close spaces to push his maddened panic aside.

He turned and looked to the opening and took a moment to catch his breath.

"Monsters…" he panted. "Monsters. In a cave. At the bottom of the sea. Lost. Alone."

He held his head and tried to keep from falling back into the beckoning arms of open panic again. It didn't work.

"*Why did I ever leave the pond!?*" he squealed. "What am I going to do now? Merantia picked the wrong person to help her in her wonderful, flawless errand."

The surface of his bubble, bulging from the crevasse in the wall, trembled. He reluctantly eased forward, took a breath, and stuck his head out into the water. At first there was silence. Then the water brought him the deep, resonant clack and crackle of claws scraping at stone. He pulled his head back into the bubble and shook the water from his hair.

"That's more than one. They're waking each other up… *What did I do!?*" he said. "Oh, think! *Think, think, think!* What does this mean? What happens now? The inscription. What did it say? There was… um… There was a bit about each one of those things being foe enough for a great hero. And… Oh! Yes! The water's edge. They will only be stopped by the water's edge! They won't go out into the air."

An almost demented smile came to his face.

"Of *course!* That's why this cave exists! That's why there's so much air here. It's to stop the thieves from getting out!"

He slumped against the wall behind him, which was now dripping dry thanks to the bubble pressing up against it.

"At least I didn't doom *everyone*." His brow furrowed. "Except… when Eddy read that tablet, the water started rising…"

He clawed his fingers through his hair. "We *did* doom everyone!"

His flight reflex briefly disregarded logic and wisdom. He rammed face first into the opposite wall in an attempt to retreat further into the tiny crevasse.

"Ugh…" he groaned. "It… It won't work this time. I can't run away from this one. Even if I *could* make it all the way to the surface without being eaten by a fish or something, what would happen to Eddy? And his sister? And everyone they know?"

He reached down to his side, where he'd secured the digging claw he'd borrowed from Eddy's glove.

"I can't flee…" He swallowed. "Which means I have to fight. Or find someone who *can*. Merantia! … No. She sent me out here for a reason. She cannot fight right now. She isn't strong enough. And not *Stuartia*. Vile and evil Stuartia. Curse her name a thousand times… But that only leaves Eddy. And what can Eddy do? He's strong, and he's more at home here in the sea. But he's still just a merman, what is a merman against one of these… these so-called thieves?"

He took a breath.

"Maybe… Maybe it doesn't matter. We'd be together. And more is better than less. And if this *is* an adventure, a story of myth in the making, then surely the end can't come until we reunite." He tightened his fist and shook his head again. "I'm talking nonsense. Madness. But this whole *day* has been madness. So maybe madness is the only thing that makes sense."

He patted his sling, and its one sweet remaining.

"Anything is better than hiding until I starve or suffocate…"

With what little courage he was able to gin up, he flitted back out into the open and began to retrace his steps. Isolated in the center of his bubble, for the first few minutes he was spared the ominous sounds of the beasts he'd unleashed.

By the time the rumble of countless clacking claws finally reached his ears, he was nearly upon them. As the only source of light in the entire cave, there was little hope he could remain unseen, but he did his best to douse his glow as much as possible regardless. This left him buzzing about in near blackness, his mystic intuition the only means at his disposal to guide himself. He skimmed low to the floor of the cave, keeping as far as he could from the clacking and crunching. Now and then he caught a glimpse of a slashing limb or a drifting hulk with a chitinous shell. The things seemed to be ignoring him, more interested in freeing their brethren than wasting a moment to squash the tiny point of light floating among them. They were also moving with a sluggishness that suggested they were anything but fully recovered.

"Good," he whispered to himself sweeping between two empty crypts, "I still have time… But who knows how much? I've got to get to Eddy fast."

His buzzing flight quickened as he approached the entrance of the tomb. When he reached the first of the three gates, he allowed his glow to return to full brightness and flew for all he was worth. His mind and body were approaching their limits. There had been a reason he'd come into this place. Was it Merantia's will? Had he thought he'd find Eddy? He couldn't remember anymore. He didn't care. For the moment the foolishness of even the divine and wise Merantia's instruction had soured him on acting on her behalf. Right now, Eddy was all that mattered.

Rustle swept together the ragged ends of his mind and focused as properly as he could on Eddy. A fairy was simple to find. They were mystically attuned, practically a part of the wind, and a bright focus of magic. Eddy, even when they were side by side, was much more subdued. And Rustle simply had never needed to hone this skill.

It was frustrating, like trying to snatch a curling wisp of smoke from the air. The mystic sensation of his soul was a blurry, half-felt ember. It was simply a weak beacon in the distance, ignorant of any walls that lay between them. He tried to trace out some path that would lead to the distant sensation, but there was no route available to him.

He was about to give up when, for the first time in too long, fate smiled upon him. He couldn't explain it, but in the blink of an eye, Eddy's soul seemed to flare brightly. There was a definite, unmistakable path to him. It was circuitous—leading deep into the system of tunnels before it looped back to him--but that didn't matter. He suddenly had a route to follow, and he would not spit in fate's eye by failing to act upon it.

#

Borgle had been digging steadily, but the lack of sea water caused a considerable amount of delay. The walls, while still cooling a good deal faster than nature would normally allow, were taking longer to cool than when immersed. No water also meant maneuverability for the huge digger was greatly diminished. Borgle's solution was to dig at a far steeper angle than normal. And after a half hour of digging, in what it appeared was becoming a bad habit for the device, Borgle suddenly vanished. The bottom of the tunnel had given out.

The digger plunked out of sight with a distinctive splash. Water rushed in to fill the bottom of the freshly dug tunnel, cooling the walls swiftly and coming to a stop about halfway up the glassy, smooth tunnel. This was fortunate, as the sight of water pouring into the tunnel was a veritable siren call for Eddy. He launched himself down the slippery tunnel and splashed into the water after Borgle without a moment's thought of if it was safe.

A few seconds later, he surfaced, sputtering and coughing.

"I forgot the water-for-air again," he said.

"I gathered," Mab called from above. "What've you found down there?"

"Good fresh water!" he said. "Not fresh in the not salty way, fresh in the not sitting around way."

"What does it matter if it is sitting around or not?"

"I don't know. Water in the sea just feels better than water in a pool. Say! Do you think that is what Rustle means when he says he knows when the air is trapped or isn't?"

"What are you on about now? Who's this Rustle?" Mab called.

"I told you all about Rustle while we were coming here."

"It's been years since I had to pay attention to yammering. Nice to have someone to talk to, but years without having to deal with nonsense talk hasn't done my attention span any favors."

"He is my—"

"I don't care any more now than I did then."

"But you just *asked*."

"A mistake I won't make again. Now what's down there!"

"I'll see!" Eddy said, Mab's bizarre attitude failing to make a dent in his unquenchable enthusiasm.

He took a breath and dove down into the water. For the first time since he came to this place, his eyes had to adjust to their own illumination.

The chamber Borgle had discovered was quite shallow, and the water was *quite* warm, almost uncomfortably so. The walls had the same glossy blackness as most of the stone, but here it was harder and more jagged. He had to be careful to keep away from the walls, lest he slice himself.

While he was taking stock of his surroundings, Borgle was keeping busy. The digger was downright graceful in the water, pivoting under the power of its tail and maneuvering toward a section of wall that was riddled with fractures. Borgle's eyes swept over the wall. It grabbed onto two rough spots with pincers and tugged. The wall shattered into chips of stone, revealing a chamber that had clearly been chiseled rather than crafted by nature. Having followed its orders, Borgle pulled back and chimed happily, awaiting the next instructions.

Eddy, whose held breath was running short, allowed himself only a brief glance at the new chamber. His eyes opened wide and he was barely able to keep himself from shouting in excitement.

He popped back out into the tunnel gasped for breath and bellowed up to Mab.

"You should see it! It's beautiful!"

"What is it?" Mab asked.

"It looks a bit like Borgle, but more! And not shiny metal like Borgle. Not mostly. It is made from *stone*."

"A digger?"

"More than a digger. A… a very *much* digger! Pointed down. It does not look like it can swim like Borgle. It is only for down digging. Thin stone things hold it up, but they look like they will break if it ever moves."

"Worthless, then."

"Worthless? It is a thing made by a hand of Tria!"

"But it is only for digging *down*. We don't want to go down. We want to go up, or aside. Anywhere but down."

"It is worth little for you or me right now. But it is worth very, very much for the world! A thing left behind by the hands of a god!"

"Bah. I'll worry about the rest of the world when I can get back to it." Mab grumbled. "You said the water felt like it was connected to the rest of the sea. Does that mean it's a way out for you?"

"I do not think so. Not for me now or for Dua then. But maybe small things. The walls are filled with very much cracks. Some I can fit my fist in, but they seem like they go a long way. Just as much digging to get out here as from anywhere."

"Fine. Then get back up here, bring Borgle, and let's dig our way out back where we should have been *hours ago*."

"We cannot go yet. This machine sleeps, waiting for someone to wake it. If Dua could not, maybe I can. Maybe it was only because she was here for so long that—"

"*It doesn't go where we want it to go, it is a waste of time!*" Mab shouted. "We are lucky digging down to find it didn't cause this whole section of the cave to collapse, if the stone was that thin between here and the water. You said the walls were full of cracks down there. That means—"

"I will go. It will be fast."

Mab shouted something rather rude after him, but he was too busy reciting the water-for-air spell to hear it. Once the words were spoken, he dunked down and replaced the stale air of the cave with a fresh, fulfilling breath of water. He swam back down to the chamber Borgle had unearthed and slipped inside.

The machine really was a wonder. It was long and sleek, simpler in design than Borgle, but more than making up for it in sheer size. It was triple the diameter of Borgle, and easily ten times longer. Rather than tentacle-like pincers, it made do with much shorter appendages, presumably the closest Dua could manage to fabricate without metal. He ran his hand over the polished stone and marveled. It was not quite like the stone around it, though. Dua may have harvested it from elsewhere, or perhaps she had changed it somehow, mystically or otherwise.

His claws clicked over intricately carved symbols. He leaned close to shed more light upon them. They were in long lines, like ribbons wrapped around the mechanism. They crossed each other, and each place they met bore the hammer and spear emblem, in metal. They had likely been harvested from a fallen digger, as was the blunt nose of the massive creation and any other parts that would strike the stone.

The great many bumps and scrapes Eddy had accumulated meant that it wasn't difficult to find a spot on his body willing to offer up a smear of blood. He anointed each emblem he found, and each time he was treated to a pulse of amber glow and a flash of mystic energy. The third and final splash of blood breathed life into the mechanism. Stubby appendages shifted and scraped. Beady "eyes" near the blunt nose lit up. Instead of the merry, lively rhythm that echoed from within Borgle, this thing had a duller, far more mechanical sound. Despite the astounding craftsmanship, it was comparatively crude. The thing lacked the spark of life, or at least of personality, that Borgle had. And it did not wait for instructions. The very moment it fully activated, it shattered its stone supports and struck the ground like a massive hammer, shattering stone like glass.

Eddy scrambled back to a safe distance and watched in awe as it sunk into solid stone as though it were mud. The pincers started to spark and heat the walls of the tunnel. This made his current distance significantly less safe as the temperature rose sharply. He retreated into the tunnel Borgle had bored. Here the temperature of the water eased upward more slowly, taking it from warm to unpleasantly warm, though not threatening to boil him alive as the water nearer to the digger had. Nevertheless, he decided to give the thing some time and distance before he ventured back to its chamber. He recited the spell once more and dragged himself back up the tube to the surface, where Mab was waiting.

More accurately, she was *fuming*.

"I don't know what I was thinking, hoping someone would eventually show up. I'd forgotten that when you talk to someone else, you may as well be talking to yourself anyway!" she barked.

Eddy hacked the last of the water out.

"I am sorry if—"

"Don't you 'sorry' me!" Mab said. "Look around you!"

Eddy blinked at the comparatively bright light cast by the stalks and ceiling. The whole cave was rattling around them. Dislodged stone danced across the cave floor. Bits of the floor had slumped downward. Some of the nearer stalks fell and slid down the slope. Distantly, chunks of the odd growth on the ceiling cracked free and sprinkled upon them, along with spritzes and showers of water from above.

"I hope your gods have some favor left for you. Mine certainly aren't listening to my prayers," Mab fumed.

"Surely this isn't as bad as the quake that came before. The cave will hold," Eddy said hopefully.

"There's a difference between shaking the earth and boring holes in it. A cave this deep, beneath the sea, is a precarious balance at best. Even if the roof doesn't fall on us, there is no telling what has kept the sea from flooding it. And *you* may be well served by having this place fill up with water, but it will be the end of me!"

Eddy's face hardened as he realized the sort of danger he'd put his new friend in.

"Borgle! Up here! Now!" he called. "Mab, you follow me."

"Where? What good will it do?"

A fault crackled up from below, splitting the edge of the pool. The stone beneath the statue of Dua cracked and the petrified figure vanished It dropped down into the shaft the massive digger was leaving behind.

Eddy dragged himself to the edge of the pool and dipped his hand inside.

"The temperature is not bad. The water from outside is cooling it fast."

"Are you not listening?" Mab said. "If the ceiling comes tumbling down, wading into a pool of water won't—"

Eddy grabbed her hand and quickly uttered the words of the water-for-air spell. Mab gasped twice, first when her lungs decided fresh air wasn't what they craved any longer, and again when Eddy heaved her forward into the water. She sunk like a stone, heavily heaped as she was with tools and armor, and came to an abrupt and uncomfortable stop when she struck Borgle approaching from below.

Stones and water rained down steadily. The ceiling was giving way. Eddy muttered the spell once more for himself, then slipped back into the water. And thumped down beside Mab, who was having some difficulty coming to terms with the fact that she was a water breather for the time being.

"Down, Borgle. Down fast, until we are safe from the collapse or I tell you to stop!" he ordered.

Borgle chimed happily. Its pincer-tipped legs reversed direction, clattering crab-wise along the smooth wall since the digger was angled such that its tail would do little good. Deep, reverberating clashes of stone on stone assaulted their ears. A thin stream of pebbles sprinkled down from the opening above. Mab clung to Borgle's blunt nose as they descended. Eddy drifted above her, darting his eyes upward to monitor the flow of debris and back again to be sure Mab was unhurt and adjusting to the jarring shift to an aquatic environment.

"Breathe normal," Eddy instructed. "I am very much a good caster of the water-for-air spell."

"I can't breathe normally!" Mab growled. "I breathe *air* normally."

"Now it is water. It is the same."

"I *hate* the water!" Mab barked.

A clatter of stones rang out from above. Eddy turned and just barely managed to deflect a large stone as it tumbled down behind them.

"Right now, you would hate the cave more."

Borgle finally reached the strange void where the larger digger had been and eagerly righted itself. As a consequence—or perhaps as a calculated act of rebellion, this dumped Mab from its nose. Eddy snatched her before she could plummet too far and worked his tail hard to tug her aside, clear of the increasing stream of jagged stones rushing down from the tunnel that had led them here.

He held her in his arms and swam over the pit the larger digger was creating. It had been mere minutes, but already the thing was little more than a distant sequence of sparking flashes and a dull orange glow of cooling stone.

"That thing digs very much fast…" Eddy said in awe.

"Never mind that! Put me down!" Mab squealed.

Eddy looked about. There was a jagged and unpleasant-looking floor to this section of the tunnel, but the low rumble of continued collapse above made it clear this wasn't the safest place to recover one's wits. Alas, the crackle and collapse had failed to open any new exits, so the only way forward was downward, where the large digger had gone. He let Mab's weight pull him down into the deepening pit. Borgle swam happily along behind them. The tunnel, while mostly glassy smooth like those Borgle left behind, had more than a few voids along its edge. The massive digger must have plunged through previously hidden tunnels running through the sea floor. Eddy darted into the largest and continued along it. Borgle followed. When the rumble of the collapsing cave either subsided or was far enough away to no longer be heard, Eddy set Mab down on the much smoother and more pleasant floor of the tunnel.

As Borgle settled down and awaited further instruction, Eddy looked over his new friend. She was, to put it lightly, less-than-mollified by the rescue. The water was doing strange things to her beard, causing it to billow and wave like an anemone. Behind it, her face was red with fury.

"See?" Eddy offered. "Safe and sound."

"Save and sound? *Safe and sound!* Is that what you call this? Before I met you, I was living a lonely but otherwise comfortable life, scraping a living out of that strange, glowing cave. Now I'm trapped underwater at the bottom of the sea, after having my former home crushed in a collapse that *you caused.*"

"It was a mistake and I am very much sorry."

"I am going to be the first dwarf to die by *starving* while wandering a maze of deep-sea tunnels, but you are 'very much sorry,' so I suppose that's fine. Nothing you do matters if you're very much sorry about it."

"I didn't know what I was doing would—"

"*I told you what it would do!*" She felt her hands over armor. "Where is my ax?"

She found the handle and pulled the gear-fabricated weapon free.

"What do you need your ax for?"

Mab answered with a vicious swipe of the weapon. Eddy darted up out of her reach.

"Get down here and take your medicine, coward!" she cried.

"What good will attacking me do?" Eddy reasoned.

"It'll make me feel better. And it'll make sure you don't cause any more cave-ins."

She swiped and slashed at him fruitlessly as he patiently waited just beyond the range of the weapon. When she was winded—or perhaps, in light of her current respiratory status, when she was currented—she dropped the ax to the floor of the tunnel and plopped to a seating position. She covered her face with her hands and, slowly, her gasping turned into angry sobbing.

"Do not be sad, Mab," Eddy said.

"What can one dwarf do in a lifetime to deserve this…"

"We will get out of this place. I will help you."

"No!" Mab cried. "Stop helping me! You are a menace, you awful fish. A curse! You are a punishment clawed up from the great below for some horrid deed I must have forgotten. Leave me be! I'll find my own way out."

She struggled to her feet and thumped along the tunnel, heading down its slope, deeper into the unknown darkness ahead.

"But you don't have any light!" Eddy called after her.

"I'm a dwarf in a tunnel. I've got all the light I need," she growled back at him.

Mab angrily grappled with her drifting beard for a moment, twisting it a bit to keep it from floating into her face, then continued on her way.

Eddy turned to Borgle.

"I had forgotten how many adventures heap terrible misfortune upon the characters who are not central to the story," he said, grateful to, for a moment, no longer rely upon his damaged translation spell. "Every good story has a village destroyed. It had never struck me how that must affect those aside from the hero."

He watched Mab stomping along until she was no longer visible, then swam along at a respectful distance behind her. Until she calmed down it was probably best to give her some space.

"Of course, she's probably one of the important helpers that show up in the more entertaining adventure stories. But it *is* unfortunate she had to lose her home. Maybe when we tell this story, we'll build her heroism up a bit."

Ahead, she stumbled and fell, illustrating how extremely well suited the dwarven language was to profanity.

"Or at least we'll make her less grumpy…"

# Chapter 18

Mira, Cul, and Cora approached the galaxy of glowing lights that marked her hometown of Barnacle. Truly, she had something to learn from the Nomads. Though they seemed to take their time, they never slowed for a moment during the journey from the rift. It helped that the current was more or less with them, but even so, Mira could never remember making the journey so quickly.

"We will ask Miss Astra for her spell book. Oh, I hope she and her family are recovered from the quake," Mira said. "And Guyver should have some spare work clothes to cope with the hot water. He has a farm farther up the rift."

"So… This is Barnacle," Cora said. "It's… nice."

Mira glanced at her. "That didn't sound terribly sincere. Not impressed?"

"Well, to be frank…" Cora began.

"We don't do business with places much smaller than West Shallow," Cul explained. "Your whole city is the size of their shopping district."

"Ah… So that would be why nomads don't stop by," Mira said.

"It doesn't say anything about *you,*" Cora said quickly. "But when you travel as far as we do for trade, you've got to think about quality, quantity, variety, *everything*. That means stopping at the largest places."

"No, no. I understand. It's just that I've always been rather proud of my home. We've been through a lot as a village and we always persevere."

She swam a bit more quickly, leading them to her home.

"Here. Stay here for a moment. If you're hungry, there is food in the pantry there. Help yourself. I'll be back as quickly as I can."

Mira swam off toward the center of the city, which while plainly recovering from the quake at least looked to have stabilized. Cora and Cul looked about in the home.

"She has so many things, Cul…" Cora said. "I've never been invited into a home before. There's nearly as much here as in the markets."

Cora picked up some of Mira's clothes, dislodged from where they had been hanging before the disasters struck. She held them against herself.

"Not my size… but do you think she'd be open for a trade?" Cora said. "It is *very* nice."

"Put that down," Cul said. "This is a home. You don't just make offers on things in a person's home."

on things in a person's home."

Cora set the garment aside and placed her hands on her hips. "So you're an expert all of a sudden?"

"It's just common sense. Shore-lovers aren't like us. Their life isn't about getting a good deal. They can afford to *have* things. To collect things. Because they have places to put them. Look at these bones…"

He swam to a small recess in a wall, where a bit of netting held a pile of assorted skulls. Cora swam up and plucked a wolf skull from the net.

"It is *sort* of impressive, I guess. Shells don't get so gnarly and full of holes. Oh, and these are the teeth, right? Intricate… But we could collect things. We just need our own whale. You could strap everything in this house to a nice big whale."

"It isn't the same. You've basically got to run your own *drift* of nomads to have a whale large enough for this much stuff. And look around. *Everyone* has a home like this."

"I suppose. But waking up every day looking at the same patch of ocean… How do you live like that? And you heard her talking. She's a *trader* and she's barely been more than a few towns over. That's no life."

"It *is* a bit stifling, I suppose."

He picked up a small frame and found what passed for a painting in a merfolk village. The color was muted, composed mostly of blacks and purples with the occasional glittery bit of powdered shell or sprinkled sand. It was skillfully rendered, though, and depicted Mira herself with a merman.

"Do you suppose this is her brother, Eddy?" he said.

"You'd better hope so."

"Why?"

"Because he's a handsome one, and if he's not her brother, then you've been fluttering your fins against the current."

"Not you, too. Why does everyone think I'm falling in love with her?"

"Probably because you're *absolutely* falling in love with her," Cora said.

"*I don't even know her!*" Cul said. "It's been just a few *hours* since she showed up. Just because I'm treating her properly doesn't mean that I'm *courting* her."

"No. It's the way you look at her and the way you fawn over her that means you're courting her."

He crossed his arms. "I'm not going to argue with you. Now, I don't know about you, but I'm famished. I'm going to take her up on her offer of food. I suggest you do the same."

"I'm going to take a look at the rest of her collection. But if she's got anything you know I like, bring me one," Cora said.

Cul swam into the pantry to carefully sift through the still-disheveled contents. While he did, Cora replaced the skull and casually looked over the mound of fallen clothes. She found another top and held it up.

"Maybe if we do a good job she'll give us some gifts. I think I might grow into this one."

#

"This is a lousy tunnel," Mab muttered.

The dwarf's temper had cooled somewhat as she'd paced along the tunnel. This was good news for Eddy. It had taken a considerable amount of will power to keep from engaging her in conversation. His unquenchable curiosity could only be denied for so long.

"What is so bad about it?" Eddy asked.

"Lousy workmanship. And look what the water's done to the walls," Mab replied.

She reached out with one of her stubby mitts and ran it along the wall of the tunnel. The black stone was riddled with cracks, some of them so deep Eddy's glow didn't reach their end.

"This is a natural tunnel. There were no workmen," Eddy said.

"Bah. What do you know about tunnels? This was dug." She crouched. "See here? Chisel marks. *Most* of this is natural. Probably a bubble in the stone when it cooled. But this stretch here was chiseled. And don't tell me you didn't notice the mounds of chips in the side caverns. Like there. See? This is a debris cavern. Dwarfs use them all the time. You've got to haul out the detritus and store it somewhere."

"But that cave where you were, and that story Dua told. She found that place while looking for a good way down. We are *much* lower than that cave now. Why would there be diggings down lower than that cave?"

Mab shook her head. "And you say you were a miner. Mining isn't just about digging down. It's about digging *quickly* sometimes, and other times it's in digging *toward* where you know something you want is. Like I said. There are these big voids down this way. And the walls are crumbly and weak. This is a tunnel dug through the weakest, most void-riddled rock available. They were after something they knew they'd find. Which is *baffling*, because in stone like this, you won't find anything but more bubbles and voids. Who would dig down looking for *nothing?*"

Eddy looked forward uncertainly. "I do not think there is *nothing* in this tunnel. This tunnel gives me bad feelings."

Mab paused and looked to him. "What sort of bad feelings..." she asked, almost accusingly.

"I feel like there is a bad thing here. A dark thing here. Not *here* here. But there. The way we are going."

She narrowed her eyes and gripped the handle of one of her axes. "So you feel that, too..."

"You feel the bad feeling? Why did you not say you did?"

"Because *you* didn't say *you* did. Why didn't you say you did?"

"Because you were mad at me and I did not want you to be more mad."

166

She shook her head, dislodging her beard to billow up again. "I was hoping it was my mind playing tricks on me. For the last few years my mind hasn't been much good for anything else *but* playing tricks. You learn not to trust it when it tells you there are monsters ahead."

"You think there are monsters?"

She nodded. "We're deep. There's a saying among the dwarfs. The deeper you dig, the surer you can be that you'll find something. It's why you don't keep digging down a hole that's not giving you something you want. Because no hole leads to nothing. So, if you keep digging where you haven't found good, you're likely to find *bad.*"

"Bad monsters? *Evil* monsters?"

"That's the feeling I've got."

"This is the best news!" Eddy crowed.

"…What?"

"I am on an adventure! The evil bad monster waiting for us *must* be the reason for the adventure. I think even maybe I was looking for it when I found you. I don't remember so good, it seems a long time ago. But now that we know there is a monster, we must go and find it!"

Eddy readied his pick and darted off into the tunnel. Borgle followed, chiming happily.

"Blast it," Mab growled. "Blast it to pieces! So my options are to remain in a dark hole in the bottom of the sea while the only person who knows how to let me breathe again dashes off to be killed, or to follow him and probably get killed with him."

Eddy turned back, his glowing eyes and fins sparkling in the distance.

"Borgle! Go get Mab. She is not so good with swimming. And she won't want to be late for the monster fight!"

"What!? No, you blasted machine!"

Borgle ignored her complaints, snatching her up with its pincers and placing her astride its back.

#

No longer limited to the speed Mab could manage, the trio streaked along the tunnel. The farther they traveled, the more certain they were that chisels and hammers had been at work here. The chip-filled voids became more frequent, and more thoroughly filled. The walls were smoother, more precise. And ahead, the looming sense of foreboding grew ever stronger. Whatever the source of the feeling was, there was no clear sign of it.

After several minutes of enthusiastic swimming, they came upon the first unique discovery. The tunnel turned sharply and began to open. Embedded in the wall, surrounded by recently fractured stone, was the statue of Dua.

"Look! Dua has been leading us!" Eddy said. "Tria is smiling upon our quest!"

"The blasted statue fell down the pit and bounced down the same tunnel we did. Not everything is an act of this god or that, you great idiot of a fish."

Eddy ignored the observation. He drifted down and marveled with wide eyes at what lay beside the statue.

"One of the hammers of Tria…" he said, reverently reaching the round-headed hammer from where it had fallen. "A gift from the gods."

"The statue's fingers broke when it hit the wall and the hammer fell," Mab countered.

"I tell you the thing the gods did. You tell me the way the gods did it. Both are true," he said. "I say it is a sign. I shall arm myself with the hammer."

He closed his fingers around the grip of the tool. He was quite strong enough to lift it, but buoyancy was another issue entirely. He had to work his tail madly to keep himself from simply sinking to the floor of the tunnel while wielding it.

"This…" He grunted. "Is maybe not a tool for carrying all the time."

"Hand it over," Mab said, hopping to the ground and holding out her stout arm.

"This is a thing of the divine. Tria is the daughter of Mer. And this is given to the hands of Tria from Tria herself. Are you a follower of Tria?"

"No. But I know how to use a hammer."

Eddy hefted it, then scratched his chin.

"I think… I think maybe Tria would rather the tool go in the hands of the better maker. Yes. It is a thing for making. And you are very much good at making. Even if you do not use it in Tria's name, you serve Tria with the good you will do with it."

"Whatever helps you sleep at night. Hand it over."

Eddy presented the hammer to her. The tool was nearly as tall as Mab was. Having carried both the hammer and Mab, Eddy knew that if they were not a match for each other's weight, they were close. Nevertheless, Mab took the tool and gripped it like she was born with it in her hands. She gave it an experimental swing, easily turning one of the larger bits of debris in a nearby alcove into powder.

"Well I'll be… It *is* a miracle. Might well be the best hammer I've ever handled, and it wasn't made by dwarfs," Mab said.

"The tales say that the hammers of the hands of Tria are forged in the earth's burning heart. They are born of a long-held agreement between the gods above, the gods below, and the gods of the sea."

"Tell your tales," Mab said. "All I know is if I'd have known it would have been worthwhile to fetch this out of the water, I'd have found a way to dig myself out of that cave without your thinking machine."

Eddy shook his head. "No. Because then it would not have been here for the fighting of the big monster."

He fetched up the chisel. Like the hammer, it was larger than seemed necessary, almost half the size of his pick. It was clearly a rock chisel, its end almost blunt, and though the dents and scrapes along its tip told the tale of centuries of usage, it looked as strong and useful as ever.

"This I will use. I do not know how. But I will use it."

"Sounds like the sort of plan I'd expect out of you."

A low grinding sound rumbled up along the tunnel. They turned to its source, somewhere in the darkness beyond the sharp turn. This grinding didn't have the subdued, muffled nature of something far off in the distance. It was sharp. Nearby. The grind ended with a metallic clack that seemed to shake the whole of the tunnel around them. Eddy's eyes literally flashed with excitement.

"I will use it now!" he proclaimed.

He darted forward. The roof and walls spread away. The ground took on a steeper slope. Without being told, Borgle snatched Mab up again and toted her along, keeping close to Eddy. The tunnel floor had turned to a vertical wall by the time they came to the evident source of the sound. It was a bar, as thick as Borgle's body, but made of a darker metal. The enormous bar was slightly curved, one end embedded into the stone of the wall. The other leading off into the darkness. Eddy and Borgle followed. The curve continued, outward into the darkness, then curving back toward the wall. Right before its opposite end embedded itself back into the stone, they found a long loop of similarly thick metal hooked around it. A second loop connected to the first one. They were the first few links of a chain, and each of them was much larger than Borgle itself.

"Look at the size of that chain…" Mab said. "If that's how much chain it takes to keep something locked down, I'd hate to see what's at the other end of—"

"You will meet your end, monster! *Yaaaaah!*" Eddy shouted.

He swam off along the chain. Borgle followed.

"I don't care if *you* want to die, but why under the mountain must you drag *me* along with you?"

Eddy's lust for monster-slaying left no room for logic or response. He followed the chain to where it connected to some manner of massive metal band. The band was embedded in a smoother column of black stone. Swimming along the band revealed another loop, and from it ran another chain. He followed this and, to his dismay, found it simply attached to another enormous metal bar. He followed it back and, when he returned to the black column, swam up along it. This section of wall was etched with long, regular grooves. A second band, not far above the first, led him to another chain and, once again, to a bar embedded in the wall of the chamber. The only difference this time was that one end of the bar had nearly been pulled away from the wall, and beyond its failing end, a tunnel not unlike the one the one that had led them here led off into the wall.

"Where is the monster!?" Eddy shouted angrily. "Why so many chains and nothing but columns and walls?"

"I don't know, and I'm not complaining," Mab said. "But now that you've taken a moment to think, have you noticed this chamber doesn't have a roof bearing down on us? We should see how far up it leads. If we're lucky—and I hesitate to even suggest it—maybe it leads all the way to the surface."

"No. It does not. We have gone very far. But not *so* very far that we are in a place that we would not have seen from my home while exploring and trading. There are no big holes with chains and columns in the bottom near Barnacle. But maybe we *can* go very far up, and from there maybe we find our way back to my mine. But I feel the bad feelings of the monster, don't you? We do not leave until we *kill* the monster. Heroes don't go home before the adventure is through."

Mab muttered through clenched teeth. "Then maybe the *monster* is further up."

"Monsters are down, not up. Everyone knows that," Eddy said.

"If you take me farther down, I will use this hammer to bash your brains out."

"That is not a nice thing to... Wait... Do you hear that?" Eddy turned to the tunnel. "It is not a big sound like before. This one is a small sound."

"Good. Let's investigate. A small sound is less likely to kill us in the meantime."

Eddy darted toward the tunnel mouth, but before he'd even ventured inside, he saw a distant glimmer of blue light. It sparked, flared, and streaked toward him. The sound resolved itself, amid considerable echoing, into a single word repeated over and over.

"Eddy, Eddy, Eddy, Eddy!"

A moment later, a bubble-encapsulated figure burst from the tunnel and thumped into the merman's chest.

"Rustle? You found me!" Eddy said, stowing both chisel and pick so that he could address the creature.

"Eddy, Eddy, Eddy," the fairy said gleefully. "I found you! I used my magic and I felt where you were and I could feel the flow of the water and *what are those things!?*"

Rustle darted up to hide among Eddy's hair, causing his hair to billow around the fairy's bubble.

"Be calm, Rustle. These are friends. That is a digging machine that thinks. It is called Borgle. It is the thing we found before things shook and I went away. And that is Mab. Mab is a dwarfmaid. Why are you in a bubble, Rustle? It is hard to hear you."

"The spell wore off. Where did you find a *dwarf?*"

"A cave with glowing sticky stalks and tasty soft-shell things."

"… Tasty soft-shell things?"

"Yes. They are like long lobsters. But that is *my* story. What is *your* story?"

"I tried to dig for you with this claw I borrowed. And then the spells started wearing off and I got scared I would die from that pain that comes from going too deep, so I went searching for help and I found the wonderful and delightful, the brilliant and kind, the magnificent and magnanimous Merantia."

"You sound like you very much like this person."

"She is divine! She is the sun and moon! And she gave me a very important task."

"She did? Was she like Stuartia?"

Rustle recoiled, drifting out into the open again.

"Do not speak that retched name! Stuartia is the enemy!" the fairy said.

"She is? She seemed nice."

"She is the enemy of the wonderful Merantia and thus she is the enemy of *all.*"

Something massive shifted nearby, causing a rumble and a rush of water.

"*What was that!?*" Rustle yelped.

"I do not know. We heard sounds, that is why we came here. But once we got here, just chains and pillars and walls."

"You can understand that whistling and squealing," Mab said.

"What did he say?" Rustle said.

Eddy looked back and forth between them.

"I think maybe my spell for knowing what people are saying works only for me. That is fine. I will explain what one says to the other. First, as I said, Mab is not 'he.' Mab is a dwarf*maid*, Rustle."

"Just a dwarf!" Mab snapped.

"Sorry. Just a dwarf."

"So it *is* a male?" Rustle said.

"No. But the maids are not maids. They are just dwarf. Not different."

"But it has a beard."

"Dwarfmaids have beards."

"Just dwarfs!" Mab growled.

"Sorry. Just dwarfs have beards," Eddy said.

"So dwarfmaids *don't* have beards?"

"They do, but they are not… They *are,* but…" Eddy paused. "I need more words to say this, I think."

Rustle shook his head. "It doesn't matter. There is more I need to tell you. Eddy, remember the story that the vile Stuartia told us? And the writing that mentioned the thieves?"

"I do! It seems so long ago, but it was not very long at all."

"I found the thieves. I didn't mean to, but I woke them up! Well, I woke *one* up. *But it woke up the rest!*"

"Good!"

"No, Eddy, not good. They are terrible."

"*Very* good, then. A quest ends when something terrible is defeated. Are they very big? Are they scary?"

"Very big. Bigger than me or you. Maybe bigger than the mechanical thing there."

"And how many."

"A thousand, I think."

"… That is very many."

"And it is *worse!* The tunnel that you started filling with water when you said those magic words? It was full of air for a *reason*. The thieves stop where the water stops. If the cave floods all the way, they'll be able to get to the rest of the sea! It will be that big battle that Stuartia talked about all over again!"

"But there was a very big thing, the Great Ancient, that was a part of that fight. We did not find *that*, so it is not the *same* fight. But it does not matter. We will fight them! You got here from there. Lead the way to the battle!"

"It isn't so simple as that. I got here squeezing through tiny cracks and fissures in the stone. Some of them were *very* long, little tubes that I could barely fit through."

"I'm still waiting for a translation of all this noise," Mab rumbled.

"Rustle says he can't show us the way out because it is through holes too small for us." Eddy turned back to Rustle. "But Borgle is very good at digging. We were going to dig out, but then we came here looking for a fight that wasn't here." The Merman furrowed his brow. "This bubble is annoying me. I will do the water-for-air for you again."

Eddy pinched Rustle's ankles lightly between his claws, carefully pronounced the words to the spell, and yanked the little fairy down out of the bubble. Rustle took a few startled breaths, then gathered his wits and let the bubble drift upward into the darkness. From the look on his face, Rustle was getting ready to give Eddy an earful about doing things like that without proper warning, but something caused him to stop. He shivered and looked about.

"Now that I'm touching the water… I don't know… Can you *feel* that?"

"What? A sort of bad feeling? An evil feeling?"

"Yes," he said warily.

"We did!" Eddy crowed. "It is why we came to this place! Can you tell where the source of the bad is? I would rather fight one very big monster than a thousand monsters that are less very big."

"I don't want to fight *any* monsters," Mab said.

Rustle continued. "It's... all around us... But it feels... It feels familiar. It feels like Merantia's magic... Glorious, resplendent Merantia..."

His eyes lost the focus. They drifted upward, to follow the chain. Suddenly any semblance of fear, or even intelligence, left his expression. He may as well have been in a trance, half swimming, half flying along the chain.

"I don't like the look on your little friend's face," Mab said.

"I do not like it either. We should follow him."

"He's tiny. Just grab him, stow him someplace, and let's find a way to get out of here."

"Rustle doesn't like to be in bags. He is afraid of small spaces."

"More afraid of them than all-encompassing auras of evil and foreboding?"

"Maybe? We will ask him when he is not so distracted. Until then, let us follow!"

#

The mesmerized fairy drifted up and up, eyes always set upon an indistinct point in the distance. They reached where the chain came to one of the narrower central columns, then continued along the column. Two more chains came and went, each attached to the column with stout metal bands. As they traveled, the column became stouter. Eventually it angled more precisely toward the center of the chamber, and some time later, it met with the other columns and combined into a massive, armor-plated shape.

"I have a bad feeling about this..." Mab said.

"The same bad feeling as before, or a new bad feeling?" Eddy asked. "My bad feeling is the same. The big bad one. The evil one. But also, I am confused. Why big columns with chains. Then a bigger one, but no chains?"

Rustle was moving more quickly now. Eddy and Borgle flicked their tails to keep up, the merman wincing through the pain. They passed two vast struts jutting out of one side of the armored shape, then watched as the shape began to narrow again. A more complex mass at the top came into view. It was a narrow fissure running along a blunt-ended protrusion. Above the fissure they found a bulge. They rose above even that, finally reaching an open chamber above the huge thing. From above, they could see that there were three bulges total, one on each side, and one centered on the top between them. There Rustle stopped, eyes set upon the central bulge.

"Rustle? Did you come here for a reason?" Eddy asked.

"I don't think your friend will be talking any time soon," Mab said.

"It does not seem so..." Eddy scratched his head. "This seems familiar. It is hard to picture, though."

He swam closer to the rocky surface of the thing and scraped out shapes with his claw on the surface just ahead of the bulge.

"It had lots of long bits down here… and then the fat bit in the middle. Then there were those two struts."

"Put two on the other side as well. The thing looks symmetric to me," Mab said.

"Yes, yes. Two struts here too. And then pinched down, and then this… and these three bulges…"

Eddy finished the rough sketch of what they'd seen.

"That looks like… That looks like something I've seen… But what? Maybe I should go and see what the end of the struts look like? Or the bottoms of the columns?"

"Oh, great creation… Oh, mighty being…" Rustle said, his voice toneless and distant.

"What's that, Rustle?" Eddy said.

"I come from far, I bring with me a thread to connect you. I link you to your master, who lingers from beyond the veil…"

"That is fancy talking you are doing, Rustle."

"That doesn't sound natural, what's coming out of your friend," Mab said. "Let's get some distance away from him."

"He's my friend. I will help him."

Rustle's natural glow, normally a vague haze that hung around him in the murky water, began to waver and contort. It's pale blue color flickered and threaded with a sharper blue. The deeper, darker color separated from the rest. It peeled away. One end threaded toward the armored shape below. The other darted off into the darkness, toward one wall.

As soon as the discolored glow separated from his own, Rustle's expression returned to a far more common frightened, confused state.

"What? What is this? Where am I? What just happened?" Rustle said.

"You were muttering something that sounded very magic," Eddy said. "And that thread happened."

The bright blue filament of light was still curling and coiling in the air. One end of it had touched the shape beneath them. The other traced a path into a tunnel far below.

Rustle shut his eyes and tried to concentrate.

"It's… it's not my magic. And it's going back the way I came. I can feel it. It's strong. It's going back to Merantia."

"Just Merantia?" Eddy said.

"Yes, Merantia! Why?"

"Usually you say nicer things around that name."

"Why would I say nice things about her? She is terrifying! A spirit, like Stuartia, but crueler. My head feels clearer now than it has since I met her. I think… I think she did something to me." He turned to the filament of light. "I think that is *her* magic! I think it was riding along with me. And it is leading back to her."

"Would you care to explain what the little chatter box is on about?" Mab said.

"The line of magic is from a dead mermaid who fought a dead mermaid *we* met and the other end is heading back to her."

"What happens when it gets to her?"

A piercing hiss split the water and the blue line of magic danced and coiled as if alive. The whole chamber seemed to shudder and quake. Then the bulge below them split. The two halves slid aside to reveal a single, massive eye.

Eddy stared in awe.

"Still want to fight the one big thing instead of the thousand smaller ones?" Mab asked.

Eddy grinned and took his pick in hand.

"Don't you dare!" Mab shouted.

*"Adventure!"* the manic merman shouted.

# Chapter 19

It takes a very special sort of person to be a true adventurer. Wisdom is important, to stay alive and to unravel the riddles on the path to glory. Bravery is important, so that the terrible threats along the path do not overcome those who face them. Strength is important, to defeat the foes that seek to bar the way. Luck is important, for sometimes wisdom and strength can fall short of the trials of a true adventure. But perhaps the most vital, and the most volatile, of those things that define a true adventurer is the precious spark of madness. The wise man is limited by his mind. A brave man is limited by his courage. A strong man is limited by his brawn. But a madman knows no limits.

In a dark chamber, far below the sea, a terrible beast had dozed restlessly for longer than memory. It was a thing of the darkest nightmares, a thing of tentacle and claw, of tooth and scale. Were it on land, it would stand as tall as a mountain. Its three great eyes were each as large as boulders. Chains large enough to bind titans held it in its place, and yet with each stirring it shook the land and sea. It was an ungodly thing. A thing from a time before grace and beauty. It was the being known only as the Great Ancient. And when the foolish spirit who plucked it from its abyss finally managed to wake it once more, it was greeted by a true adventurer. His strength eclipsed his wisdom, and his bravery eclipsed his strength. But his madness, that eclipsed it all.

"Eddy, you lunatic!" Mab cried as the merman darted toward the blinking eye.

Eddy drove his pick into the smoldering eye before him. The twisted, abused bit of metal pierced the glassy surface. Eyelids like iron shutters snapped closed, scything through the pick as though it were straw. The beast threw its head back, striking Rustle, Eddy, Borgle and Mab like a landslide. They rushed backward through the water and struck the far wall. The hapless dwarf plummeted into the darkness below as the Great Ancient roared in pain and anger. The sound was like nothing any of them had ever heard, a grinding, reverberating, thundering wail that rattled their very bones.

"Eddy, the dwarf!" Rustle called.

His voice couldn't overcome the rumble of the Great Ancient, but his terrified gleam caught Eddy's eye as he blinked away the dizziness of the impact.

"Mab!" he called. "Borgle, we have to catch her!"

They streaked down, following the flailing form of the dwarf. As the angry roar ended, they could hear the distant sound of the dwarf language serving the task it very well may have been crafted to fulfill: angry, bellowed profanity.

Eddy was the first to reach her, grabbing her arms and fighting to bring her to a stop.

"How did you live this long, you great, empty-headed fish!?" she cried, gripping him tight.

"This is my first adventure!" he said.

"And do you want it to be your last? Let's get out of here!" Mab said.

"If you don't want this to be your last adventure, Eddy, we need to get away from that thing!" Rustle said, in his own language.

Eddy flashed a smile again.

"Mab said the same just now. I think you two would like each other."

"Let's just *go!*" both Rustle and Mab shouted.

A claw lurched out of the darkness, but it reached the end of its massive chain before it could reach them. They backed against the wall, then slipped into an alcove beside the anchor of another enormous chain. The whole wall was rumbling and shaking around them.

"We've found the source of the quakes. And *you* woke it up," Mab said.

"I didn't wake it up! I stabbed it in the eye once it was already awake!" Eddy said.

He leaned into the open and gazed up. The bound beast gazed down. All three eyes were open, and the one Eddy stabbed had a brilliant glowing point. The remains of the pick were incandescent with heat, boiling away with the intensity of the monster's power.

"It blinked my pick in half…" Eddy said. "That was a good pick…"

"It was a terrible pick. You get me through this and I'll show you a proper pick," Mab said.

The creature lashed its claw forward again. Again the chain stopped it, this time with a flash of golden energy. Though the chain held firm, a fault split the wall.

"I don't think this chamber is going to last much longer," Eddy said.

"We should get back to the tunnel that brought us here! We know it goes a fair distance away. That will give us the chance to figure out what to do."

"What did he say?" Rustle said.

"She—Mab is a she—said we should go to the tunnel that brought us here to figure out what to do," Eddy said.

"Mab is very smart and we should listen to her."

"But the fight! The adventure!"

"If you want to bash yourself against a mountain that is trying to kill you, you can do it on the inside of the tunnel. It'll do you just as much good! Now lead the way!"

"Right, right," Eddy said. "We form a plan!"

He darted out into the open.

"You just wait, evil creature! We will defeat you!"

A claw swept in his direction. Yet again it was stopped by the chain, but the rush of water it brought along with it threw him against the wall. He blinked his glowing eyes and shook his head, then darted downward, quick as his tail could propel him. Rustle grabbed hold of his hair and rode along with him. Borgle swam as quickly as it could and dragged itself along with its claws for some extra speed.

"Not much farther," Eddy said. "Just a bit farther. That's the tunnel there. We'll just slip inside and—"

The air filled with an unearthly squeal. Below them a murky rush of scalding hot water sprayed from within the tunnel ahead. A flow of black stone curled from within, growing and oozing with a band of glowing red.

"Lava!" cried Mab. "But how! That wasn't there before!"

"The molten blood of the earth…" Eddy said. "The *cleansing* blood of the earth… Dua's digger struck its target!"

"What?" Rustle said. "Where are we going to go now?"

They retreated from the tunnel, moving aside so that the rising hot water would not cook them alive. The rush of molten stone grew, the flow now nearly filling the tunnel. Other nearby tunnels below began to ooze with similar streams of blackening molten stone.

"Where do we go? Where do we go!?" Rustle said.

"We stay," Eddy said, reaching for Dua's chisel.

"What can we do?" the fairy asked.

He pointed. "*That* is the cleansing blood of the earth. *That* is the Great Ancient. Borgle, Dua, the other diggers, this chamber, the others we found. They all existed for this moment. To defeat the Great Ancient who nearly ruined the sea. The Great Ancient who has shaken the sea floor in its sleep and threatened to knock my home to the ground time and time again. That molten stuff will fill this chamber. It will destroy the Ancient."

One of the shifting pillars, which they now knew to be one of the tentacles of the ancient, recoiled as the flow of stone struck it. The shifting finally pulled one of the damaged bars entirely away from the wall. Eddy's hand tightened around the grip of the chisel.

"But it will only work if the Ancient doesn't escape!"

Rustle looked all about them. Fear seized his features, but slowly something else crept in. It wasn't bravery precisely. But whatever it was, it was replacing the fear.

"The thieves," he said. "What about the thieves? They are far enough away, who knows how far the stone will flow?"

"Yes… Yes… They need to be destroyed as well," Eddy said. "Mab! Do you remember the way Rustle came from?"

"Yes! We can't escape that way because he got there though little passages."

"Yes, walls covered with little passages are weak, right? We should be able to dig through them quickly."

"Weak is a relative word, Eddy. Weaker than solid stone, but not so weak we'll be able to dig to the surface and escape before we're boiled alive."

"No. But maybe Borgle could make it to where Rustle came from to where the thieves are."

"Maybe, but what good would it do?" she asked.

"It would give us a way to get the thieves here, to be destroyed by the molten stone," Eddy said.

"But why would they *come* here?" Mab said. "If they are mindless, they cannot be led. And if they have minds, they would not come to their deaths. And besides, that thing is going to escape its bonds and bash through the roof and then what good will the molten stone do at all?"

"If you can get me back to the chamber with the thieves, I can get them here," Rustle said.

"If you can get them here, we can keep the Great Ancient here," Eddy said.

"What? What are you talking about? We should be talking about getting *out* of here. Not keeping things here!"

"We shall be *heroes,* Mab!" Eddy said.

He threw an arm around her and hauled her off Borgle's back.

"Borgle, go! Dig in the direction Rustle tells you."

The fairy darted off. Borgle followed, chiming and whirring happily now that it had orders.

Eddy worked his tail madly. With his own weight, hers, and the weight of the hammer, it was almost more than he could manage, but he grunted and swam upward.

"Where are you going? What are you doing?" Mab cried.

She knew better than to struggle, as the bottom of the chamber was already beginning to fill with molten stone and she certainly didn't want to end up there. But where they were headed wasn't much better.

"It is a monster! We are traveling up toward the *head.* You do not to the *head* of a monster!"

"You want to kill a monster, you strike its head," Eddy said.

"We weren't talking about killing it. We were talking about keeping it here. And I didn't even agree to *that!* " she said.

"Fine," Eddy bobbed aside, barely avoiding a shifting tentacle. "If we wanted to keep something here, how would we do that?"

"We'd die trying!"

"So what would we die trying to *do?*"

Mab growled. "We'll be nothing but *pests* to this thing."

"Yes. Yes! That is *right,* Mab! You are so smart! We will be pests. And it will be so busy slapping at the pest it will not get out!"

"That's not what I said at all!" Mab said, holding tight as he swam even faster.

#

Cul munched happily on some clams he'd found in the pantry while Cora snacked on a few of the sweets.

"I tell you," Cora said. "I'm starting to see how someone could get past feeling cooped up in a place like this. And that Eddy must be a good miner. Look at the jewelry she's made with the gems."

"She's very talented. I think… Do you feel that?" Cul said.

A low, ominous rumble rolled across the sea floor.

"No…" Cora said.

"Out! Out in the open!" Mira called.

Cul and Cora did as they were told, swimming out of the house and over the city. The rest of the residents had done the same. The sea rolled viciously. The merfolk, free from their homes, bobbed harmlessly. The same could not be said for their homes. The ground rattled like never before. Homes already damaged by the prior quake crumbled. It was devastating, and had the people of the village not still been alert from the last disaster, lives may have been lost. Instead, the people of Barnacle watched as homes that had stood for generations finally succumbed. But there was something different this time. The quake continued. It would not relent.

"Eddy…" Mira said, her arms clutching the equipment she'd borrowed.

Cul and Cora matched her gaze, off to the open sea, toward the rift.

"If he's still out there, he—" Cul began.

"He needs our help!" Mira said. "Come on everyone! My brother is at the rift! He could be hurt!"

Cora slapped Cul's shoulder. "Bult is there, too!"

"Are you mad, girl?" called a voice from below. "Our homes are destroyed! And the quake is still rumbling!"

"We must wait until it stops," called another.

Mira looked to the open sea again.

"I don't think it is going to stop… It feels different this time." She thrust the equipment into Cul's arms. "Come with me. Please!"

"You go with her," Cora said. "I'll go to the others. Sound the alert when you're closer, so they can find it. The drift does not leave one of their own behind if they are in peril. We'll meet you there as soon as we can get there."

#

"What am I doing, what am I doing, *what am I doing?"* Rustle squealed to himself as he squeezed through tiny tunnels.

Borgle was behind him, easily shattering the weakened stone, following in the direction he led. He was blazing a new trail now, using his growing knowledge of navigation via the flow of the water to find his way in the shortest possible path to the thieves.

"There's a machine destroying the tunnel behind me. I'm heading to a chamber filled with ancient horrors. And if I reach it, I'm supposed to lead them *back* to another ancient horror!" He squeezed through a fresh fissure. "So why am I *excited?"*

Stone shattered behind him. Ahead, he could hear the clack and claw of the creatures he'd fled just minutes before.

"Eddy's broken me. Broken my mind with his adventure business." He grinned, almost mad with glee. "But I've got to make it home. Because not even the *elder* has done something like this!"

He squirmed through the final fissure, tumbling into the open chamber that held the thieves.

"Hello!" he bellowed, his musical voice echoing off the walls. "Look over here!"

He flared his glow as bright as he could manage. Gradually, the insect-like forms gathered around him. They kept their distance at first, as if just as confused by his behavior as he was.

"Don't be scared! I know you're thieves! Hungry for fresh things to steal. Well you won't find anything fresher in these dead tunnels than me and my friends!"

Behind him, Borgle shattered through the wall. Its two functional eyes focused on the bizarre creatures before it. A curious whir was the only response.

The thieves moved closer. As confused as they might have been by Rustle, it wasn't half as enticed they were by Borgle. Perhaps it was the nature of its construction, the dash of divine in its design. Or perhaps it was that they instinctively knew just what Borgle was designed *for*. Whatever the cause, the thieves near enough to see Borgle by the fairy's glow, began to scratch and claw at the machine.

Borgle's many claws slapped and slashed at those that came close, but the press of creatures became ever thicker.

"Borgle, go back to the chamber! Go back the way you came!" Rustle ordered.

The flaw in their plan became immediately apparent. Borgle didn't understand Rustle. And Borgle did not act without orders. The orders thus far

181

had been to follow. But the press of creatures, testing the durability of the mining mechanism, was entirely blocking the way back. And as more of them arrived, it was only getting worse.

Rustle narrowed his eyes and tried to work out what to do. An idea came to mind. It was only half-formed when he decided it was the only way. He focused his thoughts and gathered to mind the words of the one spell he'd properly learned from Eddy's book. He'd cast it enough times, felt what happened with each utterance of each syllable, that he was beginning to understand just what it was the individual words meant. What each of the words did. And he knew enough of magic to know that spells were fragile things, things that could misbehave if poorly cast. But the spell as he'd learned it couldn't do what he needed from it now. So he made his best guess, inserted his own words, and spoke it aloud with all of the power he could funnel into the phrase.

With the final word, he cast the spell. As before, ribbons of energy cast from him. But this time, rather than blasting in all directions, or merely forward in a single burst, the energy sought out the thieves. It wrapped about them, coiling about their terrible limbs and encapsulating their joints. They became still, creaking and cracking against the ice, but for the moment immobilized by it.

He didn't waste any time. Moving with desperate speed and little care, he wormed his way through the press of temporarily immobilized creatures until he came to Borgle. The digger was untouched by the magic, as Rustle had intended. It was grinding angrily, slapping against the nearest of the thieves.

"Come on," Rustle said. "If all you know is follow, *follow.*"

He darted into the tunnel Borgle had left behind. The digger pivoted and followed, clicking and chiming happily, as though the greater irritation had not been the monstrosities attempting to destroy it, but the lack of fresh instructions. Borgle forced the blocking thieves aside and swam forward.

The pair moved unimpeded through the smooth-walled tunnel Borgle had produced. The tangle of frozen thieves briefly blocked the way for the rest, but already motion was returning.

"I only hope Eddy has been doing some good," Rustle said.

#

"This isn't doing any good!" Mab barked.

As Eddy adjusted to the load, he'd managed to cut closer and closer to the Great Ancient without threat of being struck. Its anger only seemed to be growing.

"What do you mean!" Eddy said, sweeping aside as a tentacle swept past. "It is not escaping, and we are not dead. These are the two things we want!"

"But look at the walls! Look at the *chains*. If this keeps up the chamber will collapse on its own. *It* might survive that, *we* definitely won't, and then it won't need to escape, because it'll already be out."

He darted into a side tunnel about midway up the chamber to catch his breath.

"It is getting very much warm in this place, too," he admitted.

"Of course it is. That lava's got to be almost to the tentacles by now, and it's flowing faster than ever. It's a wonder we aren't dead already. I think that *thing* is warding off the heat somehow, trying to keep itself alive."

"So *that* is why it is not fast enough to kill us. This is good! But you are right. Much longer and there will not be a place to hold all of the molten stone. What do we need to do?"

"We need to do some *damage*. Immobilize some of the parts that are doing the struggling."

The sound of shearing metal briefly eclipsed the boiling and rumbling. One of the chains had broken. A moment later a tentacle curled up and probed at the entrance to their alcove.

"Bad!" Eddy shouted.

He lashed at the tentacle. Though it moved like the supple limb of a squid, when the blunt tip of the chisel struck the hide, it may as well have been striking stone.

He dropped Mab to the sloped stone floor and grabbed the chisel with both hands to drive it home again. This time, amazingly, it bit into the hide. It was barely anything at all, but it was more than nothing.

"Wait. Hold it there." She drew Dua's hammer. "I think maybe your demigod may have had some tricks up her sleeve after all."

She raised the hammer high and drove it home. The chisel broke the surface and released a plume of horrible green blood into the water. The tentacle yanked from the alcove. Eddy was barely able to hold onto the chisel. The struggling beast roared.

Eddy smiled. The Great Ancient's blood was still thick on the tip of the tool.

"We are a good team! Come! I will hold, you will hammer."

"But there's nothing to stand on out there," Mab said.

"There is a big monster! Plenty to stand on."

He grabbed her and swam out into the open.

"Nothing down here. Tentacles move too much. And they're up and down. Joints. Those are the things to hit." He swam upward, dodging every attack, until he came to the point where one of the spindly arms jutted from the armored body.

He dropped Mab to the arm, then darted down and positioned the chisel right at the joint.

"Hit it!" Eddy urged.

Mab was visibly smoldering with rage and fear, but she knew better than to waste her breath. At this moment, it was better to swing the hammer, do the damage. As insane as this all was, it might well be the only thing that would give them a chance to survive.

She drove the chisel home. She had time for three sharp blows, enough to drive it hilt deep, before the Great Ancient could maneuver itself to have slack enough to reach where they were attacking. Eddy snatched her and dragged her farther up.

"What next?" Eddy said.

"Next you stop hauling me around and start treating this with the proper—"

The Great Ancient snapped at them. Eddy dropped back. The jaws fell short of the attack, but the rush of water from between them forced him farther back. A snatching claw caught them and squeezed them both tight.

Eddy propped a hand against each of the two claws. His strength was barely enough to budge them, but it was sufficient to let Mab slip free.

"No one tries to kill Mab Mill-Mason…" she growled.

She planted her boots as steadily as she could on the claw that shifted beneath her. She raised the hammer high and brought it down. The divine tool opened a fracture. Under her dwarven strength and expertise, she pummeled the monster's wrist. Five solid blows did enough to loosen the grip enough for Eddy to reach out with the chisel. A final blow from Mab drove it home and the claw opened. Eddy swam out and grabbed Mab, but the clutch had taken its toll. He could barely keep them aloft.

"This is going badly, Mab," he said, thrusting his tail against the arm as they worked their way farther upward.

"Never mind that. Get us to the head. I'm going to drive that chisel of yours right into its *brain,*" she snarled.

"I will try!"

He flopped and flailed himself, navigating up along the arm only slightly faster that Mab would have been able to climb on her own.

Mab glanced at him in time to see his sharp-toothed grin widening.

"What are you happy about?"

"If my tail doesn't get better, at least a little, then we might be in trouble."

"In *more* trouble, you mean."

He grunted, flapping his tail desperately to keep them on the shifting arm.

"If we fall, or this thing knocks us down, I don't know if I can carry us both for long. We will fall into molten stone."

Mab gripped him a little tighter.

"And that makes you happy."

"Very happy!"

The beast released a rumbling roar and shifted its arm. Eddy jabbed the chisel down into the arm, catching in a divot in its hide to keep them from falling.

"The more danger, the closer the adventure is to ending! We are almost there!"

They reached what would for lack of a better term be called the thing's shoulder. Eddy stowed the chisel and worked his free arm and tail in tandem to scale the side of the beast's neck and head. He couldn't move constantly. When the creature moved more vigorously, he had to pause and hold tighter. And vigorous motions were becoming more and more common.

The water was growing warmer. The glow from the rising lava was now enough for both his and Mab's sensitive eyes to see far more of the walls than they previously could.

"This was already happening," Eddy said.

"Talk sense or don't talk!" Mab barked.

"Look! That chain is weak. And that loop on the wall, pulled free. And you can see the breaks are old." He took advantage of a pause in motion to vault upward to his next grip. "This was breaking free. Just very slow."

"So it would have eventually gotten loose."

"And so we must be *sure* to kill it."

They worked their way up the side of its head, but as they went, the hide became harder and smoother. There was a short distance left to go, but he simply lacked the means to scale it.

"Hold the hammer tight, Mab!" Eddy said.

"Don't you dare—"

Eddy heaved Mab with all his might, lofting her up over the curve of the beast's head. She cried out, then landed with a thump. Eddy scrabbled with both hands and his tail. Just as he was sliding up over the slope of the creature's skull, she was sliding back in the other direction. He thumped into her from below, but the momentum just wasn't enough. They were both sliding down.

Then it happened. They with no firm grip, the merest twitch of the ancient's head hurled them into the open shaft to plummet down.

"Hold onto me! Hold onto me!" Mab squealed. "I swear, if you let me die, I'll kill you!"

Mab let go of the heavy hammer. He quickly caught it before it fell away.

"Are you *insane!*" she screeched. "You might be able to save us without that weight!"

"We need it! It is divine!"

Eddy's teeth clenched in agony as he tried to power through the accumulation of injuries, but the pair of them were more than his body could handle. The water was scalding, and growing more so. At this rate, they would be boiled alive before they even reached the lava. His swimming brought him to the wall, where he hoped to grab hold of something, but the surface of the stone was radiating nearly as much heat as the molten rock below. He couldn't stay near it. They were too far down now. They couldn't stay here, they couldn't drop farther. Up was the only way to safety.

He never even considered releasing Mab. That wasn't what an adventurer would do. It wasn't what a hero would do. And even if it was, it wasn't what *he* would do.

Eddy shut his eyes and grunted through the pain. Mab squealed again, then suddenly lurched upward. In a heartbeat, he found that rather than dragging him down, Mab was dragging him upward. He opened his eyes.

"Borgle!" he crowed. "You have very much good timing!"

The mechanism was holding onto Mab, who was doing an impressive job of being simultaneously relieved, terrified, grateful, and furious. Rustle was somewhat unheroically clinging to Borgle's nose, the mechanism able to swim far more quickly than he could fly. One of Borgle's other claws reached around to support Eddy directly.

Once everyone was firmly in the digger's grasp, it stopped, whirring merrily. It had no further orders. Above, one of the tunnels had begun to spew the thieves. There seemed to be no end of them, and the heroes had the very good fortune of clearly being of no concern to them. They scrabbled and scrambled over each other in their frenzied bid to be the first to tear into the Great Ancient. It was the task for which they had literally been created.

"Go! Go, go, go!" Mab urged.

"Take us up, Borgle," Eddy said. "Let's finish this."

Borgle obliged. Driven forward by the thrusts of its mechanical tail, the group surged upward, weaving between an endless horde of mindless creatures flooding the scalding hot chamber. They would either be heroes or be the first victims of a second rise of these titanic threats. But regardless of how it turned out, they would fight until the very end.

# Chapter 20

Mira swam beside Cul, matching his steady speed. It was all she could do to keep from dashing forward as fast as her tail could carry her, but she'd learned that the Nomads knew how to get from here to there far faster than she could. The water around them was still filled with the cacophonous rumble of the ground heaving beneath them. The people of the town had evacuated, hanging in the water above their homes to watch helplessly as one by one they succumbed to the quake. That was several minutes ago. If anything, the quake had grown stronger. Mira's home would be gravel by now. She didn't care about that now. The quakes always hit the rift harder than the town. And Eddy was still out there somewhere.

"It's never gone on for this long," Mira repeated to herself, almost as a mantra. "The quakes have been getting worse, but they've never gone on for this long. Something is happening, I know it."

"Don't think about what is happening now," Cul said. "You can't change what is happening. You can only change what you will do. Think about what you will need to do when you reach your brother."

"Right, right," she said. "I need the spell. So I can swim as deep as you and Eddy."

She pulled a thin spell book from her bag, a newer version of the one she'd unwittingly loaned to Eddy.

"It's too dark. I can't read it," Mira growled in frustration.

Cul wrapped an arm around her to steady her swimming, then leaned close so that the subtle glow from his spines and eyes fell upon the book.

"Yes, that's good. Thank you," she said.

She murmured words carefully. As frazzled and worried as she was, she couldn't afford a misspoken syllable. When the spell completed, she felt a sensation sweep over her, one she'd not felt in years. Not since she was a young girl and her father had taken her to the rift to see where he worked.

"Come on. Let's go deeper," Mira said. "I want to see the ground. I want to follow it, so that we can follow the rift just as soon as we reach it.

He nodded and released her waist. The two swam side by side. Mira shrugged off the strange feeling of pressure squeezing uncomfortably upon her as she dove. The spell had done its work. The pressure was unfamiliar, but it was not unsafe. Waves and ripples caused them to bob and waver in their journey, the trembling earth transmitting its motion to the water around them.

"This is no normal quake," Cul said.

"I *know*. It doesn't seem to *end,*" Mira said.

"It isn't just that. I've felt quakes before. Only one or two. But they were never like this. Quakes are constant, steady. This is different. Sudden, halting. I don't know. It doesn't feel natural."

Mira shook her head. "This is how they are in Barnacle. Now tell me. Bult might still be down there in the rift. What would he do in a situation like this?"

"If he was hurt, he would sound the trumpet."

"But no one is near enough to hear."

"The whale would hear. The trumpet can carry a long, long way. Even if we can't hear it, the whale can. And the distress call is one that no nomad drift will ignore."

She looked to him. "Make the call?"

"We don't know if we are where we need to be. They will go to where the call is sounded. If we are far from where your brother and Bult are, precious moments—"

"My brother is in the middle of this. Make the call!" she insisted.

He hesitated only for a moment. Cul produced an ornate and well-used shell and put it to his lips. A long repeating tone blared out. The tone was urgent, radiating the tone of emergency. When he was done, he stowed the shell and they continued to swim downward.

"If they have heard, they will come as swiftly as any of them can swim."

"It was hours to reach the rift from where you were before."

"They have been heading south. They will be closer now. And you've never seen a whale swimming with purpose. They will be here sooner than you might imagine. But we'll need to call again when we reach the rift so they know where the true emergency is."

Mira gazed into the murky distance.

"I think they will know where the true emergency is…"

Though it was subtle, hidden and layered among the endless rumble of the shaking ground, there was a new wound. It was sharp and tumultuous, a sound like boiling water, hissing steam. Something more was happening than a simple earthquake.

#

Borgle reached the head of the Great Ancient and the adventurers tumbled down to it. Eddy quickly pulled both the chisel and the hammer from his back. Mab snatched the hammer.

"Borgle! Dig down on the head! And if we fall, catch us!" Eddy ordered.

Borgle gave a delighted whir and clamped its claws onto the armored hide to begin rattling against it. Mab set about hammering the chisel with all

188

her might. Eddy repositioned it between each blow, keeping its tip in the place where it would do the most good.

"What do *I* do?" Rustle asked.

He buzzed about, eyes wide and trying to look in a dozen directions at once.

"I don't know. I have my hands full now," Eddy said.

"I've got to be able to do *something*."

"You are a smart fairy," Eddy said

The Great Ancient tried to shake them away. Eddy held tight to the now embedded chisel and caught Mab's leg to keep her from being thrown free.

"You can think of a good thing to do, I am sure."

"Uh… Uh…"

Rustle looked around him again. The thieves had finally finished flooding in. They were slashing and clawing at the Great Ancient, and moreover, he could feel them drawing upon its dark well of power. All around them, the walls were fracturing and crumbling. Lava poured in in great gushing black tendrils. From the cries and struggles of the Great Ancient, the rising level of the stuff had reached its tentacles. The whole, mountain-sized beast thrashed and yanked at its chains. With each motion they gave just a little bit more. If the thieves and the hammer and chisel didn't do their job, there was the very real chance that it would pull free of its bindings. The fairy weighed this into his mind, seeing what if anything he could do. A tiny fairy against a beast that had once threatened the entirety of the sea.

"I can't help you fight these things!" Rustle said.

"Then help for after!" Eddy said, yanking the chisel free and setting it in a new spot. "We will need to escape. Help us do that!"

"But how can I…"

He trailed off. The walls were sloughing into the chamber all around them. Great faults split the walls. With each new struggle, he could feel the paths around them opening. Finely trained intuition, the very thing that had allowed him to navigate first by the winds, then by the currents, drew and redrew a map in his head. There *were* paths to the outside now. And more by the minute. But with each one that appeared, others closed. Tumbling stone had thrown their surroundings into chaos. No path to the outside would last for long. They would need something to help clear the way.

Rustle turned to Borgle. The thing was visibly frustrated, still rattling and slamming its beak against the Great Ancient's hide and achieving little more than a shallow divot compared to the deep gash the divine hammer and chisel had achieved.

"Borgle! Follow me! I need you to dig this way!" he ordered.

The digger paused briefly, aiming its two functional eyes at the fairy to consider him before turning back to its present orders.

"What orders should I give? It only speaks my language," Eddy huffed, clearing some unspeakable gunk from the chisel before putting it to work once more.

"I don't know! I just… Teach me some words!"

"What words?"

"Um… Dig, and follow! And up, down, all of the directions…"

"They are very easy. Listen close."

For a few harried minutes, deep in a chamber at the bottom of the sea, merman alternated between positioning a chisel for a dwarf woman to drive into the skull of an ancient horror and giving language lessons to a fairy. Rustle absorbed the words as best he could, then turned to Borgle.

"Borgle! Follow me!" he intoned in his best approximation of Eddy's language.

The digger paused again, plinking and clacking as it considered the words, then released the ancient's head and drifted up to wait obediently await further direction.

"Good! Take it and find a way out!" Eddy said.

The fairy buzzed off toward one of the walls.

"And if it goes to sleep, put blood on the mark over its eyes," Eddy called after him.

"What are you doing? You buffoon!" Mab cried. "That thing is supposed to catch us if we fall!"

"So we should not fall! Easy!" Eddy said.

One of the thieves clattered up along the side of the Ancient's head. Eddy darted back from the gash they had been digging and pulled Mab along with him. The insect-like creature seemed to ignore them, aiming instead for the weakened point in the Great Ancient's armor.

"Out of here, you wretched thing!" A firm swing of Mab's hammer knocked the squealing thief away like it was nothing. "No one steals my hard work!"

"You see? We can do this!" Eddy said. "Keep at it. Every hit keeps the monster righting to reach us and failing to knock away the thieves. Eventually it will fall."

Mab gritted her teeth. "It'll jolly well fall when I *make* it fall!"

#

Rustle held tight to Borgle as it darted up along a jagged new fissure opened into the wall of the chamber. It was a little difficult guiding the digger when it could actually swim faster than *he* could, but the thing seemed to do well with simple directions punctuated by the mer word for "stop." They punched through weakened walls, cleared mounds of fallen debris, and gradually left the stifling heat of the Ancient's Chamber behind.

"Stop!" Rustle ordered as they tumbled into a reasonably clear section of a larger tunnel.

He shut his eyes and tried to work out the best path forward. The ever-shifting layout of the collapsing tunnels meant that the path he'd been hoping to carve when they'd started was now far from ideal.

"I think… there's a big space that's fairly open. It's this way! Dig. That way!"

Borgle chimed and hurried to comply. A few good hard bashes of its hard nose punched through to something Rustle hadn't been expecting. Light. It was a faint golden glow, a bit like the dawn sun.

"It's impossible! We haven't reached the surface yet, have we? Go! Follow that light!"

Borgle's grippers clutched stones and heaved them aside, gradually revealing the source of the light. It was most certainly not the surface. The glow came from thin stalks drifting in torn-free tufts and clumps of mushroom-like growth hanging in the water around them. It was the chamber that Eddy had stumbled onto, and that Mab had called home for so many years. Sure enough Eddy's awakening of the big digger had destabilized it. The place was mostly collapsed and entirely flooded. Rustle buzzed about, probing the place with his slowly improving mystic powers, trying to find a way out.

"We're close…" he said. "We're close to the main tunnel. It's right above us. We've got to dig upward. Dig upward, Borgle!"

The digger faithfully swam to the ceiling and clamped on. Unfortunately, the weakened stone had already come raining down. What remained in the ceiling was good, thick stone that slowed the digger terribly. He turned to look where he'd come. The ease of reaching this place was tempered by the fact that much of the digging they'd done along the way had already been closed in again by further collapse. On one hand, they were nearly to a tunnel that could lead them out of the tunnels. On the other hand, he'd have to do nearly as much digging to get back to them as he'd done to get here. And as the rumbling intensified, it was only going to get worse.

"Think, Rustle. Think," he muttered to himself.

One of the glowing stalks drifted nearby. A bit of the fluid within had seeped out, giving the water around him a wonderfully sweet flavor. He darted to the stalk and sampled some of the fluid directly. It was nourishing. Far more so than Eddy's sweets. After a few grateful swallows, he noticed something else in the dimly lit cavern. Something was shiny. He flitted down to find what looked to be a second Borgle. Not far away there was a third, and a forth.

"That's it!" Rustle proclaimed. "Let's see. They're fueled by blood, right?"

He nicked himself with his borrowed claw and smeared a bit of it on the mark near the glass globes of the inert digger's eyes. It shuddered and flickered but did not awake. He tried a second one. It shifted a bit more but seemed unable to move. One after another he dabbed blood onto the marks.

Eventually he found a second digger able to pull itself from the rubble. Then another. One by one he stirred them to life and gave them their orders.

"Dig up! Open the way to the tunnel!"

Rustle worked his way deeper into the cavern until he found a particularly tall mound of stone with a gleaming bit of metal beneath. He swam between the cracks in the stone, following the curves and shapes of the thing until he finally found an appropriate mark. He smeared it with blood.

Instantly the whole mound of stone seemed to lurch around him. He swam to the relative safety of the open and watched as the device he'd awakened started to shed the debris. As it revealed itself in full, he smiled.

"*You* are coming with *me*," he said.

#

Eddy and Mab had been hard at work. They were both doused with whatever purple-blue goo it was that flowed through the Great Ancient's veins. The thing had ceased to do anything but try to shake them free. With each successive wound they opened, the ancient diverted more of its efforts ridding itself of them. It was no longer clawing at the thieves. It was barely trying to keep itself from the rising lava. If not for them, it might have escaped by now, but they'd succeeded in eclipsing every other threat. It wanted them dead. Nothing else mattered.

"I think we're about to hit a rich vein on this one, Eddy," Mab said, heaving the hammer for another blow.

Despite their terrible predicament, she seemed almost gleeful in her wielding of the hammer, as if she was a fish who for the first time in ages had been allowed to swim in the open ocean. She raised the divine hammer high and brought it down.

There was no telling what exactly they'd managed to pierce, but the moment they did so, the ancient released a deafening, shrill roar. All four of its arms heaved at their chains. The motion drove the beast down into the lava, completely immersing its tentacles, but also tore it free of its shackles. The four arms raised high and thrust at the pair of adventurers.

"We go now!" Eddy cried.

He grabbed Mab, coiled his ailing tail, and sprung from the thing's head just as it raked its hideous claws over where they had been.

Eddy hadn't had much time to recover, so he still lacked the strength to keep the pair afloat, but he was at least able to drag them toward the walls. The rising lava had forced the thieves that hadn't been destroyed to cluster all the more thickly. They still couldn't care less about the merman and the dwarf. He caught their legs, bounced off their backs, and otherwise used them as stepping stones to keep himself and Mab from falling to their doom.

The now-freed limbs of great ancient slashed and swatted at the horde of creatures around it. It was too far buried in the lava to free itself, but it was dead set on ensuring it wasn't the *only* thing to succumb to the molten stone.

It bashed the walls and gripped thieves by the handful. The mounting damage to the chamber caused the ceiling to fail. Boulders rained down. Eddy flopped and bounced between them just as he had between the thieves.

Finally, amid a hail of crumbling roof, he spotted a section of wall that seemed to have given way to one of the many natural tunnels. He heaved himself toward it and worked his tail for all it could give. They reached it just as the stones raining down became a full landslide. Eddy threw himself over Mab and held her close against the wall of the alcove the section of tunnel they hoped would hold strong. For what seemed like an eternity, the thundering rain of stones continued. Jagged pebbles and stones rattled and bounced off Eddy's back, mounding up. Then, gradually, the rumble ceased. Not just the tumble of the stones, but the quaking motion of the creature's struggles and his attempts to escape.

"Mab?" Eddy asked, pulling back and allowing the heap of debris atop him to sprinkle way. "Are you hurt?"

"I've been better," she coughed.

He rolled aside and the pair surveyed their situation. The tunnel both ahead and behind were utterly and hopelessly blocked with fallen stone. A few large chunks of the ceiling had dropped down around them as well.

"We are very much lucky!" Eddy said. "Any of these big pieces could have crushed us."

"Yeah," Mab said, climbing to her feet and brushing herself off. "I'm not convinced we are all that lucky."

"We could be dead!" Eddy said. "And the shaking is done, so the big monster is dead! That's how an adventure should end."

"I hate to puncture your happy ending, Eddy. But there are a few things you need to keep in mind. We're still trapped."

"Rustle will rescue us."

"From what I've seen of him he's mostly good for fretting and getting us in hotter water. But let's assume you're right. That lava is still rising, with plenty of cracks just big enough for it to seep through. This tunnel is getting hotter by the moment. So he's not only got to rescue us, he's got to rescue us *fast*. We don't know how far he got, and we know how fast Borgle can dig. There's a chance we're already dead, we just haven't been boiled alive yet."

Eddy crossed his arms. "He will save us."

"Fine. But that's not all. Listen close."

The merman waited.

"You are not saying anything," he said.

"Not to me, you great bubble-headed fish! Listen to everything else!"

Eddy nodded and shut his eyes. The rumbling was done, certainly. The distant—but approaching—whistle and spit of water meeting cooler water— was constant. Subtly interspersed, though, was a clatter and scratch. It wasn't just settling stone. It was motion. Motion of things smaller than the Great Ancient.

"The landslide didn't kill all of the thieves..." Eddy said.

"Right. So where are we? Either the lava rises and the thieves are either roasted or boiled. Not ideal. We get rescued, but the surviving thieves escape, too, which is no skin off my nose, but seems like it would cause some problems for you and your kind."

"We could be saved and the thieves could die! That is a thing that could happen! We just need to be very much lucky, and we have *been* very much lucky."

"Maybe you have. I've been trapped in an air pocket for years, and the first so-called 'intelligent' beast to come along drags me into a fight with an ancient horror and gets us trapped in a pot that's about to boil over."

"I think my good luck is better than your bad luck... But maybe we dig up a little. To help the luck find us."

She hefted the hammer. "Now you're speaking my language."

#

Mira and Cul had reached what should have been the beginning of the rift not long before. What they'd discovered was horrific. The rift was gone, or at least it was no longer recognizable. Vast sections of it had crumbled in on itself. Others had deepened. The farther they went, the deeper the rift went. What had been a deep gash in the sea floor, softened by untold ages of constant currents, now was a jagged, fresh wound that continued downward seemingly without end.

"No... No, no, no..." Mira muttered as she held tight to Cul.

His natural glow was still the only useful source of light. In her haste to be on her way, she'd neglected to bring a light of her own beyond the shells that hung from her necklace. At another time, they would have done some good, but not here, and not now. The devastation had kicked up copious amounts of silt. The water around them was milky with the stuff. It choked them with every breath and made it necessary to nearly be on top of something before their light cut far enough through it for them to see.

"We look for a merman's glow," Mira said. "Eddy isn't a fool. He would have gotten as near to the surface as possible if something like this was happening. We'll see him. I know we will..."

They swam onward, following the path of the devastation. Gradually it became more substantial. The rift was no longer a sharp, defined thing in the floor. It was merely the deepest part of a sinkhole.

"He'll be alive. He'll be alive..." She repeated desperately, as though through repetition she could make it true.

A short, wavering blast of sound came from below. Mira recognized it as a weak attempt at the same distress call she'd convinced Cul to sound not long ago. Cul reacted to it as though his body were moving of its own accord.

194

He darted directly toward it, moving faster than Mira had ever seen him move. Mira worked her tail to catch up.

"There… What color was your brother's glow?" Cul said, pointing as he swam.

"Blue-green. A bit lighter than yours."

"Not your brother then. I see… I see two colors. Do you see? There, below. And something red farther ahead. I recognize that sharp green. That's Bult!"

They dove toward the gravely dross piled beneath them. The vague glow resolved into what was clearly the spines of a merman. Cul gripped the largest of the stones and heaved them aside. Mira had mystically borrowed the pressure resistance of the males, but lacked their higher strength. Instead, she consulted the spell book, squinting at the page and holding her faintly glowing necklace closer. When she was satisfied she'd found the proper words, she murmured them with eyes shut tight.

The water around them coiled and churned. A tight swirl drew the silt around them up and away, then slowly strengthened to begin lifting away the smaller stones and pebbles. Between the two of them, Mira and Cul unearthed Bult. When he was clear of the heaviest of the stones that had trapped him, Cul put his arms around his fellow nomad and pulled him free.

"Bult! Speak to me! What happened?" Cul said.

The rough-looking merman was dazed, but his injuries were mercifully minor.

"I was looking through the overhangs. The sort of places that I thought a shore-lover might like. Then the ground started shaking. Half the sea floor came down upon me."

"Are you hurt? Do you need aid?" Mira said.

"Nothing a couple loaves of pannet couldn't cure," he said, blotting some of his thick blood from his forehead.

"Did you see my brother?" she urged.

"Didn't see anyone."

She darted up and away, straining her vision for the other glow they'd seen.

"You've got to help us then."

With Cul's aid, Bult joined them and they swam down along the slumping ground. As they'd traveled they'd come to forget the whistling, churning sound that had concerned them when they'd first drawn near. It was constant, an unnatural but unchanging part of the disaster that had happened here. As they approached the hazy, smoldering glow, they found the sound was growing louder. The water was turbulent, and had grown sharply warmer along the way.

"I know this. This sound. The way the water is so lively," Bult said. "Remember? When we followed the stout current out past Deep Swell to see if we could get some good weapons for trade?"

"The Glowing Pools," Cul said. "Yes. This *does* feel like that. But there are no glowing pools here."

"There are now…"

They paused and gazed down. The collapsed sea floor dropped sharply down. Constant rippling currents stirred the water even more powerfully, keeping the water heavy with silt. And deep below the silt, a deep, constant glow.

"The blood of the earth…" Cul said. "All of that trembling… It must have opened a wound deep enough to reveal it."

Mira's expression took on a hard, defiant look. A realization was dawning upon her, but she seemed to be physically fighting it.

Cul approached her.

"Has your brother… Has he worked with the Glowing Pools before?" Cul asked.

"He hasn't," she said quietly.

"Done for, then," Bult said.

Cul thumped him in the arm.

"We don't know that," Cul said.

"We do! Takes all sorts of magic and equipment to work near the glowing pools. If they just showed up, and he wasn't ready—" Bult continued.

"Shut your *mouth*," Cul barked.

"Do you hear that?" Mira said, shutting her eyes and turning her head.

The others did the same. Amid the roiling tumult, there *was* something more. A clatter and crackle. Moving stones. Not settling. Not dislodging. Shifting with purpose. Something was digging, and not far below.

"Come on! It could be him! It *is* him. I know it!" Mira shouted.

She dragged Cul and Bult deeper. They followed the sound, eventually locating its source along one of the shallower parts of the sloping wall. She tugged madly at the stones. Cul did the same.

"We're coming, Eddy! We're coming!" she cried.

They shifted as many stones as they could, sending them tumbling down into the glowing pit. But for every stone they moved, the sound seemed just as far away.

In the distance above them, a blast of a shell rang out.

"They're here!" Bult said. "The rest of the drift is here!"

"So quickly?" Mira replied.

"I told you. Nothing covers a long distance quicker than a good healthy whale and a dedicated drift of nomads," Cul said. "Bult, go to them. Send down the strongest mermen and see to it you get your wounds tended to."

"I can work."

"They're fresh, you were buried for an hour. Now go!"

Bult muttered under his breath, but finally obliged. Mira re-cast the spell that began to clear away the smaller stones again and pull the silt from the water.

"Hold on, Eddy!" she called. "Help is here!"

#

Beneath the sea floor, Mab and Eddy worked at the stone. The heat was becoming unbearable. Though the lava's rise seemed to have slowed, or even stopped, the temperature continued to creep higher.

"I don't..." Eddy wheezed. "I don't know how much longer I can go on..."

"I've seen worse heat than this. Just keep at it," Mab said.

"It isn't... It isn't the same for mermen. We do fine with cold. But hot. Not so fine."

He cleared a bit of stone that they'd chiseled away and packed it into the cracks behind them. If they'd not been sealing off the tunnel behind, the flood of hot water probably would have finished them minutes ago.

"Just imagine nice cold water on the other side of the next stone. Look, see? There's just a bit more. I can see a big gap on the other side of it."

"I will work until I can't... But you do me a favor."

"Fine, fine. What's the favor," Mab grumbled, hefting the hammer as he found a proper place to position the chisel.

"Tell my story. The adventure. I told it all to you, the parts before you got here. And you have been here for the rest."

"Tell it yourself."

"If I die, you tell it."

"Just hold the chisel."

She raised the hammer up and brought it down. The chisel punched cleanly through the stone ahead, shattering it. The rest of the wall before them fell away. Sure enough, there was a void behind it.

"There! See? Never doubt the mining intuition of a dwarf! We just need to..."

The pair clambered over debris to find that they'd revealed not an open tunnel, but a small chamber blocked on the far end with a massive, entirely intact stone. Mab ran her hand over it. Boring through it wouldn't be like they'd been doing until now. It wouldn't be shifting fallen stones and chipping through bits of collapsed roof. It would be like starting a fresh tunnel from scratch.

"All right..." Mab said. "Any bits of the story you'd like me to emphasize?"

"Make sure you talk about Rustle. Find him and learn his part. I think he thinks this adventure wasn't for him. But it was for him. It was for both of us. For all three of us."

A subtle rumble started to rattle around them. Likely some of the thieves scrabbling between bits of debris in their own bid for freedom. Eddy raised his voice to be heard.

"Tell people about the big fight. How we poked holes in the head of the monster. That was good."

The rumble grew louder.

"Tell them about the place we found you! And how you helped fix Borgle."

Now the rumble was almost painfully loud. Eddy swam back and held the chisel defensively. Mab stood beside him and held her hammer.

"Probably this is a part you should tell, too," Eddy said.

Rhythmic pounding sent fractures splitting along the surface of the wall before them. Finally the wall seemed to turn to powder all at once. Mab and Eddy shielded their eyes. When the jagged bits of shattered stone settled, what stood before them was a massive, complex assembly of gleaming metallic parts.

"That's… That's my *house!*" Mab said.

Indeed, they were staring into the front door of the structure Mab had built from the diggers. The mechanism settled a bit lower, like a crab taking a seat, and a blue gleam of light flitted from within. Rustle appeared. Once again he greeted Eddy by darting into him and hugging his neck. The force of the pounce was enough to knock Eddy back a bit.

"Yes, *definitely* remember to tell this part," Eddy said.

Mab stepped up to the thing she'd called her home for so many years. "You woke it up?"

"Yes. I found a few marks and put blood on them."

"Rustle says yes," Eddy explained.

"I guess the metal carcass still had a mind in it somewhere." She grinned. "I'm glad I made sure the thing could still move!"

"Come on," Eddy said, flitting inside. "I woke up other diggers. They've been digging upward. We should have a way out by now. I want to get *out* of this place right now!"

The three entered the 'house' and found places to brace themselves.

"Maybe you could tell this thing what to do. It was having a very hard time piecing together useful orders out of what I remembered you taught me."

"Take us to the surface!" Eddy said. "The most direct route!"

Gears spun, chains shifted, and the mass of machinery pivoted in place to retrace its steps.

"Did you do it? Did you kill the Great Ancient?" Rustle asked.

"Yes! We broke its head, and then stones pushed it down into the blood of the earth."

"And the thieves?"

"Um… Less yes…"

#

Six of Cul's fellow nomads, including a reluctant Sitz, were hard at work clearing away the stones nearest to the scratching sound. It had seemed tantalizingly near to the surface when they'd begun, but the smaller, easier to move stones had quickly sifted aside to reveal much larger slabs. Fortunately, there were few things that couldn't be moved by a sufficient number of mermen working together.

"On three," Cul said. "One, two, *three!*"

All six of them propped their tails against the ground and heaved with all their might. A glassy block of black stone tipped up and tumbled down into the glowing pit. Below was nothing but darkness. They'd broken through the debris.

A roar began to rise up, but it was cut short when *something* came rushing out of the gap they'd opened. Had they been present for Rustle and Eddy's adventures thus far, they would have known it was a thief, and a badly injured one at that. The insect-like form was missing several limbs, and its carapace was fractured and oozing. But it was still very much alive, and without the irresistible target of the Great Ancient, the thing picked a fresh target. As there was but one creature present with a mystical aspect, Mira became that target.

The thing launched at her. She darted nimbly aside, but it scrabbled along the debris and thrust itself after her. Shouts rang out among the mermen to kill the beast, and soon the six of them had converged upon it, driving stout knives into the creature, tugging at its limbs, and generally attempting to break it to piece. It snapped and slashed at them, and though they were strong, they couldn't seem to put an end to it. Worse, while they grappled with it, another emerged from below. Then another.

"Head up! Find the rest of the drift. Tell them to take up arms!" Cul shouted.

"If I go, they'll follow! They're after *me!*" Mira shouted.

The ground began to rumble.

"What did you get us into!?" shouted Sitz.

Fresh pits began to open all around them. From some, more of the horrid monsters flitted out. From others, something *else*. Gleaming metallic mechanisms. Then the ground practically exploded beneath them and a massive final beast emerged. It was Mab's house, and in it, the three adventures.

Eddy darted out from within as the thing crept crabwise to a stop.

"Eddy!" Mira called.

"Mira!" he shouted back.

His eyes swept about, trying to make sense of what was going on around him. Then, in a snap decision he shouted.

"Diggers! Destroy the thieves. Borgle, Mab, Rustle, you come with me, help me defend Mira!"

The metallic mechanisms released a chorus of obedient chimes and quickly assaulted the thieves. Eddy swam painfully to Mira's side and raised his chisel. Mab trotted over and readied her weapon. Rustle flitted between them, eying the water behind.

"What is all of this?" Mira asked.

"A very long story," Eddy said. "An adventure!"

Mab swung the hammer and smashed one of the thieves aside.

"A bloody nuisance from beginning to end," she growled.

For a time, chaos reigned. It seemed to do so rather frequently when Eddy was around. He and the others faced off against the remaining thieves. A thousand of them had been enough to challenge the Great Ancient. Even a hundred would have probably been enough to kill the whole of their little group. But when the hole stopped spewing them, there were barely a dozen, and they were all suffering from a massive landslide, a near-cooking, and a prolonged battle with the Great Ancient. It was by no means an easy battle, but when all was said and done, the creatures were defeated with little more than a few extra scrapes and gouges suffered by the heroes.

"I knew you'd still be alive... I *knew* you would be," Mira said, hugging Eddy tight.

"Easy," he said. "I've taken some bumps and bruises. Who are these nomads?"

"This is Cul and his drift," she said. "After the first quake I was worried about you. I hired them to help find you. Who are these... creatures?"

Eddy smiled broadly. "This is Rustle. He is a fairy. A *water* fairy from the forest on the other side of the mountain. He is clever and helpful and brave. And this is Mab. She is a dwarf from the mountain. *She* is clever and *hardworking* and brave. And that is Borgle! Borgle is a digger, and Borgle is helpful and hardworking. Brave, too, but I do not know if the word applies to a machine. The other diggers are like Borgle, but Borgle is the best, if you ask me."

"And the largest thing?"

"That is Mab's house."

"... Dwarves live in great mechanical crabs?"

"Not all of them. But Mab did. Like I said. It is a long story. And I cannot *wait* to tell it to you..."

# Epilogue
*Four Months Later…*

Rustle padded along the moist ground beside a small lake not far from his home pond. It had been a long, long time since he'd visited this shore. In all measurable ways, this lake would be a wonderful improvement as a home for him and his people. It was quite a bit larger. The fields surrounding were dense with winter-hardy foliage, plenty of delicious nectar and more than enough cover to hide them from predators. But it had its downsides as well. Those downsides were significant enough that no fairy had come to this place alone. Not until today, that is.

Today the elder had decided Rustle was the one to see if maybe the time had come to see about readying the lake to be their new home. Though their home wasn't very deep into the north, there were still many plants that bloomed only for a few weeks a year, and for several months the surface was frozen solid. They were in the depths of the warm season. The forest was blooming with more food and more shelter than there would be for the rest of the year. If they were planning to move all of his people, now was the time.

He slowed as he approached the water's edge. The cool soil beneath his feet felt strange. He seldom set foot on the ground so near to a body of water as large as this. A ripple along the surface reminded him why.

A slick gray form dragged itself from the water. A toad, large enough to make a meal of a fairy as small as Rustle. He buzzed his wings and began to weave his mind into complex shapes. The creature blinked its bulging eyes one at a time. Rustle took a breath.

The toad made its move. Its maw flipped open. A lethal tongue lashed in Rustle's direction. The fairy spat a single word and thrust his hands forward. A swirl of magic lanced from his hands and swept over the predator. The air crackled. Frost and glimmers of light filled the air. When the settled, the toad was encased in ice, its tongue a mere whisper from touching Rustle's face.

He took a shaky breath and buzzed over to the frozen creature, knocking on its head.

"There. Not so scary anymore, are you?" he said.

Rustle took to the air and looked over the lake in satisfaction.

"Good," he remarked. "If we keep our eyes open, and a few more of us learn the ice spell, then we won't have to worry about the toads anymore."

Over the last few months, Rustle had been meeting with Eddy regularly to swap stories, trade goods, and practice magic. Eddy was slow to pick up the more complicated spells, but Rustle was beginning to get the knack of stripping away all but the absolute essence of spells. Fairies were *very* well suited to magic, and he'd found that a tiny nudge from the original spell mixed with his own instinct was often enough to get what he needed from the merfolk magic. At first, he'd not expected very many of the sea-centric spells to be of much use to him in the woods, but among his other talents, Eddy was peerless at finding unintended applications for the spells in his book.

Rustle looked to the sky.

"The toad showed itself more quickly than I'd expected. I'll have time to make my meeting with Eddy after all. I can't wait to tell him about this!"

#

Barnacle was a very different place these days. Gone were the shabby, tumbledown homes that had endured so many quakes. The town had been rebuilt from the ground up, and though it was still small, it was glorious. Four months isn't much time to rebuild a city, but then, most cities don't have the help of machines built by demi-gods. It turned out that diggers, if given the proper instruction, were equally good as builders.

A pair of children swam up to a gong beside the doorway of one of the humbler but better-built homes of the city. The gone was a curious one, made from a shiny metal gear.

"One moment," called a voice from within.

Eddy swam out from the home. He had a few more scars, a few more notches missing from his fins, but he was otherwise none the worse for his adventure.

"What is it, children?" he said, his eyes sparkling and his smile wide.

The pair whispered amongst themselves, awed by his presence. Finally, one worked up the courage to swim a bit closer.

"Can we see the hammer and chisel?" asked the little merboy.

"Of course!" Eddy said.

He led them inside to something akin to a shrine set up in the entryway. It held the hammer and chisel of Dua. The mergirl swam up and gawked at them.

"Are those *really* the tools of the Left Hand of Tria?"

"No, no," Eddy said. "The Right Hand. These are the hammer and chisel of Dua."

"And, and, and they are the things that Eddy and his friends used to defeat the Great Ancient!" the boy said eagerly.

"That is *right!*" Eddy said.

"What ever happened to them?" the girl asked. "Wasn't it Mad that had the hammer at the end of the story?"

"Her name was Mab. And she gave it back," Eddy explained.

202

"Because she is gentle and kind, right?" the boy said. "She wouldn't need the hammer."

Eddy reminisced about the moment. Mab's exact words were, "I can't keep this. If the others find out a *dwarf* had to rely on something made by *fish*, I'd never live it down!"

He grinned a bit more. "Yes. Very gentle, and very kind. But *fierce* when circumstances demanded it."

"And what about Rustle?"

"He went back to his home pond. *Much* more learned and powerful than when he left. He visits the shore every few weeks, and I go to meet him."

"And what happened to the wizards?" The girl asked.

"… The wizards?" Eddy said.

"Yes! In the story, you say that they both woke up. And their power was being used to keep the thieves and the Great Ancient trapped. And now the Great Ancient and the thieves are dead. So what are the wizards doing?"

"Oh, yes." Eddy paused for a moment. "They are back asleep."

The girl looked relieved. "That is good to know."

"You two should run along now," Eddy said. "Soon I have to go back to the glowing pools and tend to my new farm."

They merrily swam back out to the city square. Eddy swam a bit deeper, to Mira's study.

Presently, the room was a bit bare. When the house collapsed, a good deal of her skull and bone collection was damaged or destroyed. She'd taken it in stride, though. For one, the important thing to her was that she got her brother back, safe and sound. And now that the quakes had stopped and her and Eddy's home was more stable, Mira could begin rebuilding her collection *and* displaying it more elegantly. The centerpiece—unlikely ever to be dethroned—was a carefully cleaned and bleached skull from one of the thieves.

At the moment she was at her work bench, tapping at her latest piece of jewelry by the light of a netted jellyfish.

"Mira? I am going to go to the farm. Do you need anything?" he asked.

"If you are going to swing past what is left of the mine, see if you can find any more of that good white stone. The last necklace I made with it fetched us three amber gems in return."

Eddy scanned a nearby shelf until he spotted the book he was looking for.

"I certainly will. I know just where to find some," he said, subtly slipping a brand-new spell book from the shelf."

"I may be a little late. I have some ideas for how to better prepare the farm for using the glowing pools more effectively."

"Take extra food, then," Mira advised. "Remember the stomach ache you got when you ate nothing but snails last week."

"I will. See you later."

He slipped back to his own room and swiftly packed his things, including the purloined spell book. When his pack was filled with food and equipment, he slung it over his shoulder and swam out the door. After a moment, he darted back in and fetched Dua's Hammer and chisel.

One never knows when one might need such things…

###

# From The Author

Thank you for reading! If you liked this story, or perhaps if you found it lacking, I'd love to hear from you. For **free stories** and important updates, join my newsletter or keep in touch at:

www.bookofdeacon.com/contact

## Discover other titles by Joseph R. Lallo:

### The Book of Deacon Series:

Book 1: *The Book of Deacon*
Book 2: *The Great Convergence*
Book 3: *The Battle of Verril*
Book 4: *The D'Karon Apprentice*
Book 5: *The Crescents*

### The Big Sigma Series:

Book 1: *Bypass Gemini*
Book 2: *Unstable Prototypes*
Book 3: *Artificial Evolution*
Book 4: *Temporal Contingency*

### The Free-Wrench Series:

Book 1: *Free-Wrench*
Book 2: *Skykeep*
Book 3: *Ichor Well*
Book 4: *The Calderan Problem*

### Collections:

*The Book of Deacon Anthology*
*The Big Sigma Collection: Volume 1*
*The Free-Wrench Collection: Volume 1*